ANCIENT SPIRITS

SPIRITS, FEATURING
DAISY GUMM MAJESTY

ANCIENT SPIRITS

ALICE DUNCAN

FIVE STAR
A part of Gale, Cengage Learning

GALE
CENGAGE Learning·

Detroit • New York • San Francisco • New Haven, Conn • Waterville, Maine • London

GALE
CENGAGE Learning

Set in 11 pt. Plantin.

LIBRARY OF CONGRESS CATALOGING-IN-PUBLICATION DATA

Duncan, Alice, 1945–
  Ancient spirits : spirits, featuring Daisy Gumm Majesty / Alice
Duncan. — 1st ed.
     p. cm.
  ISBN-13: 978-1-4328-2570-6 (hardcover)
  ISBN-10: 1-4328-2570-4 (hardcover)
  1. Majesty, Daisy Gumm (Fictitious character)—Fiction. 2.
Spiritualists—Fiction. 3. Pasadena (Calif.)—Fiction. I. Title.
PS3554.U463394A84 2012
813'.54—dc23
                                                        2011035648

First Edition. First Printing: January 2012.
Published in 2012 in conjunction with Tekno Books and Ed Gorman.

For my Rebelwriter sisters. I don't know what I'd do without you guys. Thanks also to Deb Brod, a great (and understanding) editor. And for Anni and Robin, my wonderful daughters. You made me realize that family members don't automatically detest each other. How'd that happen?

CHAPTER ONE

Sometimes the months of June and July are foggy and overcast in Pasadena, California, my hometown. However, the fifteenth day of June in that year of 1922, the day of my Billy's funeral, the sun shone brightly, the sky glittered blue as a sapphire, and high, puffy clouds decorated it at perfect intervals. The day was as beautiful a one as I'd ever seen. Didn't seem fair somehow.

I'd wanted my friend and Billy's, Johnny Buckingham, to conduct the graveside service, but I didn't argue much when my family told me the minister of Pasadena's First Methodist Episcopal Church, North, should conduct the service. After all, the Gumms and the Majestys had gone to the Methodist church for decades. Johnny, while a good friend, was a captain at the Salvation Army.

Much to my relief, Johnny and his wife Flossie stood beside me at the service. So did Sam Rotondo, a Pasadena police detective and Billy's best friend. And so did my good friend Harold Kincaid, a costumier at a motion-picture studio in Los Angeles. Harold had come with his . . . oh, nuts. This is always so hard to explain.

You see, Harold was what Billy and Sam called a faggot. Harold's longtime companion, Del Farrington, had taken the day off from his duties at the bank to attend Billy's obsequies. I thought that was nice of him. Whatever Sam and Billy called them, *I* called Harold and Del dear friends, and I was grateful for their support on that ghastly, glorious day.

My parents and my aunt Vi, who lived with us, both cried, holding on to each other, throughout the service. I noticed for perhaps the first time that they looked kind of alike. That really didn't make much sense, since Vi was Pa's sister-in-law and his late brother's widow, but it struck me then. Ma and Pa wouldn't allow me to bring Spike, Billy's dachshund, to the service, although I think Billy would have liked to have had him there. Billy didn't have any family left by the time of his death. Both his parents had died during the flu pandemic that swept the world at the end of the war, and he'd been an only child.

Nevertheless, the place, Morningside Cemetery in Altadena, California, was packed with friends of the family and concerned clients of mine. I, you see, earned a living for Billy and myself working as a spiritualist medium. That day, more than any other day before or since, I wished I honestly *could* communicate with the dead.

Naturally, everyone wore black, including me. What do they call a flock of crows? A murder of crows? I think that's it. Well, as I gazed upon the assembled mourners, they appeared to me to be a murder of crows. That seemed totally appropriate, since my Billy had been, in effect, murdered.

You see, Billy was yet another casualty of the late Great War. Yes, I know the war had been over for years by 1922. That doesn't negate the fact that it and the forever-cursed Kaiser killed my husband. Slowly, painfully and horribly. By the way, in spite of the fact that Billy actually did himself in on purpose by taking an overdose of the morphine syrup Dr. Benjamin had prescribed for his pain, his death was documented as accidental. No one who really knew Billy's story believed that, but Dr. Benjamin, one of the most wonderful men in the world, had filled out the death certificate.

Doc Benjamin was at the funeral, too, small and dapper and without one of his almost-constant cigarettes between his lips. I appreciated his tact and consideration in regard to Billy's death certificate almost more than I could say, and he knew it, but he never said a thing about it. But his kindness spared my family and me a whole ton of trouble. Why, I don't think the minister of our church would have presided over the funeral if it was known Billy was a suicide. I wonder who made up that stupid rule. Whoever'd done it must have been unfamiliar with the lingering cruelties of war.

In April of 1917, right after Billy joined the army, he and I were married. We both thought his joining the army in the effort to free Europe from the Hun plague was a great, even a romantic, idea. Boy, were we wrong. He never got the chance. He hadn't been in France for more than a month or two before he was gassed out of his foxhole on the French frontier and shot when he tried to crawl to safety. He spent nearly a year in hospitals overseas and came back to me a ruined man. I knew he wished he'd died over there in the mud and blood of the battlefield, because he often told me so.

He hated the way he was. He hated that he hurt all the time. He hated that he couldn't take a deep breath, go for a walk, sing as he used to be able to sing or take the dog for a walk unassisted. Most of all, he hated that he couldn't earn our living for us as he'd planned to do, as a mechanic at the Hull Motor Works, but had to rely on me. Yes, he got his monthly soldier's benefit, but that wouldn't have kept Spike alive.

About the only thing Billy could still do at the time of his death was play gin rummy with my father and Sam Rotondo and let me push him in his wheelchair when we took Spike for walks on pleasant days. Oh, and he could read. He loved to read *National Geographic*, probably to see pictures of all the places he'd never be able to visit, and he enjoyed reading the *Tarzan* books by Edgar Rice Burroughs and various detective thrillers. I kept him in reading material by visiting the library at least once a week. Naturally, because the library had steps, he couldn't pick out his own books. Do you blame him for feeling hopeless and helpless?

I didn't blame him one little bit. I felt hopeless and helpless myself. This was especially true when Billy criticized the way I earned our living. I tried to pass his negative comments off as a result of his war injuries and general state of melancholia, but they hurt me anyway.

By the time of Billy's funeral, four years after the war ended, casualty reports still appeared in our local newspapers at least once monthly. I used to run down to City Hall to see the names posted daily on the lists while the war lasted. For over a year after the conflict ended, the lists were still posted outside for people to glance through, hoping to find—or not to find—the names of loved ones. By 1922, I guess most people scanned the printed lists in the newspapers, praying the remains of their missing husbands, sons, cousins, lovers, etc., might have been identified. The only worse fate I can think of than the way my Billy died was never to know for certain what had became of a loved one. I knew exactly what had happened to Billy.

The funeral service was lovely, I guess. At the time, my spirits alternated between benumbed to enraged. If I'd had the Kaiser at my disposal at the moment, he'd have died a slow and painful death. The same kind of death he'd dealt my Billy. Mostly, however, I stood between Johnny—tall, lean and handsome—and Flossie—shorter, pretty and loving—and stared at the hole in the ground into which the undertaker was going to lay my husband Billy, the only man I'd ever loved—and I'd loved him pretty much from the time I could walk.

My name, incidentally, is Daisy Gumm Majesty. Billy and I lived with my parents and Aunt Vi in a neat little bungalow on South Marengo Avenue in the fair city of Pasadena, California. I'd got into the spiritualist business when I was a kid one Christmastime, pretty much by accident. Aunt Vi's employer, who was then named Mrs. Kincaid, had given her an old Ouija board, and everyone else in the family pretended to be afraid of it. I, being ten and having no scruples about much of anything at that age, manipulated the board with my cousins and my sister Daphne. I got quite the reputation at that family gathering, and it eventually paid off rather handsomely. I'm not saying Billy couldn't have made more money at the Hull Motor Works than I did doing my spiritualist act, but I made considerably more money than other women who had to hold down jobs in the 1920s. Well, except for movie stars. They only have to look good on the silver screen. Life isn't fair now, never has been, and probably never will be. I know all about it, believe me.

Billy left me a note, in case you wondered. In it, he told me that he could no longer stand to live the way he had to, and he asked me please to forgive him. He said he'd waited until June because June was the middle of the year and didn't correspond with any particular family holidays. He didn't want me to be sad at Thanksgiving or Christmas or whatever because he'd died then. As if I wouldn't think of him on holidays, no matter when he died! Still, it was a nice note: he told me he loved me and that he hoped I'd understand.

I did understand. For a long time, by then, I'd been fighting for my Billy's life and fighting against his desire to leave it. He'd waited until I was out of the house, working on a motion-picture set for a bunch of Hollywood people. Ma was at her job as chief bookkeeper at the Hotel Marengo, and Aunt Vi was at her job working as a cook for Mrs. Kincaid, who was by that time Mrs. Pinkerton. Pa had gone for a walk with Spike—Pa used to be a chauffeur for some of Pasadena's wealthy residents, but had been forced to quit working because of heart problems. In other words, Billy had planned well for his demise. Pa came home while he was still barely alive and called an ambulance, but by the time I got to the Castleton Hospital, driven there by Sam Rotondo who'd come to the set to deliver the news, he'd stopped breathing.

As much as I didn't want to admit it to myself, I knew Billy was better off dead. There'd been no hope that he'd ever get better. As he'd told me over and over again, he was merely marking time. At the time of his death, he was twenty-four years old.

I'd come to the conclusion shortly after Billy returned from the war that the people who start the cursed things ought to be the ones to fight in them. If the world were governed by me, here's what would happen: President Wilson, Clemenceau, the Czar of Russia, the King of Serbia, the guy who assassinated Archduke Ferdinand, Prime Minister Asquith and the Kaiser would get into an arena together and slug it out, thereby doing their own dirty work and leaving the young and healthy men of all their countries at home, alive and well.

As ever, I had no say in how the world ran. Heck, although I was twenty-two at the time of Billy's death, I hadn't even voted yet because the last election had been held when I was twenty.

"You holding up all right, Daisy?" Flossie whispered in my ear.

She was worried about me, which I thought was sweet, since she was "with child," as the quaint saying goes, and all this standing by the graveside probably wasn't very good for her. I squeezed the hand she'd laid on my arm. "I'm all right. Thanks."

I felt someone put a hand on my shoulder, and was surprised to look to the right and discover it was Sam Rotondo, tall, the least little bit heavyset, and looking worn out and unhappy that day. Sam and I hadn't got off to a very good start together when we'd first met. He'd thought I was a crook, and I'd thought he was a bully. I guess we were both more or less . . . well, not right exactly, but not exactly wrong, either. I earned my living fooling people, and he earned his dealing with criminals. For some reason unknown to me, on that day I lifted my other hand and put it over his. I'd overheard a conversation between Sam and Billy shortly before Billy died, during which he'd asked Sam to look after me if anything happened to him. Even then, I knew he was planning something.

Heck, one day, while looking for a shoe in our closet, I'd found a box full of morphine syrup bottles. His suicide wasn't a surprise when it came, but it certainly was painful. I felt as though I had a huge, gaping hole in my heart as I stood in the cemetery that gorgeous June day, staring at that hole in the ground and at the coffin next to it, which contained the mortal remains of my beloved Billy.

I don't have any idea what the minister said. I'd been to funeral services before, and I presume he said what preachers always say. Then it was over, the minister prayed, I laid some red roses on Billy's coffin—by the way, there were floral arrangements by the score there, sent by my wealthy clients who are occasionally good for something besides making my living for me—and Sam, Ma, Pa and Vi laid some white roses on it, and then we all turned around and began walking away. I guess funeral directors don't like to have family present when their loved ones are lowered into the ground and covered with dirt. I don't think it would have mattered much to me. I knew where Billy was, and where he would always be, from that point until the end of the world.

Have I mentioned that I hate the Kaiser? If it weren't for him and his mustard gas, Billy would probably have recovered enough that he wouldn't have felt the need to do away with himself. His bullet wounds might have always caused him some pain, but at least he'd have been able to breathe.

I didn't cry on the way to the motorcar as we walked from the grave. I didn't cry when people came over and hugged me and wished me well and told me how sorry they were. I just thanked them and invited them to our house for a little post-funeral get-together, which was a tradition in our family. I guess it is in most families.

I didn't even cry on the way home from the funeral. Sam Rotondo drove us in his big Hudson. Ma, Pa and Aunt Vi sat in the backseat, sniffling, and I sat next to Sam, numb. Sam, whose black eyes and olive complexion didn't ever give much away, was hurting that day; I could tell by the set of his jaw and the way his hands tightened on the steering wheel. A long line of automobiles followed us from Woodbury Street in Altadena, where the cemetery is, to our home on South Marengo.

The moment I cried was when we opened the front door and Spike flew into my arms. Then I more or less collapsed onto the floor, hugged Spike, wept and rocked back and forth for what seemed like forever but probably wasn't, since Ma and Aunt Vi and Johnny Buckingham shuffled me away to what had been Billy's and my room off the kitchen.

"Don't come out unless you feel well enough, Daisy. You've been through enough today." This sympathetic advice came from Johnny. My mother probably would have told me gently that I should try to hold myself together and do my duty by my guests, but she didn't get the chance because Johnny spoke first. Anyhow, I preferred Johnny's advice, which I believe came from his service with the Salvation Army. Those Salvation Army folks have seen it all, done it all, and they love their fellow human beings anyway, which was a lot more than I was able to do most of the time.

Anyhow, Spike didn't mind.

CHAPTER TWO

Spike and I made it out of my bedroom eventually, although before I joined the crowd milling about in the living room and dining room, I made a detour to the bathroom to bathe my eyes in cool water. It didn't help much, but I doubted anyone would criticize my appearance. Puffy eyes for the sake of a deceased husband weren't considered unfashionable, and the rest of me was quite fashionable, mainly because I made all my clothes.

Goodness gracious, but people had been generous with the flowers! There were floral arrangements everywhere, on every surface, on the fireplace mantel, on the china hutch, on the piano, and even residing in the odd corner. When I looked at the side porch, I saw flowers there, too. I determined to ask Mrs. Wilson, our neighbor to the north, if she'd like to relieve us of a couple of bouquets. She probably would be pleased. After all, it wasn't every day a person got store-bought flowers.

My floral thoughts were interrupted when Mrs. Pinkerton rushed up to me. "Oh, Daisy, I'm so terribly sorry!" She burst into tears.

"Thank you, Missus Pinkerton."

Harold and Del followed on her heels, and as Harold gently guided his mother away—she can be a rather trying woman even at the best of times—Del said, "I know it's trite to say so, Daisy, but the service was lovely."

"Thanks, Del. The day is lovely."

He heaved an enormous sigh. "Yes. It is. Too pretty for the

funeral of such a young man."

Del had been a soldier during the Great War, too. In fact, when I'd first seen him at Mrs. Pinkerton's house, I'd almost suffered a spasm because he'd reminded me so much of my Billy when he was well and whole.

"You doing all right, Daisy?" asked Harold, who'd deposited his mother somewhere and come back to give me his support.

"Thanks, Harold. As well as can be expected, I guess."

"In a way," said Dr. Benjamin, who'd sidled over to join us, "you know this is the best thing that could have happened, don't you, Daisy?"

I smiled at him through my tears. What I wanted to do was hug him. "I know. And I want to thank you for always being available to us, Doc. I don't know how we'd have survived these past years without your help and advice."

The good doctor shook his head. "It's a crime, is what it is, what that war did to the young men in our country."

He was right, we all knew it, and so we only nodded our agreement.

"May I bring you something, Daisy? Some punch or something?"

Dear Flossie looked quite worried about me. She was a sweet thing, a former gangster's moll who'd seen the error of her ways and managed to end up in the loving arms of Johnny Buckingham. Johnny, by the way, was another casualty of the war, although he'd survived his descent into alcohol and melancholy and come out a better man. He'd helped me a lot over the years, too.

"Maybe some punch, Flossie. Thank you."

"You need to eat something, my dear," said Dr. Benjamin.

The mere thought of food made my stomach rebel. It had never done that before when confronted with the notion of eating. How odd. "I'll have something a little later," I promised.

"See that you do." He sounded stern for effect. I don't think there was a true stern bone in that man's body.

"Is there anything I can get you, Daisy?"

When I looked up to see who'd asked the question, which had sounded tentative, I was surprised to find it had been Sam Rotondo. I wouldn't have pegged him as having a tentative bone in his body, but I guess none of us really knows another person completely. I decided, on this day that was clearly painful for the both of us, I'd treat Sam as a human being and not an enemy, which was something of a departure for me. On the other hand, I wasn't trying to get away with anything that day, either, so maybe it worked both ways.

"Thanks, Sam. Flossie's getting me some punch. I don't really care for anything else right now."

A furrow appeared between his eyebrows. "You need to eat something," he said.

Oh, boy. Here was I, Daisy Gumm Majesty, who, while not fat, was about as far from the slim and boyish model of young womanhood then in fashion as a woman could get, being pressed to eat by a doctor and a police detective. "I won't starve, Sam. You know that." The good Lord knew he'd eaten Aunt Vi's delicious food often enough to have seen for himself that I wasn't about to die of hunger. Sometimes I thought Sam spent more time in our house than in his own, wherever that was.

"Good," he said. Then he shuffled around for a second or two and blurted out, "When Margaret died, I couldn't eat for weeks. Got so skinny, my mother feared for my life. Just be sure you eat, whether you want to or not." And with that, he turned and marched away, leaving me blinking.

Evidently Sam Rotondo was taking to heart Billy's request that he take care of me. This might turn out to be a problem given the state of our relationship, which was rocky at best.

"Who's Margaret?" whispered Harold as Sam walked off.

"His late wife. She died of tuberculosis shortly after they moved to Pasadena."

"I didn't know he'd ever been married." It sounded as though the notion of Sam having a wife came as a surprise to Harold. I couldn't fault him for that. Sam didn't go around spreading warmth and cozy feelings right and left.

"Yes." I sighed. "He's not such a bad person, I guess."

"Hmm. Well, it's nice that he's trying to look out for you," said Harold doubtfully. He and Sam weren't best buddies, because Sam disapproved of Harold and Del.

"I suppose," said I, giving the matter no more thought. Heck, I didn't have the energy to think. Enervated probably best describes my overall state of being.

Mrs. Bissell, who had given me Spike after I'd performed an exorcism on her basement—a long story I won't go into here—came over just then and said, "I'm so terribly sorry, dear. I think the Kaiser should be tried and hanged for war crimes."

"I absolutely agree with you, Missus Bissell. Thank you for coming."

"Spike is looking well, dear. You're doing a wonderful job with him."

That was nice to hear, and I was about to tell her so, when a honking voice spoke up at my right elbow. If I'd had the energy, I might have jumped. "She certainly is. Why, that dog of hers and Mister Majesty's came in first at my last obedience training class."

This piece of information was delivered in her characteristic loud, hollow voice by Mrs. Pansy Hanratty, who had indeed instructed Billy and me in how to train our dog at the Pasanita Dog Obedience School. In fact, our last lesson, the one in which Spike had ended up at the head of his class, had been held only a week before Billy's death. It seemed like a lifetime ago, and it hadn't even been two weeks. Funny how time has a habit of speeding up and slowing down when you aren't watching.

"Excellent," said Mrs. Bissell. I got the impression she and Mrs. Hanratty already knew each other, because they moseyed off together, leaving me with my friends. Both ladies were deeply involved with dogs. Mrs. Hanratty taught people how to make them obey. Mrs. Bissell bred dachshunds. Her major ambition in life was to show a dog at the American Kennel Club's Westminster Dog Show one day.

When you have enough money, I suppose your ambitions alter to suit your circumstances. Most of the Gumms and Majestys of the world were only concerned with making a living from one day to the next.

Flossie appeared with my punch and Johnny, who eyed me with sympathetic understanding. "Any time you need a shoulder, Daisy, you know mine's available," he told me with a smile.

"Thanks, Johnny. I'm surprised you can still hear out of those ears of yours, I've poured so much junk into them."

"Nonsense. That's what I'm in this world for. If you need us for anything at all, Flossie and I will always be available for you."

He meant it, too. That's what I mean about the Salvation Army. They don't care if you're rich or poor or considered "good" or "bad" by society at large; the Army loves you anyway, and will help you with anything from food and clothes to counseling. Great organization, in my opinion, which isn't universally shared by my Methodist cohorts.

"Thanks, guys. I couldn't ask for better friends." My tearstained gaze encompassed Flossie, Johnny, Harold and Del . . . and Sam Rotondo, who had suddenly reappeared, my father at his elbow.

Pa was clearly as upset as I. He had loved Billy like another son. My brother Walter was there that day with his wife Jeanette, as was my sister Daphne and her husband Daniel. Daphne and Daniel's two daughters, Polly and Peggy, were staying with a friend for the day, since neither Daphne nor Daniel thought a funeral appropriate for children their age. That suited me just fine. I love my nieces, but I didn't want to bother with them that day, of all days.

"You doing all right, honey?" asked Pa, looking as if he was about to have another heart attack.

His pallor worried me. "I'm all right, but I think you need to sit down and rest, Pa. Here, why don't you and Sam chat with Walter over there on the sofa? I'll bring you a plate of food." I took Pa's arm to lead him to the sofa. Sam, taking his other arm, meekly followed my lead. This seemed most unusual behavior for Sam—until I remembered that he'd just lost his best friend. If I could only keep that salient fact in mind, I'm sure I'd not be so suspicious of Sam all the time.

Walter jumped to his feet when he saw us approaching. "Daisy! Are you doing any better now?" He'd witnessed my collapse at the door, I presume.

Jeanette slapped his arm. "How can you ask such a question?" She rose to meet me and give me a hug, joggling my glass of punch slightly. "Don't pay any attention to Walter, Daisy. I know you must be perfectly miserable. I know I would be."

It's nice she understood. "It's . . . hard," I said, and then my throat closed up and my eyes filled with tears again. Rats!

She put an arm around my shoulder, dislodging Pa and Sam, and sat me on the sofa. I sipped some punch, which more or less reopened my throat. I forgot all about getting Pa a plate of food, but I don't think he remembered I'd offered to get him one anyway. We were all fumbling around in a state of confusion that day.

"Daisy, I just wanted you to know how very sorry I am for your loss."

When I glanced up, I saw Miss Emmaline Castleton, of the fabulously wealthy Castleton family. Heck, it was in a hospital named for her father in which Billy'd died. She'd once explained to me how her father and his partners, after grinding the competition under their heels and killing thousands of Chinamen and Irishmen on their railroads, had retired to do good works, evidently believing a number of good works could erase their past misdeeds. As she'd told me: folks hadn't called Mr. Castleton and his cronies robber barons for nothing. Now people called them philanthropists. Life's funny that way.

I took the hand she held out to me. "Thank you for coming, Emmaline."

She shook her head, looking close to tears herself. "I couldn't stay away."

Miss Emmaline Castleton had lost the man she loved during the war, too. Only his life had been temporarily saved by—of all unlikely creatures—a German soldier. But that's another story I won't tell here. I just wanted you to know that, however disparate our circumstances, the war had leveled social barriers between Miss Castleton and me.

"I understand," I said honestly.

"I know you do." She heaved a sigh. "But I suppose I'd best be getting along. Please come to me if there's anything at all I can do for you." With a shake of her head, she said, "Although I don't know what that might be. I certainly can't erase the past."

"None of us can," I said, appreciating her a lot in that moment.

As Emmaline Castleton maneuvered through the crowd toward the front door, Jeanette said, "Who was that, Daisy?"

"Oh," I said. "I'm sorry. I forgot to introduce you."

"Never mind that. But who was she? She looked . . . rich."

I almost chuckled. "She is. Very. That was Emmaline Castleton."

Jeanette's eyes went wide. "Castleton of the . . ."

"Yes. Emmaline Castleton of the Castletons."

"My goodness. I didn't know you knew each other."

"Yes. Well, we met not long ago and under . . ." I paused. I really didn't want to go into it all there and then. "Well, it was kind of a surprise to meet her. But she's very nice."

"She must be," said Jeanette dubiously.

How was I ever going to get over Billy's death? Had Emmaline Castleton managed to overcome the death of her own love, Stephen Allison, who'd died in Flanders about the same time Billy was wounded? Does one ever truly "get over" the death of the love of one's life? I wanted to ask someone how long the exquisite pain would last and wished I'd asked Emmaline when I'd had the opportunity. Would the intense agony subside one day, leaving me merely aching inwardly? Unfortunately, the only person whom I knew had lost a marriage partner was Sam Rotondo, and I didn't feel comfortable asking him questions like that. Well, Aunt Vi's husband had died years ago. Maybe I'd ask her. But no. She'd also lost her only son in the war, and I didn't want to bring *that* awful memory to her mind again.

Oddly enough, Sam plunked himself on the sofa next to me so that I was sandwiched between him and Jeanette. Even more oddly, he said very softly in my ear, "You're going to hurt for a long time, Daisy. You'll feel like somebody's ripped out your heart and stamped all over it for weeks and weeks. Maybe months. Hell, maybe even years. Eventually you'll stop hurting as much as you do right now."

I turned to gape at him. "I beg your pardon?"

"I've been through it."

His words gave me pause. "Yes. I know you have. You know

exactly what I'm feeling right now, don't you?"

"Definitely. You'll never stop . . . missing him, but you won't feel this bad forever."

"Thank you, Sam," I said, meaning it sincerely. "I was pondering the answer to that exact question just now. How long will I hurt this badly, I mean."

To my utter astonishment, his face flushed. Sam Rotondo. A man whom I hadn't believed possessed a single human emotion until quite recently.

"Well, I know what it's like. When I lost Margaret, I . . . well, it was hard to go on, I guess is what I mean. But you do what you have to do in this world, I reckon."

"I reckon." Which meant I'd have to get back to raising the dead for rich people eventually. At that particular moment, I couldn't bear the thought.

"But take your time. You're not hurting for money, are you? Because if you are—"

"No!" I hadn't meant to say the word so loudly. Sam's eyebrows lowered into a V over his nose. "I'm sorry, Sam. But we're not hurting for money. Thank God," I added, both because I meant it and because it was the truth.

He maintained a stony silence for a few moments. I heard bits of conversation wafting around us: soft, dignified, subdued. No laughter anywhere in the room. When Billy and I first began "courting"—I believe that's the appropriate word, even though I'd known I'd marry him when I was four years old—there had always been laughter and good humor wherever we were. How times changed.

"You'll go back to your regular line of work?" Sam asked eventually. He didn't approve of what I did for a living any more than Billy had. No surprise there, since the police department tried to keep "fortune-tellers" off the street. But I wasn't a fortune-teller. I was a spiritualist medium, and there's a big difference. Neither Sam nor Billy could ever be made to acknowledge the difference, but that didn't mean it didn't exist.

I didn't want to think about work, even though I would have to go back to it eventually. Still had to help support my folks and Vi, and my income was greater than anyone else's in the family. So, yes, I'd go back to work. But I didn't want to talk about it then.

Nevertheless, I said, "Yes. It's what I do best."

"Huh."

"Don't 'huh' me, Sam Rotondo. You know it's my work. And it helps people."

"Yeah?"

"Yeah."

"Well, if you decide to talk to Billy, let me know, will you? I have a few things to say to him."

He got up and walked toward the dining room, leaving me gawking after him.

CHAPTER THREE

For some reason, I couldn't get myself to climb out of the pit of depression that seemed to engulf me. I really tried to do so. Honest.

After about a month or so, I decided I was fit enough to return to work whether I wanted to or not—and I did not. Anyhow, Mrs. Pinkerton had been calling me daily for a week or more, ostensibly asking about my state of mind and health, but I knew she was teetering on the edge of hysteria and wanted me to commune with the spirits for her. I'd known her more than half my life, after all.

So one day, after toying with some oatmeal—not my favorite breakfast at the best of times because it made me feel kind of sick to my stomach, even when I was feeling perky—the phone rang, it was Mrs. Pinkerton, and I gave up dawdling.

"How are you doing, Daisy?" she asked. She started off all of her telephone calls that way.

Always, before, I'd said something like "I'm still feeling pretty blue, but I'll be up and around again pretty soon." Darned if I was going to let her dictate my life, even though she'd been my best and most dependable client for years. That day, something inside me seemed to tilt sideways, and I decided what the heck. Nothing else seemed to be taking me out of my melancholy; might as well work.

Therefore, I said, my voice sounding dull to my own ears, "I'm still not feeling awfully chipper, but I'm ready to get back to work if you need me, Missus Pinkerton."

Her sigh over the telephone wire nearly blew my eardrum out. "Oh, Daisy!" cried she. "I'm *so* very *glad* you feel well enough to work again!"

"Is something the matter?" I asked politely. My policy is that one should always be polite to one's clients, no matter how stupid, foolish, insane or inane they are, and sometimes I thought Mrs. Pinkerton was all of those things. I don't know how she managed to end up with a son like Harold Kincaid, who was a true, staunch and imminently sane friend. On the other hand, she'd also ended up with a daughter like Anastasia "Stacy" Kincaid, who was a complete and utter poop.

Mrs. Pinkerton sobbed, and I rolled my eyes. Ever since Billy's death I'd noticed that my temper seemed to be exceptionally short. I told myself that I needed to keep a rein on it or I wouldn't have any business left. It was good advice, if I could only follow it.

"It's *Stacy!*" wailed Mrs. Pinkerton. She was a first-class wailer.

Oddly enough, I felt a little better. Stacy Kincaid had always been a stinker. About a year prior, however, she'd undergone something of a transformation, joined the Salvation Army, given up her wicked ways, calmed down, and stopped drinking and smoking and hanging out at speakeasies. I'd been pretty sure the "new" Stacy would crumble eventually. That morning I wasn't sure whether to be happy I'd been proved correct or sorry that poor Mrs. Pinkerton, an ineffectual parent if ever there was one, had to suffer through Stacy's ghastly behavior some more.

"Um . . . I thought she was firmly ensconced in the Salvation Army," I said, trying to lead Mrs. Pinkerton out of her perpetual state of befuddlement and onto coherent ground. This was tough going at the best of times; that day, still mourning my

Billy and with a temper that felt as brittle as a dry twig, it was more difficult than usual.

"She's slipped." Mrs. Pinkerton spoke the two words in a melodramatic whisper.

Gee, what a surprise, I thought. Naturally, I didn't say those words. I was a true professional. What I said was, "I'm so sorry. What happened?"

I noticed again that my voice seemed particularly flat and decided to try to put some animation in it, although I felt about as animated as a dead moth.

"She came home last Saturday, and she'd been *drinking!*"

Big deal.

I knew that wasn't the correct thing to say and scrambled for more appropriate words. None came to mind at once, so I tutted. Tutting and saying things like "mmmm" and "hmmm" and "I see" and "my goodness" can carry you a long way in the spiritualist business.

"And then," continued Mrs. Pinkerton in a gasping whisper, "something even worse happened!"

Golly. How alarming. After not yawning with boredom, I decided to try something different after my next tut. "Have you tried speaking with Captain Buckingham? I'm sure he'd be happy to talk to Stacy and counsel her."

"Captain Buckingham!" Mrs. Pinkerton screeched. She whined, screeched and wailed better than anyone else I'd ever met. "But . . . but he's with the *Salvation Army!*"

"Yes," I said. "I know. It's the Salvation Army and Captain Buckingham that led Stacy in the right direction a year ago. Don't you think he might be of help this time, too?"

"Well . . . I just don't know."

It had long been my contention that if Stacy had been rescued by an Episcopalian, Mrs. Pinkerton would have been pleased as punch. The Salvation Army was beyond the pale to a woman like her, however, no many how many good deeds the organization performed. Still, I knew better than to believe Mrs. Pinkerton might actually behave in a sensible manner for once in her life. What she wanted was for me, a phony if ever there was one, to go over to her house with my tarot cards and my Ouija board and my crystal ball and predict a bright future for her pain-in-the-neck daughter, who had seemed to me to be on a crash course with destiny since the day of her birth. The absurdity of people sometimes amazes me.

Generally, while it amazed me, it didn't annoy me. That day I wanted to reach through the telephone wire and slap Mrs. Kincaid around until she saw the light. However, my annoyance was merely one more impediment that I aimed to swallow. I had a living to earn, after all. My family needed the money I made.

"Would you like me to come over, Missus Pinkerton?" I asked sweetly, bowing to the inevitable.

"Oh, Daisy! Will you? I'd *so* appreciate it!"

"Of course I will." If I were any sweeter, I'd gather flies. I glanced at the clock on the wall. It was only nine o'clock. Pa had taken Spike for a walk, Ma and Aunt Vi were at work, and I didn't feel like rushing around for the idiot on the other end of the wire. "I'll be able to be at your house at ten-thirty, if that's all right with you." If it wasn't, she could just go hang herself.

I shook my head when that thought entered it. I really had to get my unpleasant impulses under control. Mrs. Pinkerton couldn't help it if she'd been born rich, pampered and stupid, any more than I could help having been born into the struggling lower-middle classes and with something of a brain. The fact that I empathized with bomb-throwing anarchists in those days following Billy's death, I told myself, could be chalked up to my state of bereavement. I didn't believe it, but I kept telling myself so anyway.

"Ten-thirty?" Mrs. Pinkerton sounded disappointed. What she wanted was for me to drop everything and rush to her house.

To heck with that. And never mind that I wasn't doing anything in particular. I refused to rush for someone who preferred to believe in the supernatural trash I dealt out rather than in the realities of life.

"I'm afraid that's the earliest I can be there," I said, still so sweet, my teeth were in danger of rotting away.

"Well, if that's the earliest . . ." Her voice trailed off.

"It is," I said firmly.

"Very well. Thank you, Daisy. I'm so worried, don't you know. I really need you to talk to Rolly for me."

"Yes. I know." Shoot, if I'd had a child like Stacy, I'd have been tempted to kill her long since. Or myself. Maybe the both of us. Once the Kaiser got through with Billy, however, children had been out of the question for us. One more bitter pill to swallow. I tried to comfort myself by reminding myself that if Billy and I *had* been able to have children, we might have had another monster like Stacy, but I didn't believe it.

"Well, thank you, Daisy. I can't wait to see you."

"I'll be there at ten-thirty on the dot," I told her and hung up the 'phone.

Feeling blue and tired and draggy, I dumped out the rest of my oatmeal, something that gave me pause since we Gumms didn't go about wasting food as a rule. However, the mere notion of finishing it made my stomach lurch, so I threw it away. I probably should have saved it and mixed it in with Spike's dinner, but I didn't want Ma or Aunt Vi to know I hadn't eaten.

Then I took a bath, went to the room I used to share with Billy and tried to decide what to wear that day. By that time, August was almost upon us, and the weather was hot as blazes. Mrs. Pinkerton's home was generally cool inside—she was rich enough to be able to afford thick, insulated walls and lots of electrical fans—but I didn't want to burn to death inside our Chevrolet. Another thing: I'd been proud of that automobile when I'd bought it after a happy client had given me a huge bonus for doing something kind for her daughter. Ever since Billy's death, I hadn't been proud of anything at all.

I decided to wear a pretty dark-gray voile dress with a black-embroidered wide boat neck and elbow-length sleeves and a dropped waist, both of which also sported black embroidery—if sported is the right word. The black suited both my position as a grieving widow and my mood. I wore black, low-heeled shoes and a gray straw hat.

There. Nobody could fault me for not being in the pink of fashion, and even if I wasn't clad entirely in black as mourning would dictate, at least I wasn't the least bit colorful. This was particularly true as I hadn't ventured out of doors since the day of Billy's funeral except after evening fell, when I'd take Spike for walks. Therefore, any color had fled my cheeks long since. I didn't feel like talking to the neighbors, which is why I went out only after dark. Silly, I suppose, but that's how I felt about things.

Our neighbors to the north, the Wilsons, had a little boy named Pudge, who was a Boy Scout. Pudge was about as pudgy as a fence post, had freckles that would probably mark him for life as a genial soul, and took to heart the Boy Scout pledge to do a good deed every day. Therefore, every single blasted day since Billy's demise, he'd been coming over and begging me to allow him to do me a good deed. I didn't want to wound the boy, but I didn't want him hanging around, either.

That morning, right after I'd dressed myself for going out, Pa and Spike came home, bearing Pudge with them. I fear I didn't suppress my sigh of annoyance as well as I should have, because Pudge stopped in the doorway, staring at me in dismay. I hadn't meant to hurt his feelings. Curse my bad mood!

Spike, bless him, didn't notice things like people's moods—or if he did, he didn't blame them for them. He bounded up to me, wagging and leaping as if he hadn't seen me for weeks and weeks, rather than the approximately twenty minutes that had elapsed since Pa'd left the house with him.

"I didn't mean to bother you, Missus Majesty," said Pudge in a small voice.

"You're not bothering me, Pudge," I said softly. Heck, it was summer vacation. What else did the kid have to do? Pudge had been "sweet" on me for a long time, and he meant well. "But I really don't need you to do anything right now."

He brightened up a bit. "I thought I could give the dog a bath. Mister Gumm said I could."

I glanced at Pa, who winked at me. In some ways, Pa was like Spike. He knew I was going through a personal sort of hell and didn't hold it against me or tell me to buck up, or say any of the other inane things people say to other people when they're feeling devastated and crushed.

"Then that sounds like a fine idea, Pudge." I also knew, because I'd deduced it a long time ago, that Pudge liked to get his good deed out of the way early in the day. That way, he'd have the rest of the day left to do whatever he darned pleased with his pals. Smart kid, Pudge.

"Want me to use the bathtub?" he asked.

I shrugged. "Sure. Why not? Just be sure to scrub the tub when you're through." I knelt beside Spike and gave him a hug to make up for the indignity Pudge aimed to inflict upon him. Still, a bath wouldn't hurt Spike any.

"I sure will. Thank you, Missus Majesty."

"Thank *you*, Pudge." I think I even managed to smile at the kid.

After Pudge led a bewildered and stubbornly reluctant Spike toward the bathroom at the end of the hallway, Pa said, "You

31

look like you're going out."

"I am." I gave Pa a significant look. "Missus Pinkerton. Stacy's slipped from the straight and narrow path, and Missus P wants to consult Rolly." Rolly was my spirit control. I'll explain more about him later.

Pa rolled his eyes at this news, but only said, "It was good of you to let Pudge do his good deed, sweetheart."

"Well, I suppose Spike can always use a bath."

I was pulling on my gray gloves when Pa said, "Daisy, if you ever need to talk about anything . . ."

He didn't finish his sentence, but I did notice him looking at me with grave concern.

My stupid eyes filled with tears. I wiped them away with the tips of my gloved fingers. "I'm all right, Pa. It's just . . . so hard. You know?"

"I know, sweetheart. You and Billy never even had a chance. But . . . well, your mother and I are a little worried about you, you know. You don't seem to be . . ."

"Pulling myself together and getting on with my life?" I finished for him since he seemed to be stuck.

He shook his head impatiently. "No! For God's sake, you can't just *get over* something like that. You just seem too pale and wan, and . . . well, you seem sad all the time."

I gave his words some serious thought before I responded. Then I said, "I guess you're right. I am sad all the time. For so many years, I honestly thought we'd be all right, Billy and me. Not all right in the normal sense, but . . ." My words gave out, too.

Pa didn't answer in words. He only came over and gave me a hug. "Maybe getting back to work will help lift your spirits a little."

I gave him a wry smile. "Aptly put."

Pa grinned.

It was still early for a ten-thirty appointment, so before I wended my way to Mrs. Pinkerton's mansion on Orange Grove Boulevard—called by some folks "Millionaire's Row" back then—I betook myself to the public library. I remained in charge of getting library books for my family. Now that I didn't have to search out books for Billy, I could still amuse myself by rummaging through the shelves for books my mother, father and aunt might enjoy. And me. I always read mystery novels, although I hadn't been reading much of anything since Billy's funeral. I couldn't seem to concentrate.

Miss Petrie, my special librarian friend, smiled sadly at me when she saw me walk through the front doors of the library. I love that library. It's big and wood-paneled and smells like furniture polish, leather and books. I smiled back and decided it would be polite to speak to Miss Petrie, who always kept books for me that she thought someone in my family might enjoy. She'd been at Billy's funeral, too, and I'd appreciated her attendance.

"Good morning, Daisy. It's good to see you out and about again."

It was? Hadn't I been to the library recently? Thinking about it, I realized I hadn't. Oh, my. That was a lapse indeed. I shook my head. "I guess nobody's been reading much in our house recently. But I aim to make up for that today." I tried to sound jolly and didn't succeed.

"I've saved some books for you. I know your father likes Mister Burroughs' books, as your . . ."

"Yes," I said, seeing she thought she'd blundered. "Billy loved Mister Burroughs' books, and so does Pa. What do you have?"

She brightened slightly. "Well, it's not a Tarzan book, but *The Chessmen of Mars* has just come out, and I have that here behind the desk." She handed me the book. It had a ripsnorting cover, and I was sure Pa would love it.

"Thank you. You're very nice to do this for us."

"It's my pleasure, Daisy. I just love it when an entire family enjoys reading."

"We sure do," I said, wishing the conversation was over. It wasn't. "And here. I've got something for you, too. *Captain Blood.*" She glanced around furtively. "It's a very romantic adventure. I hope you enjoy it as much as I did."

"Thank you. I probably will. I like romantic adventure stories. Um . . . do you have any mysteries?"

This time her smile seemed perkier. "Oh, my, yes. I've saved you *The Red House Mystery*, by A.A. Milne—"

"I've never heard of him."

"I believe this is his first book. He's written articles for *Punch,* which is a British magazine, and I believe he writes plays, too." She giggled softly. "Anyhow, as the title says, this book is a mystery story, and I enjoyed it very much. And I also saved you *The Man Who Knew Too Much* and *The Adventures of Sally.*"

G.K. Chesterton and P.G. Wodehouse. Add those writers to A.A. Milne, and one would think a person had to use only his initials in order to get a book published those days. "Thank you very much," I said again. "I truly appreciate your help." I hesitated for a second or two and then added, "Especially now."

Miss Petrie's eyes filled with tears, and I felt like a brute. But I'd meant my words sincerely.

I was beginning to feel as though I couldn't do anything right.

CHAPTER FOUR

The feeling didn't last. The moment I pulled up to the huge wrought-iron gate in front of the Pinkerton estate, Mrs. Pinkerton's gatekeeper, Jackson, said, "Good to see you again, Miss Daisy. The missus has been feeling right poorly of late."

Jackson hadn't come to Billy's funeral, although I'd have been glad to have him there. But he was a colored gentleman, and I suppose he'd have felt out of place amongst all the white folk in attendance. He did send me a note, though, and I cherished it along with all the other cards and notes I'd received from friends and family.

As the huge gate creaked open, aided, I'm sure, by Jackson having pushed a button from inside his gatehouse, I said, "I'm sorry to hear it, Jackson. She told me Stacy's started acting up again."

He shook his head. "That girl needs a switch, is what she needs."

"I'm afraid it's too late for that now. She needed a switch when she was five or six. Now I think she needs a bullet."

Good Lord! I don't think I'd ever uttered so ruthless a comment aloud—although I'd thought that and worse more than once.

But good old Jackson only grinned, his white teeth a sparkling contrast to his dark face. "You got that right, Miss Daisy."

The gate was open, and I drove on through, waving back at Jackson and feeling minimally better that at least somebody agreed with me about the Stacy Kincaid situation. Well . . . Billy had, too, but he was dead.

There went my mood, crashing through the floorboards of our Chevrolet. I cursed myself for thinking about Billy just then.

A surprise awaited me when I parked the car in the circular drive in front of the Pinkertons' massive front porch. Feather-stone, who had been Mrs. Pinkerton's butler for as long as I'd known her, had the door open and was waiting for me even before I climbed the porch steps. This boded ill, in my opinion. Featherstone, the most correct and erect butler I'd ever seen, and who had appeared to me to be the epitome of the butlerine arts for decades, never did anything that might be considered unusual. The fact that he'd anticipated my arrival and had actu-ally opened the door before I'd rung the bell worried me.

"Good heavens, Featherstone, has the sky fallen?" I asked. For some reason, I always joked with Featherstone—probably because he never, ever reacted. As I said, he was the perfect butler. I think butlering was in his genes or something.

"Missus Pinkerton has been eagerly awaiting your arrival, Missus Majesty," said Featherstone in his upper-crust English accent. He was ever so much more upper-crust than I, a fact that used to make me laugh when I was home. But in those days after I lost my Billy, nothing could make me laugh.

"Lead me on, then, Featherstone. I'll brace my nerves on the way."

This was another thing that always happened: although I'd been coming to that mansion on Orange Grove forever and knew pretty much where every room in the house was, Feather-stone always led me to the front parlor. Or, rather, the *drawing room,* as Mrs. Pinkerton called it. Looked like a big living room or parlor to me, but I'd been born a Gumm. We Gumms didn't have *drawing rooms.*

Even before Featherstone opened the door to the drawing room, I knew I was in for trouble because I could hear Mrs. Pinkerton weeping. Oh, boy. Just what I needed. An hysterical woman whose daughter was misbehaving. Shoot, she should be used to Stacy's rotten antics by that point in time. She must have got out of practice during the year or so Stacy had behaved herself.

When Featherstone opened the door, however, I realized things were a good deal worse than I'd imagined they'd be. Harold Kincaid, who, as I've mentioned, was a great pal of mine, was there, trying to comfort his mother.

Harold wasn't the problem. The problem was that Sam Rotondo was also there. Oh, dear. If Sam was there, Stacy must have done something particularly bad.

As soon as he saw me, Sam rolled his eyes. I resented that. I scowled back at him.

"What are you doing here?" Sam asked in a curt grumble.

"My mother called her and asked her to come," said Harold, sounding every bit as curt and perhaps even more angry than Sam had sounded.

Mrs. Pinkerton wrenched herself out of her son's arms and made a dash at me. I fortified myself by grabbing hold of a medallion-backed chair before she flung herself upon me. I'm not sure if I've described Mrs. Pinkerton, but she was a nice-looking, if slightly overweight, lady in her middle years, and she was a good deal taller than I, who am only five-three or thereabouts. At any rate, I managed to keep us both upright by clinging like mad to the chair. Fortunately, Harold was right behind her, and he managed to haul her away before she, the chair, and I could all fall over backwards.

"Mother. Take it easy. Daisy's here to help you. She can't help if you damage her."

"*Damage* her! Oh, Harold! Oh, Daisy! Oh, I'm so, so sorry!"

And she plumped herself on the same chair to which I'd been clinging, buried her face in her hands and continued to sob. I blew out a breath and glanced from Harold to Sam and back again.

"All right," I said, forsaking my well-modulated spiritualist's voice for the nonce. "Somebody had better tell me what's going on here. Has Stacy done something truly criminal this time?"

I probably shouldn't have said that, since it precipitated a loud wail from Mrs. Pinkerton, but, as I've said more than once already, my temper wasn't awfully steady in those days.

"She was picked up in a raid in a speakeasy," said Harold bluntly. "Drinking is illegal in the first place, but this time she managed to slug a copper as she tried to escape. There was quite a to-do before they finally got her under control and into the paddy wagon."

"Oh, Harold!" sobbed Mrs. Pinkerton. We all ignored her.

"Criminal assault against an officer of the law," said Sam in his policeman-like voice, which was very crisp and severe, "is a serious violation."

"She punched a cop? What was the idiot thinking?"

Another anguished wail from the chair. Again, we all ignored it.

"She wasn't thinking. She was drunk," said Harold, rather baldly, considering we were in the presence of his mother, of whom he was generally quite considerate. I guess he was as sick as I was of Stacy and his mother's incompetence in dealing with her.

"She was belligerent and didn't come peacefully. After she punched the officer, she tried to run away. Then she kicked and scratched until another police officer managed to get handcuffs on her. When we finally got her to the police station, she kicked a policewoman and knocked her down."

"Good Lord. Even for Stacy, that's pretty bad," said I, not

guarding my tongue as I should have done. After all, my living depended on idiots like Mrs. Pinkerton, and the more trouble her daughter gave her, the better off my finances would be. If you wanted to look at the matter from that point of view, which I didn't, mainly because Stacy Kincaid made me sick.

"Oh, *Daisy!*" cried Mrs. Pinkerton. "Whatever shall I *do?*"

Harold, Sam and I eyed one another for a moment, and then we all looked at Mrs. Pinkerton. Harold tilted his head to one side. Sam scowled. I decided it was up to me. "My suggestion is that you leave her in jail and not bail her out this time, Missus Pinkerton. She'll never learn how to behave if you keep taking care of things after she breaks the law and ends up in the slammer. She needs to learn to be responsible for her own behavior someday. She's no longer a child. And I still believe you need to place a telephone call to Captain Buckingham. If anyone in the world has any patience left for your daughter, it's Johnny Buckingham."

Mrs. Pinkerton howled. It made an interesting change from wailing, although it was hard on the ears.

"Exactly what I told her," said Harold. "You have to stop letting her get away with murder, Mother. Or one day, she might just think she *can* get away with murder."

Wow, that was brutal. I was being ever so much more candid about Stacy and what I thought of her than I usually was, but even I, in my bad mood, wouldn't say anything like that to Stacy's poor mother, whom I didn't respect, but whom I liked a lot in spite of herself.

"*No!*" cried Mrs. Pinkerton, horrified into shrieking her denial.

"But yes, Mother. If you don't believe me, ask this nice detective here." Harold gave Sam a sugary smile.

Sam returned Harold's smile with another grumpy frown. "Your daughter has been in trouble for breaking the law and been arrested four times, Missus Pinkerton. It's time somebody did something, and I agree with Missus Majesty and Mister Kincaid. Let her pay the consequences for her actions for once." He shot me a grimace. "And it probably wouldn't hurt to call the Salvation Army. They helped her before."

I could tell it galled him to say those words, but they were the truth.

"Oh, my goodness!" howled Mrs. Pinkerton, although less loudly than before.

I was curious. "What set her off this time? I thought she was really happy at the Salvation Army. Her association there seemed to have turned her life around. How'd she slip?"

"I think some of her old friends kept ribbing her about her change of habits, and she finally succumbed," said Harold. "No strength of character, my sister."

"*Harold!*" screeched Mrs. Pinkerton. "How can you *say* such a thing?"

"Because it's the truth, Mother," said Harold in a voice I'd never heard him use to his mother before.

As little as I approved of the way Mrs. Pinkerton allowed her daughter to run roughshod over her, even I winced at his tone. When I glanced at Sam, I noticed he had a small, unpleasant smile on his face, as if he agreed with Harold and was glad someone besides he himself was telling Mrs. Pinkerton the ugly truth. Being a policeman in a rich woman's house, he couldn't be as brutally honest as Harold.

It seemed to me that all this chitchat wasn't getting us anywhere. I made a decision to move things along. "Missus Pinkerton, please try to calm down. Stacy's in jail, and there's nothing you can do for her at the moment."

"Oh, Daisy!" At least this wail was softer than her prior several.

I knelt beside her and put a gentle hand on her shaking

shoulder. Although I didn't feel like it, I donned my spiritualist persona and made my voice a soft murmur. "It's time to calm down and allow the spirits to guide you." I could practically feel Sam rolling his eyes again, curse him. Nevertheless, I persevered. "I think what you need to do is consult the cards and perhaps the Ouija board. Harold and Detective Rotondo are absolutely right, you know. Stacy needs to learn how to control her own behavior and take the consequences when she does bad things. You know that in your heart, don't you?"

She sniffled pathetically. "That—that's what Algie said, too."

Her new husband's name was Algernon Pinkerton. He was a very nice man and most unlike Harold and Stacy's rat of a father. Still, I don't think I'd like anyone to call me Algie, which sounds like something you'd scrape off the bottom of a river rock. However, he was rich and I wasn't, so there you go. I'm not sure what that means, but it's always been sort of a guiding principal in my life, mainly because I make my living dealing with gullible rich people with more money than sense.

"So are we through here?" asked Sam, as if he was impatient to get going. It occurred to me to wonder why he was there. It seemed to me that a regular old policeman could have told Mrs. Pinkerton about her wayward daughter. On the other hand, the police treated the wealthy people in town differently from the way they treated the rest of us, whether they wanted to admit it or not, so maybe that explained his presence.

I glanced up at Harold, being still on my knees trying to comfort his mother. Harold answered Sam. "Yes. I think so. Daisy will be able to help you better than anyone else in this situation."

I think Sam said, "Good God," but the words were so soft, I'm not sure.

"Let me see you to the door, Detective Rotondo, and we can leave my mother to Daisy's tender ministrations."

My knees creaked a little when I rose, and I nodded to Harold. He made a gesture indicating I should telephone him when I was through dealing with his mother, and I nodded again to indicate I'd understood. After I stood, I didn't have to rearrange my dress, which slid neatly into place. That had never happened before due to the unseemly curves my body possessed. Maybe I'd lost a little weight since Billy's demise. Wouldn't hurt me, I supposed, as the fit of my dress proved.

"I'll be in touch, Missus Pinkerton," said Sam in his official policeman's voice. "I'm glad Missus Majesty is here to assist you." He gave me a look I didn't appreciate one bit, although I couldn't tell him so right then.

The two men left the room, and I was left with the quivering emotional jelly that was Mrs. Pinkerton.

I don't suppose you've ever wondered about what I'm going to say next, but it was important to me: why in the name of God are people more willing to accept trash from someone like me, a phony spiritualist medium, than they were from an experienced police officer? Although I'd been doing my spiritualist routine for more than a decade, I still couldn't figure it out. It was just as well they did, or I'd probably have to get a job as a clerk at Nash's Dry Goods and Department Store, but it points out a curious aspect of human nature.

Mrs. Pinkerton, with much assistance from me, managed to get herself from the chair to the sofa, where she more or less fell into a seated position. She looked up at me with swollen, watery eyes, and I mentally cursed Stacy Kincaid from Pasadena to Kingdom Come.

Why was it, I asked myself—and perhaps God—did a good man like Billy, who was hardworking and responsible, have to die, when foolhardy, worthless specimens like Stacy Kincaid remained to pollute the earth with their ugliness and bad actions? As ever, I received no answer, either from myself or from

God. It pains me to say so, but I resented God a good deal in those days. According to all the folks who claimed to know such things, God is always with us, and He supposedly answered prayers. So how come I couldn't get a simple answer to a simple question? Oh, never mind.

Therefore, I pulled the medallion-backed chair over to the table in front of the sofa so that I was face to face with Mrs. Pinkerton. "I believe we should consult the cards first."

"Do you really think so, dear? I did so hope Rolly could offer me some aid and comfort."

See what I mean? She wanted to hear from Rolly, my totally imaginary spirit control whom I'd thought up when I was ten years old. What's more, in my youthful eagerness I'd given him a history and a Scottish accent. Back then, I'd thought it would be romantic if Rolly and I had been soul mates and he'd followed me through all my incarnations since eleventh-century Scotland, where he'd been a soldier and we'd been married and had five sons together. I'd managed the Scottish accent thanks to the little Scottish girl who went to grade school with me. Since my tenth year I'd sometimes wished I'd given him a more sophisticated name, but what can you expect from a ten-year-old? Anyhow, most of my clients thought his name was spelled Raleigh, so I don't suppose it mattered much.

"We'll consult with Rolly after I read the cards for you," I said firmly. Drat the woman; she wasn't going to dictate *my* actions. If she took hell from her daughter, she could take spiritual advice from me the way I chose to deliver it.

I guess I was still in a pretty rotten mood, huh?

CHAPTER FIVE

Naturally, since I was the one manipulating the cards and the Ouija board, both the cards and Rolly told Mrs. Pinkerton exactly what Sam, Harold and I had already told her.

The cards, which I dealt out in a Celtic Cross pattern, told Mrs. Pinkerton that she would have to endure some rough days ahead, but that if she did what she needed to do—it didn't pay to be too specific about these things—her life would resume a pleasant course again soon. Anyhow, Sam, Harold and I had already told her what she needed to know. She wasn't the brightest woman on earth, but she must have got the picture by that time.

"Oh, dear. Oh, dear," said Mrs. Pinkerton after the reading. "I don't really know how to make Stacy behave, Daisy. I truly don't."

Good Lord. "I think the cards are saying you need to be firm with her," I said, knowing even as I did so that Mrs. Pinkerton was about as firm as whipped cream.

"I suppose that must be it," she said.

So then I hauled out the Ouija board. I always kept it in a little drawstring bag I'd made for it and, while it was probably one of the very first Ouija boards ever marketed in 1903 or thereabouts, I'd polished it up some. Mrs. Pinkerton always loved chatting with Rolly, although I sensed she wasn't going to enjoy that day's session as much as usual, mainly because I was in such a lousy temper. As a rule, the Ouija board spells out the answers to people's questions and Rolly only showed up to speak during séances, but since we weren't in séance mode that day, I had him speak, through me, to Mrs. Pinkerton. I pulled the draperies so the room would be dark in order to further the pretense. Then I got to work.

"Och," I had Rolly say in my Rolly-voice, which was about an octave lower than my normal speaking voice, "the poor woman shouldn't have to take grief from her child. Her child should be an aid and comfort to her. Tch, tch. 'Tis a shame, that is. She needs to learn a lesson, that daughter of hers."

"Oh, Rolly!" wailed Mrs. Pinkerton. "But she's my *daughter!*"

"She don't act much like one," said Rolly with more candor than usual.

Did I mention that Rolly's grammar wasn't the best and that he didn't spell very well? Well, he didn't. Remember, he came into hypothetical being when I was ten. I might have been a fairly smart kid, and I'd liked to read even then, but . . . well, I was only ten, you know?

"Rolly," I said, feeling I ought to even though I didn't want to, "Missus Pinkerton needs a dose of comfort."

"She needs comfort from her children, not me," said Rolly, although I really didn't want him to. I couldn't seem to help myself. I had him add, "At least she has a good son," because I thought I should.

"True. Harold is a staunch support to his poor mother," said I, back to being Daisy Majesty again.

"Her daughter needs to take lessons from him, then," Rolly said, once more surprising me. Gee, I didn't recall ever being as viciously honest in a spiritualist session before. I hoped this cranky mood of mine wouldn't last, or I'd be out of work.

Mrs. Pinkerton sobbed. "I know! I know! Oh, I don't know what to do!"

Something occurred to me that I decided Rolly should broach

with Stacy's mother. Therefore, I had him ask, "Does the girl have an income of her own?"

"An income?" repeated Mrs. Pinkerton, blinking.

"Aye. Does the girl have an income of her own? Or does she rely on you for her money?"

"Oh, I see. She gets an allowance."

"From you?"

"Well . . . yes, of course. I'm her . . ." Her voice trailed off. I suspect she'd been about to say she was Stacy's mother—as though that might explain everything—but didn't because she didn't want to hear Rolly say any more bad things about her daughter. If so, she was out of luck.

"Och!" cried Rolly in triumph. "There you have the solution. Withhold her allowance unless she agrees to comply with the rules of your house. This is your house, is it not?"

"Y-yes."

"Then there you have it," said Rolly firmly. "It's your house. You set the rules. Quit paying her for behaving badly. If she kicks up a lather about having her funds cut off, she can get a job and move out."

A job. A place of her own that she had to pay for. Wow. I doubt that Stacy Kincaid had ever considered the possibility that she might actually have to earn the bread she wasted on a daily basis or pay for the room she took up on this green earth. I'm surprised I'd had Rolly voice such a revolutionary suggestion—but I was kind of proud of myself for having done so.

"A-a *job?*" said Mrs. Pinkerton in a quavery voice. "A place of her *own?*"

"Aye. A job. A job of work. Like the rest of the people in the world. Why should she be given money by you, when all she does is get herself into trouble with it? If she don't abide by your rules, she can get a job and a flat somewhere that she pays for with money she earns."

"But . . . but, a job? What could she do?"

"She's not worth much, eh? Has no useful skills? Can't sew or cook or sweep floors?"

Boy, I *really* had to get myself under control. Never, in all my years as a spiritualist medium, had I been so cruelly honest with a client.

Therefore, I, Daisy Majesty, said to my Rolly-self, "Rolly, Stacy was reared as the daughter of a wealthy man and woman. She doesn't know how to do any of those things. That's not really her fault."

"Och. It's as I said: she's worthless."

"Rolly!"

"Oh, dear," said Mrs. Pinkerton in a ragged whisper. "I'm afraid what Rolly is saying is the absolute truth, Daisy."

She feared that, did she? My goodness. Would wonders never cease?

"We were too easy on Stacy. Harold was expected to do chores and help out, but I'm afraid we allowed Stacy to run a little wild."

A *little?* Huh.

" 'Tisn't too late to change that," said Rolly, sounding gruff but kindly. It was about time. I was beginning to despair of myself. "You ought to talk to that minister of hers. That fellow who runs the Salvation Army."

"Um, he doesn't really run it," I felt compelled to say in my Daisy voice.

"Don't matter. He probably has more influence over her than you do at this point."

Egad. What a terrible thing to say to a fond mother!

But Mrs. Pinkerton clutched her hands to her bosom as though Rolly had revealed a miracle, although both Sam and Harold had told her the same thing not a half hour earlier. "You really think so?"

"Aye," said Rolly firmly. "It's not too late. Speak with your husband about it, and take a firm stand, the two of you. In the meantime, my darling Daisy don't know how long your daughter has to stay in jail without being bailed out, but let her stay there. You've bailed her out too many times already. And be sure to talk to that minister of hers."

A silvery tear slid down Mrs. Pinkerton's no-longer-powdered cheeks. She'd cried all her powder off during Sam and Harold's reign, I reckon. "Oh, dear," she whispered. "It's so difficult to treat one's children harshly."

"Harshly?" Rolly gave what I fear was a rather sarcastic laugh. "She's the one who's been treating you harshly, from what I've heard over the years. It's past time she began to behave as a dutiful daughter should. Och, if one of our boys had given us such grief, I'd have switched his backside raw."

Mrs. Pinkerton swallowed audibly. I was kind of appalled myself. As a rule, I didn't favor corporal punishment for children. On the other hand, we were talking about Stacy Kincaid here, and as far as I'm concerned, the only things she deserved were maybe a silver bullet or a stake through the heart.

"Oooh," she cried wretchedly. "I wish Algie were here. He's my strength, you know. I'm sure he'll help me remain firm with Stacy this time."

"If he don't," I had Rolly say in the voice of Doom, "you probably won't get another chance. Your child is playing with fire as a moth is drawn to a candle flame, and she won't be the first bright young thing to burn up as a result of her own stupidity."

Very well. That was it. I couldn't do this any longer, at least not that day. Poor Mrs. Pinkerton was in as feeble a state as I'd ever seen her, and I'd been the one to put her in it. Worse, I was glad of it. Perhaps because I was wallowing in grief, I wanted everyone else in the world to suffer. I don't know, really.

"But my time here is through for today," Rolly said hastily, before I could blurt out any more hurtful words. "Take heart, m'dear. You talk to your Algie and form a plan to deal with your daughter. You needn't let her rule the roost any longer. This is your home, and you should be comfortable in it. You shouldn't have to worry about a spoilt child."

Shut up, Daisy! I commanded myself.

"Thank you for helping us today, Rolly," I said, vowing that he'd say not another word.

"Yes," said Mrs. Pinkerton. "I . . . you've been honest with me, Rolly, and I appreciate it. Although . . . oh, it's so hard!"

Rolly struggled to emerge once more, but I wouldn't let him. Mrs. Pinkerton had never had to work a day in her life, and this postwar world we lived in was nothing like the easygoing days of yesteryear. Well, they'd been easygoing for the likes of her. We Gumms and Majestys had still had to work like the dickens for our livings. Not that I was bitter or anything.

Um . . . I think I just lied about that part. But never mind. I'd known for a long, long time that the world wasn't fair, and that there were the haves and the have-nots populating it. The fact that I fell into the latter category wasn't Mrs. Pinkerton's fault, even if she was a silly woman.

"I'm afraid Rolly has gone back to the Other Side," I said softly, hoping to make up for some of Rolly's earlier harshness. "I hope he hasn't upset you."

She heaved perhaps the largest sigh I'd ever heard and said, "Well . . . yes, he did upset me. But I suppose it's no more than I deserved to hear. He told me the truth."

As sympathetically as I could, because I felt guilty, I said, "I'm afraid he did, but he didn't have to be so mean about it." *Bad Daisy.* "But I think he had a good idea. I'm sure your husband will help you come up with a plan for dealing with Stacy. It can't be easy for him to have her upsetting you all the time. He loves you, after all."

And then, as stupid as it sounds, I almost started crying myself.

However, my words seemed to buck Mrs. Pinkerton up slightly. She squared her shoulders. "Yes. Yes, Algie does love me. And I love him. And he shouldn't have to suffer from Stacy's behavior."

"That's the spirit," I said bracingly.

And then I got out of there as fast as I could. Because I still felt rotten about having upset Mrs. Pinkerton so badly, I made a detour to the kitchen to have a chat with Aunt Vi and see if there wasn't some tea and maybe some cookies there that might make the lady of the house feel better.

When I pushed open the swinging door, Vi had her hands in a bowl of dough, punching it down with a vigor that signified to me she was taking her frustrations out on it. She turned and frowned at me.

Pressing a hand to my heart, I said, "I'm sorry! I didn't mean to upset her so badly."

Vi's expression changed to one of bewilderment. "What are you going on about, Daisy? Upset whom?"

I sank down into a kitchen chair. "Oh, dear. Missus Pinkerton called me because Stacy—"

"That horrible, awful *brat!*" cried Vi, surprising me. "I thought maybe she'd changed her wicked ways for good, but now she's gone and got herself arrested again, and poor Missus Pinkerton is beside herself! To think that good boys like your Billy and my Paul—" But her voice caught on a tear and she couldn't go on.

"Oh, Vi." I leapt from my chair, rushed over to her and threw my arms around her, flour be darned. It had never occurred to me that she might resent Stacy's behavior for the same reason I did: Stacy was alive, and Vi's son and my husband were dead.

Irrational, I suppose, but who ever said human beings were rational?

Vi pulled herself together after about thirty seconds of that. "Oh, dear. I don't want to get flour all over your pretty dress, Daisy."

"Don't worry about my dress, Vi. I don't care about the dress. I feel the same way about Stacy that you do."

Vi wiped her eyes on her apron, smearing flour across her face. Poor thing. She worked *so* hard. Not only did she cook for the Pinkertons and the wretched Stacy, but she also cooked at our house. That was fortunate for us, because neither Ma nor I were very good cooks. Oh, very well; the truth is that I am probably the worst cook in the entire world.

Then I confessed to my aunt, "I'm afraid Rolly told Missus Pinkerton some stuff she didn't want to hear today when he visited from the netherworld."

"Pshaw," said my aunt, who knew as well as I did that Rolly was a figment of my imagination. She didn't mind that, since he earned the family a good deal of money. "Well, I guess it's time somebody told her the truth about that child of hers."

With a heavy sigh, I said, "I hope I wasn't too hard on her. But Stacy shouldn't be allowed to get away with all the stuff she gets away with. And if Missus Pinkerton keeps paying her bail and stuff like that, she'll never learn."

"Missus P is a gentlewoman, Daisy. I don't think they see these things as clearly as us commoners."

With a grin, I said, "Good way to put it. Anyhow, she was pretty upset, and I thought maybe some tea and cookies might cheer her up some. I'll be happy to take a tray in to her."

"Never you mind about that," said Vi, eyeing me critically. "You're the one who needs the cookies. I swear, Daisy Majesty, you're fading away."

I was? I glanced down at my now-floury dress in astonishment. "I am?"

"Well, I don't know how much weight you've lost since your poor Billy died, but you're beginning to look downright scrawny."

"I am?" Boy, that would be a change! Although I faithfully followed the fashions—nobody wants to hire a dowdy spiritualist—I'd always despaired of my curves, which simply couldn't be hidden, even though I wore the requisite bust-flattener.

"But never mind about that. Here. Take this to Missus P. Tell her to buck up and stick to her guns."

Vi handed me a tray, which she must have had ready before I entered the kitchen because I sure hadn't seen her boiling any water or anything, and I took it. "Thanks, Vi."

"Those are Swedish cream cookies. They're full of butter, sugar and cream. Eat a few. They'll put some meat on your bones."

"Thanks, Vi. I sure will."

As I carried the tray back to the drawing room, I eyed it. The Swedish cream cookies were quite pretty and flaky-looking, but the notion of eating one made me feel squeamish. Gee, maybe Vi and the fit of my dress were both right about me losing weight. If they were, it was the only good thing to have come about after Billy's short life ended.

Mrs. Pinkerton was grateful for the tray. She brightened when I entered the room, although she still wore a haggard, careworn expression on her face, and her eyes remained swollen and red-rimmed. I hated Stacy Kincaid in that moment. Not that I didn't generally hate her, but to put a woman like Mrs. Pinkerton—who was kindhearted and nice (even if she was a bit dim)—through such troubles went beyond what any child should inflict upon a parent.

Unclenching my teeth and swallowing the bitter words dancing on my tongue, I smiled at the forlorn mother suffering on her wildly expensive sofa. I guess it was true that money couldn't buy happiness—although I'd just as soon be unhappy in, say, France or somewhere, than in our little bungalow on Marengo. But that's neither here nor there.

"After what Rolly put you through, I thought you might need a bracer," I said softly, effortlessly assuming my sympathetic spiritualist persona in spite of my animosity toward this poor woman's daughter.

"You're always so thoughtful, Daisy."

Tell my mother that, thought I.

"I'm afraid Rolly was a bit . . . ah . . ." For some reason, I ran out of soothing words.

"He told me the truth," said Mrs. Pinkerton.

I set the tray down as silently as a trained servant would have done. "I suppose so, but he was a bit rough about it."

With a wan smile, Mrs. Pinkerton said, "Well, don't forget he's used to being a soldier in Scotland during the Dark Ages. I don't suppose he ever learned how to convey unpleasant news gently."

Maybe he hadn't, but I sure had. If I were rude to an adult whilst growing up, my fanny would know about it for days afterwards. Neither Ma nor Pa stinted on the discipline, although they loved us all—which, come to think of it, might be the reason they were strict. Anyhow, did the Dark Ages include the eleventh century?

What a nonsensical thing to think about right then. I was really off my game. I decided to ignore her comment, even though I suppose it might have been pertinent. "Here, Missus Pinkerton. I understand hot, sweet tea helps people when they're feeling down in the dumps. And these cookies Aunt Vi made look delicious."

"Your aunt is the best cook I've ever met, Daisy. I'm so fortunate to have met both of you."

Now I *really* felt guilty.

I was so relieved when I finally got out of that mansion, I had to lay my head on the steering wheel of the Chevrolet in order to get my wits together before I could drive home.

CHAPTER SIX

I'd taken a cup of tea with Mrs. Pinkerton, although I couldn't handle a cookie, sure that if I ate one of the incredibly rich confections, I'd disgrace myself and throw it up again. What was the matter with me? I'd never in my life had this reaction to food.

Spike's ecstasy upon my return home nearly made me collapse at the front door and burst into tears, exactly as I'd done after Billy's funeral. Boy, there was truly something wrong with me. Not only had I begun to reject food, but I cried at the drop of a hat. When I glanced up from greeting Spike, I saw my father gazing at me with a worried frown on his face. I gave him my best approximation of a smile.

"Hey, Pa. Everything's fine. Well, everything's not fine, but I think Missus Pinkerton has managed to gather the courage to leave her daughter in the clink for once."

The briefest of hesitations preceded Pa saying, "How'd you make her do that? I didn't think she'd ever stand up to that kid of hers."

To Spike's dismay, I stood and brushed off my dress, noticing that flour still clung to it, which might have been the main reason for Spike's disappointment. He loved food the way I used to.

"I didn't do it. Harold, Sam and Rolly did. They all told her the truth. Stacy will never learn to behave if Missus Pinkerton keeps bailing her out when she gets herself into trouble."

"Good for Rolly!" Pa's voice was a little heartier than the occasion called for. "And Sam and Harold, of course."

I recognized an attempt to perk me up when I heard one. Good old Pa. He was the dearest man. "Of course."

"Sam's coming to dinner tonight, by the way," Pa said, peering at me from the corner of his eye as if he expected me to object.

I didn't. "That's nice." Glancing down at my dress, I said, "I'd better get this thing off. It got all floury when I went to the Pinkertons' kitchen to fetch some tea for Missus Pinkerton."

Pa squinted at my dress. "How'd that happen? You don't generally get close enough to flour to get dirty."

I almost chuckled. "You're right about that. But . . ." Oh, dear. I didn't want to tell Aunt Vi's tale for her. But what the heck; I didn't think she'd mind, and I was pretty sure Pa wouldn't let on that I'd ratted her out. "When I got to the kitchen, Vi was punching dough as if it were Stacy Kincaid's face. When I asked her what was wrong, she . . . well, she kind of broke down."

"Vi broke down?" asked Pa with incredulity.

"Yeah. She said she didn't know why people like her Paul and my Billy had to die when vicious idiots like Stacy Kincaid still lived. I got a little flour on my dress when I hugged her."

Pa shook his head sadly. "I understand why she feels that way. And you, too. Your mother and I have wondered the same thing more than once."

I heaved a huge sigh. "I guess we'll never know the answer to that one."

And I departed to my room, which used to be Billy's and mine as I've mentioned several times before, to change clothes. Luckily for me, Spike followed me. I don't know if he was after more flour or more hugs, but I was glad for his company.

Sam arrived for dinner at six that evening, bearing with him a bouquet of flowers. I blinked at him as he stood in the doorway waiting for me to move so he could enter the house. He'd never brought flowers before that I could remember.

"Wow," I said stupidly. "Flowers."

He let out an exasperated grunt and thrust the bouquet at me. "I figured you could use them after having to deal with the Pinkerton woman this morning."

Flabbergasted, I managed to mutter, "It wasn't all that bad."

"I don't believe it. She was hysterical when I got there, and she was hysterical when I left. And she hasn't sent anyone down to the PD to bail her blasted daughter out, either. I figured, since she didn't seem to be listening to her son or me, it was you who convinced her to let Stacy stew in her own juices for once." Then he said irritably, "Can I come in, or do you want us to stand at the front door all evening?"

Good old Sam. Every time I thought he might actually possess a softer side, he set me straight with a vengeance. I stepped back. "Sure. Come on in. I'll . . . find a vase for these. Thank you very much. We'll all enjoy them."

"You're welcome." I don't think I've ever heard a grouchier acceptance of thanks.

Ma and I had already set the table—neither of us could cook, but we did our best to make Vi's life as easy as we could—so I rummaged around in the china cabinet for a vase to put the flowers in. Or in which to put the flowers. I know that latter sentence is correct, but it sounds funny. Anyhow, the flowers were very pretty. There were some yellow roses and some white daisies and some blue something-or-others, and they helped to perk me up slightly. Because I couldn't think of a better place to put the vase once it was filled, I set it in the middle of the dining-room table and stood back to observe the effect. Ma caught me in the act.

"What are you—oh! What pretty flowers. Where'd they come from?"

"Sam brought them."

"How very kind of him. And they look perfect with the tableware, don't they?"

They did. We Gumms didn't have fancy china, but we did have a matched set of dinnerware, augmented with mismatched serving pieces. The tablecloth was white, the plates were white with a little blue floral pattern around the edges, and most of our serving pieces were either white or blue. The flowers looked great.

Sam had studiously avoided me after we met at the door, but when Vi called him and Pa in after Ma and I set dinner on the table—roast pork, mashed potatoes and Brussels sprouts, generally one of my favorite meals—Ma said, "Thank you so much for the flowers, Sam. They're beautiful."

Looking embarrassed, Sam said, "You're welcome. Daisy had a tough job to do this morning and . . . I figured she could use a pick-me-up."

Ma turned to me, her eyes wide. "Oh, dear. What happened, Daisy? I didn't know."

"It was Missus Pinkerton," I said, not really wanting to go into details, mainly because I feared Ma would scold me for being so rough on Mrs. P.

"Good heavens, I thought all was well with her now that she's married that nice man and her daughter has changed her ways."

Sam huffed. "That's the problem. Her daughter has slipped from the straight and narrow. Got herself arrested in a raid on a speakeasy, punched one copper, kicked two others, and got locked up."

Ma's hand flew to cover her mouth. Vi, who sat at the head of the table because she was in charge of the food, huffed. "That daughter of hers ought to be horsewhipped. But Daisy took care of her." The look she gave me appeared suspiciously like a smile of victory.

Goodness. I hadn't expected such a commendation, even though I'd already known Vi appreciated my work that day.

"You did?" Ma sat, too, and picked up her napkin, gazing at me the while. "How'd you do that? I thought the woman was impenetrable."

Sam stifled a guffaw. "Good way to put it."

I sat, too, next to Sam. Ma sat across the table from us, and Pa sat at the foot of the table. I know the arrangements aren't what the etiquette books demand, but they worked for us. "I . . . well, I'm afraid Rolly was pretty hard on her, actually."

"Nuts. She needed to hear the truth."

My eyes narrowed. It wasn't like Sam Rotondo to leap to my defense. Heck, he was generally trying to get me to give up my evil ways—evil meaning my spiritualist line of work. However, I knew better than to question his motives at the table. I'd argued with Sam once or twice in the past, and it always worked out poorly for me because Ma blamed me for being rude to a guest. Huh. By that time, Sam darned near lived at our house. But that's neither here nor there.

"I suppose she did, but you and Harold had already told her the truth."

"People like her don't take sensible advice from legitimate sources. They prefer phony ones like the kind you dish out."

Good old Sam. He never let a compliment linger in the atmosphere. As soon as he delivered one, he followed it up with a body blow.

"Thanks a lot, Sam," I muttered.

"Well, whatever you did, Daisy, it really opened Missus Pinkerton's eyes," Vi said, carving pork and, I think, attempting to steer the conversation away from conflict. "I left the house at three-thirty, and she and Mr. Pinkerton were in the drawing room, having a powwow about Stacy. I heard him tell her she ought to do exactly what Rolly told her to do."

"And you think she'll listen to him?" I asked, hearing the hope in my voice, mainly because I didn't think I could cope with another session at Mrs. Pinkerton's place any time soon.

"She'd better," said Vi with conviction. "That girl is a menace. In fact, she isn't even a girl any longer. She's old enough to know better than to get into trouble the way she does."

I sniffed. "Maybe, but don't forget she's a rich person. She doesn't have anything useful to do."

Vi pursed her lips. "She was doing something worthwhile when she was with the Salvation Army. She even got you to teach that cooking class earlier this year at the Salvation Army."

I shuddered involuntarily. "I'd rather not be reminded of that." That class had been a disaster. The only reason the entire Salvation Army didn't burn down was that Flossie kept a close eye on me, and the book from which I took the dishes we made, *Sixty-Five Delicious Dishes,* was so simple, even I couldn't ruin them. Well . . . actually, I had ruined one, but it wasn't while I was teaching the class, so nobody who mattered ever found out about it.

"Nevertheless, she was being useful. I don't know why she ever left that church."

"I don't either. I hope Missus Pinkerton takes everyone's advice about speaking with Johnny Buckingham, although I don't hold out much hope for that."

"I don't know," said Sam. "Stacy's really stepped in the sh— mud this time. Missus P might decide to talk to the devil himself if she thinks it will do her daughter any good."

"I think Stacy's already too well acquainted with the devil to do Missus Pinkerton any good. She'd be better off talking to Johnny." *Stop it, Daisy!*

But Vi didn't take me to task. "You're right. I hope she does." She passed a plate loaded with roast pork to Sam, who handed it to me, who handed it to Pa. That's how we worked things at our house.

Since I knew I was next on the food chain, so to speak, I said, "Just a little for me, please, Vi. I'm not awfully hungry."

Vi gave me a squinty-eyed stare. "You're wasting away to nothing, Daisy Majesty. You need to eat. You're becoming downright gaunt."

Gaunt? Me? Good heavens. "I'll eat. I promise. I'm just not awfully hungry." A brilliant excuse struck me. "I had cookies and tea with Missus Pinkerton." Okay, so I'd just lied to my wonderful aunt. It wasn't my fault the thought of food made me sick to my stomach, was it?

"That was hours ago," said Vi. "You clean your plate tonight, young lady."

I saluted my aunt. "Yes, ma'am." What the heck. I could sneak pieces of pork to Spike if I felt myself in danger of exploding. Spike even liked Brussels sprouts, bless him. I used to. Until Billy . . . well, never mind.

"Get along with you, Daisy," said Vi. She said that a lot, and I'd never quite understood what it was supposed to mean.

I watched with dismay as she heaped my plate with roast pork. Oh, dear. But I'd deal with it somehow.

She finished serving the rest of the family with pork, and we passed the side dishes around: mashed potatoes, gravy, Brussels sprouts, some of Vi's feather-light dinner rolls and butter. She was an amazing cook.

Then Pa said a short prayer—we didn't go in for long, involved blessings, but preferred to eat our meals hot—and we all dug in. Everyone but me. I toyed with my pork, cutting it into small pieces. I ate a few bites when I felt the eyes of my aunt or my mother on me. And I downed three whole Brussels sprouts and about a tablespoon of potatoes with gravy. I passed on the dinner rolls, hoping nobody would notice.

Good old Spike had a great meal that night. If my appetite didn't improve soon, he'd be fat as a pig.

After supper, Ma and I washed up while Aunt Vi went to the living room to relax and read the newspaper, which she never had time to read in the mornings. It was only fair that she get some time to take it easy. Heck, she cooked all day long. And Ma and I didn't mind washing the dishes, mainly because neither of us could cook a lick and didn't want to learn.

"You didn't eat much, Daisy," my mother said, her voice severe.

"Did too," said I, sounding and feeling like a chastised child.

Ma heaved a sigh. "I don't know what's to become of you."

I didn't respond to that remark because I didn't know what to say. Anyhow, I didn't know what was to become of me, either. If I didn't regain at least a modicum of my spiritualist vigor, I might be waiting tables at the Castleton Hotel's fancy dining room soon.

After I'd dried and put away the last dish, Ma and I took off our aprons, hung them on their hooks, walked back through the dining room and betook ourselves to the living room, where we saw that Pa and Sam had set up the card table and were playing gin rummy.

My heart gave an enormous lurch at the sight. It used to be that Sam, Pa and Billy had played gin rummy of an evening after supper. But now there were only the two of them left. My eyes filled with tears, and I made an abrupt about-face and retreated to the kitchen again.

"Daisy? Are you all right?"

It was Ma. I said, "I'm fine, Ma. Just wanted to get . . . something from my room." Fortunately, I remembered the library books I'd checked out earlier in the day and amended my statement. "I mean the car. I went to the library today."

"Oh, did you?" Ma was pleased. The whole family liked to read.

"Yup."

"Did you find anything for me?" Pa asked, his attention diverted from cards for the moment.

"Sure did. I'll be right back."

Our house had a side door leading to a porch, and I'd parked the Chevrolet in the drive right there in front of the side porch. Glad I'd remembered the books, which I'd shoved into the backseat earlier in the day, I climbed into the machine and gathered them in my arms. Then something inside me seemed to crack open and, laying my head on the top book in the stack, I broke down and cried and cried.

I don't know how long I was in the car ruining library books when the back door of the Chevrolet opened again. Darn it! I hadn't wanted anyone to catch me.

"Move over, Daisy," Sam's gruff voice commanded.

I was so startled, both by the command and the fact that it had come from Sam, that I did what he told me to do. "I . . . I just couldn't stand to . . ." My voice gave out.

"You couldn't stand to see your father and me playing cards when it used to be the three of us. I understand." He put a hand, rather tentatively I thought, on my shoulder.

Wiping my face with the back of my own hand, I glanced at Sam, who looked blurry through my tears, and said merely, "Yes."

"I know." He nodded. "I remember what it was like." Then, shocking me profoundly—I wasn't yet accustomed to Sam being a good guy in my life—he took out a neatly folded handkerchief from his jacket pocket and handed it to me. "Wipe your face." He eyed the books. "And then wipe the books. If you want me to, I'll take the books inside while you go and wash your face."

Astounded, I wiped my face and the books. "Thanks, Sam. Um . . . that would be very nice of you. To take the books in while I try to recover, I mean."

"Happy to help," he said. And, as I waited for him to add something snide or cutting to his announcement, he picked up the books and left the Chevrolet.

Boy, you just never knew, did you?

CHAPTER SEVEN

I never got the chance to thank Sam properly for rescuing me that night, because by the time I felt well enough to rejoin my family, it was bedtime. Then, of course, I felt guilty and decided maybe I should visit him at the police department the following day. He'd hate that. I'd visited him there before, and he always took umbrage. But that day, I'd be there to thank him, and that was different, wasn't it?

The telephone rang as I sat at the breakfast table with Pa, mulling over the problem of Sam and pretending to eat the delicious egg-and-potato casserole Aunt Vi had created for our delectation. She was already at work at Mrs. Pinkerton's house, and Ma had gone to her job, so it was only Pa and me. And Spike, of course. There had been hundreds of time during the last five years when Billy, Pa and I had carried on lively conversations at the breakfast table.

That morning, Pa read one section of the newspaper and I pretended to read another one as I secretly fed portions of my eggs and potatoes to Spike. I took a sideways glance at him and noticed the indentation in his sides where his waist used to nip in didn't nip as much as it used to. Shoot. If only for Spike's sake, I simply *had* to stop feeling sick at the thought of food.

Rescued by the telephone—although I feared it meant another call to Mrs. Pinkerton's house—I got up to answer it, saying lightly, "It's got to be for me." Our telephone hung on the kitchen wall, so wasn't a long walk.

Pa chuckled. "I'm sure it is. Good luck." He knew what a pain in the neck Mrs. Pinkerton was.

I was surprised to hear Harold Kincaid's voice on the other end of the wire. "Daisy Majesty, you were supposed to call me after you left Mother's, but I'm not calling to scold you. You performed a miracle yesterday!" he said without even a "good morning" to start off the conversation.

"I did?"

"You did. Mother has refused to bail Stacy out, and she's not going to appear in court when Stacy's arraigned this morning, either. What's more, she's visiting the Salvation Army Church today to have a chat with your friend Mister Buckingham."

"Good gracious."

"You could say that. What's more, according to your pal Sam—"

"He's not my pal," I said instantly, interrupting Harold.

"I don't know why not. He's not such a bad man. You could do worse."

Speechless, I held the receiver away from my ear and stared at it for a second or two until I heard Harold's sharp "*Daisy!* Are you listening to me?"

Snapped back to attention, I lifted the receiver to my ear again. "I'm sorry, Harold. I . . . dropped the receiver." Lie, lie, lie. Sometimes it seemed all I did back then was lie to the people I loved.

"I said Detective Rotondo told me Stacy's probably going to get three months for her antics this time."

"Three months? You mean three months in jail?"

"Right-o. Three months in the Pasadena City Jail. It's right there behind the police department. I'm so proud of Mother, I'm taking you to lunch today, because it was you who made her stand up to my rotten sister."

"Um . . ." Oh, God. More food I couldn't eat.

"Lunch," said Harold firmly. "I'll pick you up at one."

Hmm. Maybe by one, since I couldn't eat my breakfast, I'd be hungry. Based on the experience of the past month or so, I doubted it, but at least if I went out to dine with Harold, I wouldn't be contributing to turning my formerly slim and trim dachshund into a tugboat.

So I said, "Thanks, Harold. It'll be good to see you under circumstances more pleasant than yesterday's were."

"You betcha, kid."

"Got a date for lunch?" Pa said after I'd replaced the receiver. He knew what Harold was—that is to say, he knew there was no romantic link between us and never would be—but Pa, unlike Billy and Sam, didn't seem to care.

"Yes. Harold says he wants to take me to lunch as a thank-you for getting his mother to see reason as far as Stacy goes." I sat in my chair with a thump. "Sam told Harold he thinks she's going to be sent to jail for three months!"

Oddly enough, I found myself struggling not to feel sorry for Stacy, who had been, until a year or so ago, the bane of my existence. Well, along with Sam. Heck, even after she'd joined the Salvation Army, she'd still managed to plague me in one way or another.

"No more than she deserves," said Pa, who'd always taken a dim view of Stacy's antics.

"I guess you're right. It's just difficult to imagine somebody my age—and a female, to boot—being locked in the jug."

Pa shook his head and turned the page of the newspaper. "Act like a crook, get treated like a crook, rich female or poor male. Most of the time, anyway." Pa knew as well as I did that rich people could get away with bad behavior a lot more easily than poor people could.

"I guess you're right." Since Pa's attention was otherwise engaged, I seized the opportunity, whipped my plate off the table and carried it to the kitchen sink. I heard the newspaper rattle and feared Pa had lowered it to look at me.

"I hope you ate that wonderful breakfast your aunt prepared." Pa's voice seldom sounded severe as Ma's occasionally did, because he was too much of a softy. That morning, however, I detected a definite hardness of tone.

Fortunately for me, I'd been able to scrape my plate's remains into the sink before Pa noticed, so I turned, smiled and showed him my empty plate. "See? I cleaned my plate." There. I didn't even have to lie that time. He couldn't see what was left of my breakfast lying in the sink, from which I aimed to scoop it up and throw it away.

His eyes narrowed. I braced myself. Pa wasn't one to lecture, but he sometimes had a word or two to say about the behavior of his children. "Daisy, I know you miss Billy like fire, but you aren't doing yourself any good by starving to death."

"I'm not starving to death!"

With as stern a look as I'd ever seen on his face, he said, "Go take a good look at yourself in the mirror, Daisy. Your aunt is right. You're wasting away."

"Nuts, Pa. I was too fat before. I'm just having . . . a little trouble eating as much as I used to, is all."

He shook his head, and I could tell he despaired of me, which made me want to cry again. Nuts. How come life was so blasted hard?

Nevertheless, I decided that the whole world couldn't be wrong about my altered appearance, so after I washed up the breakfast dishes, I decided to do what Pa had suggested, and took a good gander at myself in the bedroom mirror. Spike, bearing with him his expanded waistline, trotted along with me, probably in the hope of getting more food. I stripped to my combinations and stared at myself. Then I frowned.

"Heck, Spike, I don't think I look so darned skinny. I look

like I'm supposed to look."

Spike snuffled, and I frowned down at him.

"I do, too. All the fashion magazines claim ladies are supposed to have a slim and boyish figure these days. I've never had one until now."

My image in the mirror did make me think, though. It had only been a little over a month since Billy's funeral. I had no means of weighing myself, but I had to admit that I did look kind of, maybe, *possibly*, the least little bit gaunt. My cheeks seemed to have caved in somehow, and my eyes looked back at me from hollows I'd never noticed before. The faded gray day dress I'd popped on that morning hung on me kind of like it did on the clothesline out back after it had been washed.

"Oh, brother. How can I eat if food makes me sick, Spike?"

Spike wagged his tail. I swear, if that dog couldn't actually talk, he sure could communicate. What he was telling me then was that he'd be more than happy to help me out, and that if I didn't want my food, he'd be delighted to eat it for me.

"But you'll only get fat, Spike, and then Missus Bissell will never forgive me. And neither will Missus Hanratty."

Spike took that opportunity to sit on his hind legs and wave his paws at me. I caved in, plunked myself down on the floor and hugged him. "I do love you very much, Spike. And so did Billy. I think you were the very best present I ever got for him."

With a lick on my chin, Spike agreed with me.

I tried to gussy myself up a bit for Harold. I didn't need another lecture on how skinny I was getting from Harold, of all people, who was supposed to be one of my best friends. My choices were limited since I was still in mourning, the weather remained hot, and I hadn't felt like sewing lately. But I managed to find a lightweight navy-blue suit with a long, straight jacket that went quite a way to disguise the fact that I actually had a waist by that time. Not to mention ribs that stuck out like a skeleton's. With any luck and a dab of powder and paint, Harold wouldn't notice the change in me.

Then I recalled that he'd seen me only the day before.

But he hadn't said anything then, and it wasn't like Harold not to tell me when I looked like hell—not that I ever did. As a rule, Harold only complimented me on my attire. I was a darned good seamstress. I also, as I've said once or twice already, kept strict tabs on the fashion magazines for the sake of my image as a spiritualist. None of your nonsensical Gypsy-type trappings for me, thank you. I not only dressed to perfection, but I'd studiously cultivated the pale-and-interesting look—and that was even before I'd begun avoiding daylight like Count Dracula. I'd also mastered the art of wafting. I tell you, I was *good* at my job.

At least I had been.

But I didn't want to think about that. The doorbell rang at about five minutes past one, and Spike and I raced each other to get to the front door. I didn't want Pa to have to bestir himself. While Dr. Benjamin had recommended him taking walks with Spike, he still had a bum ticker and I didn't want him having any heart attacks on my watch. After losing Billy, I couldn't even bear the thought that Pa might be next.

"Spike, sit," I told my dog. God bless the dog, he sat. It was no fluke that he'd come in first in Mrs. Hanratty's dog obedience class. "Good boy. Stay."

Spike stayed. He was *such* a wonderful dog.

I opened the door, said, "Hey, Harold," and stepped aside so he could enter the house.

He did. Then he said, "Daisy Majesty, you look like hell."

As he bent to pet Spike, whose tail swished across the floor like a dust mop, I felt like applying the sole of my foot to Harold's hind end. "Thanks a lot."

Harold straightened. "I'm serious, Daisy. You're not eating, are you? You must have lost fifty pounds."

"In a little more than a month?" I said, huffy as all get-out. "I don't think so. But thank you so much for the compliment."

"It's not a compliment," Harold said with a frown that appeared more worried than mean-spirited. Harold himself was a bit on the plump side and had been for as long as I'd known him. "I know you're grieving, but you have to take care of yourself, Daisy. You won't do your family any good if you fall ill, you know."

My shoulders slumped. "Oh, Harold, don't you lecture me, too. Please. I've heard it all from my mother and father and aunt and Sam. The thought of food makes me sick to my stomach. I can't help it."

"You can, too, help it," said Harold firmly. "If you can't, who can?"

It was a good question, I supposed. Hanging my head, I whispered, "I don't know. But it's the truth, Harold. I can't seem to force myself to eat. Ever since . . ."

He hugged me. "I know, sweetheart. You miss your Billy."

I nodded, unable to speak.

"But he'd hate it that you've let yourself go so badly."

That snapped me to attention. "I haven't! I haven't either let myself go, Harold Kincaid. Billy's only been gone for a little more than a month, for heaven's sake! Give a girl a break, can't you? Shoot, Queen Victoria mourned her lost Albert for the remainder of her life!"

"In case you haven't noticed recently, you're not Queen Victoria."

I gave him a sharp smack on the arm. "You know what I mean!"

"Yeah, I know what you mean. But this discussion is getting us nowhere. Fetch your hat, and I'll drive us to the Castleton

Hotel. They've got a great lobster salad there that might tempt even you."

My stomach took that opportunity to heave in revolt at the thought, but I didn't let on. Rather, I released Spike from his enforced seatfulness, went to get my hat, said good-bye to my father, gave Spike a farewell pat and left the house with Harold, Spike gazing mournfully after us. *He'd* be more than happy to eat a lobster salad, his big sad eyes seemed to say, and three more after that, along with all the dinner rolls anyone cared to toss him.

Harold owned a bright-red, shiny, snazzy, low-slung Stutz Bearcat, and it stood out like a peacock in a flock of sparrows on our staid, pepper-tree-lined street. I was grateful he'd put the top up on the machine, because I didn't fancy having my hat blown off or my hair messed up. Mind you, since I'd had my hair bobbed a year or so prior, it was a good deal easier to take care of than it had been when it was long, but I still didn't want to be blown to bits.

In spite of Harold's eagle-eyed watchfulness, I couldn't eat too much of my lobster salad, although I did manage several bites. I guess it was tasty, except that it made me want to throw up. The Castleton provided its diners with delicious rolls as an accompaniment to their salads, and I buttered my roll after I tore it into pieces, mainly so Harold couldn't fuss at me anymore about my lack of appetite.

He did anyway. "I know what you're doing, Daisy, and I'm not going to let you get away with it. You're moving the food about on your plate. You're supposed to stick it in your mouth, chew it and swallow it."

Feeling oppressed and beleaguered, I said, "I'm really sorry, Harold. But, honestly, I can't seem to eat very much anymore. I'm sure I'll get over this loss of appetite one day. But for some reason, ever—"

"Yes, I know," he said, cutting me off. "Do you know I even spoke with your pal Johnny Buckingham about you?"

I felt my eyes go round as saucers. "You did *what?*"

"I talked about you with Captain Buckingham. Mother asked me to speak to him about Stacy, even though she'd already done so, so I decided what the hell and told him you were turning into a wraith before everyone's eyes and asked him what he thought might be done for you."

I pressed a hand to my forehead, aghast. "I can't believe you did that, Harold! Johnny and Flossie are going to have their first child any week now, and they don't need my problems heaped on their heads."

Giving an irritated shake of his head, Harold said, "Nuts to that. He volunteered to devote his life to dealing with other people's problems. And we came up with a great idea."

"You did?"

"We did."

The expression of triumph on Harold's face worried me. A lot.

CHAPTER EIGHT

"Harold wants to *what?*" asked Ma, fork held before her in shock, as we sat at the supper table that evening. When I glanced around the table, I saw that Pa and Vi were also staring at me, open-mouthed with astonishment.

Oh, goody.

After heaving a less-than-ecstatic sigh, I explained. "Harold wants to take me to Egypt to get me away from home. He—and he talked to Johnny Buckingham, who agreed with him—thinks that a change of scenery might be what I need to perk me up." As if anything could perk up a grieving widow.

"How nice of him," Ma said at last, her voice faint. She allowed her hand to carry her fork the rest of the way to her mouth. That night it had stabbed a bite of cold roast pork.

Vi had turned the leftover mashed potatoes into potato patties, fried them in butter, and served the pork and potatoes with a nice green salad. And I still could barely tolerate the idea of food, much less eat more than one or two mouthfuls of it.

"That's . . . amazing," said Vi. "Um, why did he decide to take you to Egypt?"

I shrugged. "He says he remembered that Billy always wanted to visit Egypt, and that his mother and Mister Pinkerton enjoyed their visit down the Nile. Or is it up the Nile? I can't remember. Billy would have known." Harold had also said he wanted to see me ride a camel, but I decided not to tell my folks that.

After a deal of thought, Vi said, "I bet you anything this is a thank-you for helping his mother see the light about that daughter of hers."

"Maybe." I nodded, although I doubted Vi's scenario. I'd believed Harold when he'd told me he was going to whisk me away to foreign ports in a mission to heal my heart. The scenario he'd presented at lunch didn't make a lick of sense to me, but I supposed it might be interesting to be sick of food in England, where we'd land first, and then in Egypt. Heck, maybe I could be sick of food in France and Turkey, too, along the way. But our main destination, according to Harold, was Egypt.

"When is this trip supposed to take place?" asked Pa, looking as befuddled as everyone else.

"Next month."

"In *August?*"

"Well . . . yes. Next month is August."

Pa shook his head and shoveled in another bite of potatoes and gravy. "It's going to be hotter than heck in Egypt in August."

"Mercy, yes," said Ma. "Don't most expeditions to Egypt take place during the winter months?"

"Yes, they do," said Pa, who used to enjoy the same articles in *National Geographic* that Billy had. Well, he still would. Until Billy's subscription ran out. I shook my head, not wanting to think about that.

"Hmm," said Vi. "But it's hot in Pasadena during the summer months, too. Why, it gets to be over a hundred degrees here quite often."

"That's so," said Ma thoughtfully. "Egypt probably won't be so bad. And you can always take summery clothes with you. Knowing Harold Kincaid, he'll demand the very best of accommodations, so even if it's hot, you probably won't suffer from heatstroke or anything like that."

"That's true," said Vi. "Harold is quite a wealthy man."

"I guess so, but it doesn't matter. I told him I wouldn't let him do it."

"You *what?*"

Ma again, this time with a piece of lettuce spiked on her frozen fork.

"I can't let him spend all that money to take me to Egypt, Ma. It wouldn't be fair to him. I mean, it was very nice of him to offer, but . . . well, I just can't accept."

"Don't know why," said Pa, after he'd swallowed a bite of whatever he'd forked up. "He's got all the money in the world, you and he have always been great friends, and it would give you a chance to see the world. The good Lord knows you'll never be able to see it any other way. We Gumms aren't the traveling kind."

What he meant, of course, was that we Gumms—and me, as a Majesty—were hardworking peons who couldn't afford to do any traveling.

"I think your father's right, Daisy," said Vi after giving the matter some thought. "Harold is a good man, and he has your best interests at heart. Besides, I think he might well be right. His mother will probably agree, too. In fact, she'll probably start telephoning here and bothering you about taking the trip with her son as soon as she hears about it. All you're doing here is moping around and missing Billy. You need to expand your horizons."

There had been a time in the recent past when I'd have joked that my horizons had expanded plenty enough already, thank you, but that wasn't true any longer. In fact, my bottom hurt as I sat in the hard wooden dining-room chair because it was no longer padded as it had once been.

"I think so, too," said Ma. "You don't get offers like that every day. You'd be throwing away a wonderful opportunity if you refuse. Besides, it would hurt his feelings."

Hurt Harold's feelings? I doubted it. Granted, his suggestion had been kind and generous, but . . . Vi's words finally struck home. "Have I really been moping around?"

"Lord, yes, child! You don't do anything from sunup to sundown but crawl around the house like a ghost. I was so pleased when you finally agreed to work for Missus P. again. I'd hoped it might help you feel better if you got back to work."

Talk about guilt! I lowered my eyes and said penitently, "I guess I haven't been pulling my weight around here recently, have I?" I knew my family needed the money I made. Had I been self-indulgent and childish for the last month and a half? Should I have shoved my grief aside and charged back to the spiritualist trade, even given my bad attitude, which had me wanting more to chuck my clients out of high windows than help them cope with their trivial problems through idiotic spiritualistic means?

"Nuts to that," said Pa. "You're hurting, and you have every right to hurt. Your Billy was a good man, and what happened to the two of you was a tragedy of the modern age. Anyhow, thanks to your generosity, we can manage fine for a few months without you working. But you'd be better off not working in, say, Cairo, than here, looking at the same old walls day and night for another six months or so."

"You're all against me!" I cried pettishly. "I don't want to go to Egypt." What I wanted was to sulk and put flowers on my husband's grave every couple of days or so.

Very well, so perhaps I had been a little self-indulgent in recent weeks.

"We're not against you, Daisy. We're worried about you."

When I looked at Ma, who'd spoken the words, I was appalled to see tears in her eyes. Oh, Lord, I was breaking my parents' hearts. It didn't seem fair that I had to think about their hearts when my own had been so recently plucked from my chest, stamped upon repeatedly, and dumped back inside my body, where it ached and throbbed constantly.

"Why don't you go down and talk to Johnny yourself, Daisy?" suggested Pa. "He's a good man. I don't think he'll steer you wrong."

"Probably not," I admitted reluctantly.

"Harold is such a dear man," said Vi. "So unlike his sister."

"And remember, too, that if you're hoofing it all over Egypt with Harold, Missus Pinkerton can't call and wail in your ear," said Pa, grinning.

That's what decided me.

I sat in a chair opposite Johnny Buckingham's desk in his office at the Salvation Army. "I know you're doing the right thing, Daisy," said Johnny, smiling at me.

As for me, I was mopping up tears with my hankie. I swear to you, I never used to cry all the time. But in those days after my Billy died, I was a blasted watering pot.

"Thanks, Johnny. Harold has been quite insistent, and even my folks and Vi think it's a good idea." I remembered the past Saturday, when Sam Rotondo had again come to dinner and played cards with Pa afterwards, and added grumpily, "And so does Sam."

Johnny's smile turned into a grin. "Billy told me he asked Sam to watch out for you after he passed, you know."

Flabbergasted, I blurted out, "He did?"

"He did."

"Good Lord. I overheard a conversation between Billy and Sam about a week or two before he died, and I heard him ask Sam to take care of me after he was gone."

Johnny nodded. "It looks as if Sam is trying to do his best to follow Billy's wishes." He added with what I considered an unnecessarily sly glance, "If you'll let him."

Ancient Spirits

"I don't need anyone to look out for me," I said irritably.
Then I remembered the incident in the car, when Sam had
found me blubbering on a stack of library books, and sighed.
"But, yes, Sam has been . . . nice lately." Boy, it hurt me to say
that! But Sam and I had been enemies for so long, it was difficult to give up my animosity toward him.

"He is a nice person, Daisy. Give him a chance. He'll be a
good friend to you."

"You think so, do you?"

"Sure. And it never hurts to have a copper on your side. Just
ask Flossie. Heck, just ask me."

I think I've already mentioned that Johnny'd had a terrible
time after the war ended. "I thought it was the Salvation Army
that saved you."

"It was, but I was steered there by a good old Pasadena copper. George Halstead. We still keep in touch, George and me."

"I didn't know that."

"For the most part, policemen join the force because they
want to help people by taking crooks off the street. Sometimes
you'll find one who's willing to go the extra mile—or two, in my
case—to help someone who has problems. I thank God every
day for sending George to me."

I thought about all the people in my life and wondered if
God had put them all there for a reason. It didn't seem likely.
After all, why should God pay that much attention to little old
me? He had bigger problems to solve. I didn't say so to Johnny,
who claimed God had His eye on every single individual in the
entire world. Sounded like a mighty big job to me.

"I guess I should start thanking Him for you and Harold."

Johnny's grin widened. "Wouldn't hurt. I thank Him for you
every day."

His words so startled me, I jumped in my chair. "You do?

79

Why, for heaven's sake?" Apt phrasing, although I didn't plan it that way.

"For connecting me with Flossie."

"Aw. Thanks, Johnny." It had been through my influence that Flossie and Johnny had got together, although I hadn't originally planned that they should marry and have a family together. I was only trying to help Flossie at the time.

"Thank *you*, Daisy."

And then he made me pray with him. He always did that. It embarrassed me a little, but I appreciated him a whole lot and didn't argue.

I called Harold that evening without even bothering to shoo our nosiest party-line neighbor, Mrs. Barrow, off the line. I didn't care if she eavesdropped on this conversation. Harold, by the way, lived in a lovely home in San Marino with his special friend Del. I'd done a séance there for them once. It had gone very well. I feared this telephone call wouldn't.

"Have you talked it over with your parents?" he asked as soon as he knew it was me on the other end of the line.

"Yes."

"You don't sound overjoyed. Does that mean a yea or a nay?"

"I don't mean to sound ungrateful, Harold. Billy always wanted to go to Egypt, but I . . . well, everybody in my family thinks I should take you up on your very kind offer, and so does Johnny Buckingham. Heck, even Sam thinks so."

"It's not a kind offer. It's a gift to a dear friend in need. I've always wanted to see Egypt, too, and we'll start off in England, where I have friends."

Oh, boy. Just what I needed right then: a bunch of rich English friends of Harold's to make me feel poor and inadequate. "You have friends in England?" My voice quivered slightly.

"Don't worry. They'll love you, and you'll like them. Most of them, anyway. Piggy Fallowdale is a bit of a snob."

I drew my head back and stared at the 'phone on the wall. "He's a snob, and his name is *Piggy?* I should think being called Piggy would cure anyone of his snobbishness."

"The British are different that way. They give each other nicknames. You know, like Bertie Wooster in the Wodehouse books."

"Oh. Yes. I read one of his books. Had a butler in it who was smarter than his boss." I didn't tell Harold, but I'd identified strongly with Jeeves, although I wasn't the genius at getting people out of trouble that Jeeves was. Still, I must be smarter than most of my clients if only because I didn't believe in the garbage I spewed at them.

There went my attitude again. I simply *had* to overcome my present state of impatience and irritability. According to my family, Johnny and Sam, the cure probably lay in Egypt. The notion didn't appeal a whole lot.

"But that's beside the point," said Harold, sounding moderately impatient himself. "Are you going to go with me to Egypt or are you not?"

I hesitated and drew in a deep breath. Then I let it out in a whoosh and said, "Yes. I'm going with you to Egypt."

"Bully, as our late President Roosevelt might have said! That's wonderful, Daisy. We'll have a glorious time. I promise you that you'll feel one hundred percent better about life when we get back."

I doubted that. "I still won't have Billy," I reminded him. Then, naturally, I felt guilty for throwing the corpse of my dead husband at Harold when all he was trying to do was be a good friend to me. "I'm sorry, Harold. I didn't mean to say that out loud."

"Piffle. You did so mean it, but it doesn't matter. You have every reason to feel bitter and resentful about life. But two or three months away from home, seeing and doing new things and meeting new people, will prove the cure. You'll never get Billy back, but you might regain your spirit. So to speak."

"Right," I said. "I'm sure you're right, Harold." Then part of what he'd said made my head snap straight up. "Did you say two or three *months?*"

"Well, yes. First we'll have to take the train to New York City, changing trains in Chicago. Then we'll take an ocean liner to Southampton. That's in England. From there we take the boat train to Marseilles. Then we take the Orient Express from Paris to Istanbul—"

"What?" I interrupted. "Where's Istanbul?"

"It's what people are calling Constantinople these days."

"Oh. I didn't know that." Learn something new every day, I guess.

"You can call it Constantinople if you want to," said Harold generously.

"That's all right," said I, thinking my life was confusing enough already without people going and changing the names of cities on me.

"Anyhow, we'll go from Paris to Istanbul—or Constantinople, if you prefer—"

"I don't prefer either one." What I really wanted was not to go at all, but I knew I'd better not say that.

"Anyhow, then we'll take another train from Constantinople to Cairo. Then I'll book us on a Cook's Tour down the Nile. Or up the Nile. I can't remember which way the boats go."

"Good Lord," I said, feeling rather faint. "I've never traveled anywhere before in my life except for when we went back to Massachusetts to visit my parents' families." You wouldn't catch anyone in Auburn, Massachusetts, changing its name, I'd bet. Istanbul, my foot.

"This will be a broadening experience for you."

I suppressed about a thousand and three jokes about broadening experiences and only said, "I guess so. What kinds of clothes should I bring?"

"Ah, now you're talking my language!"

Have I mentioned Harold was a costumier for a motion-picture company? Well, he was. The rest of that long and exhausting telephone conversation was taken up with talk of clothing. Harold didn't believe in packing light, but I didn't see the point of taking more clothes than I'd need.

"Fiddlesticks. You won't be the one carrying the luggage. We'll have servants to do that for you."

"Good Lord," I said, faint but game. But honestly. Me? With servants waiting on me? Never in my whole life had anyone ever waited on me. Well, not since I was out of diapers, anyway.

"You'll need at least four evening gowns, my dear," he said reprovingly when I told him I didn't want to be overburdened with clothing on that gigantically long trip, servants or no servants. "Think of the evenings you'll spend in Paris on the way there and in London on the way back. I know you have evening duds, because I've seen you in plenty of them. So bring four or five gowns for evening wear."

In an attempt to assuage his gusto regarding my wardrobe, I tried to steer the conversation to a salient point. "Egypt is sure to be burning hot, Harold. I presume I should bring lightweight frocks and hats and a couple of parasols or something to shield my face from the sun." If I aimed to resume my career as a spiritualist one day—and I did—it would never do to appear rosy-cheeked and robust.

"Yes, that's so. Actually, it'll be warm during the entire journey, I suppose. But don't worry about that. Bring lightweight clothing for everywhere, and if you need something else, we'll get it abroad."

Yeah? You and who else? thought I. Naturally, I didn't say that to Harold. Still, the fact remained that he was rich and I wasn't.

"And don't worry about the expense," he hastily added, as if he were reading my mind. "Mother is going to give you a huge wad of money tomorrow or the next day."

"She's going to *what?*"

"She's giving you a big bonus for dealing with Stacy. Oh, that's right. I forgot to tell you that your Captain Buckingham went down to the Pasadena City Jail, talked to Stacy, and Stacy has repented of her evil ways and is going back to the Salvation Army as soon as she's finished her term in the pokey."

"Good Lord." I was feeling fainter by the second.

"You might phrase it that way," said Harold with a wry bite to his voice. "But it's true. She's been re-saved, if such a thing is possible, and even Mother doesn't care if she goes to church at the Salvation Army. She's decided not to hold out for an Episcopalian this time. I think she's decided Stacy's too far gone for the staid Episcopal crowd anyway. She's only glad Stacy claims she's going to tread on the straight and narrow path from now on."

"I'll believe it when I see it," I said before I could think better of my words. That happens a lot with me.

But Harold didn't mind. He only laughed and said, "Yeah. Me, too."

CHAPTER NINE

By August first, Harold had made sure I had all the proper travel documents, and Dr. Benjamin had made sure I had all the proper travel inoculations, one of which made me *really* sick for a day or two. They were the only two days out of the entire month of July during which my family didn't rag me about not eating enough. Heck, I wasn't dying or anything. I was clearly eating plenty enough to stay alive. I figured that was sufficient. I even began taking Spike for walks during the daytime. So there.

The notion of this trip with Harold—this two-or-three-month-long trip—daunted me a good deal, though. I knew I'd miss my family, and I already missed Spike. He was there on the front porch, along with my entire family, Sam Rotondo, the Wilsons from next door to the north and the Longneckers from across the street to the south when Harold arrived in a chauffeured limousine to take me to the station in Pasadena, where we would catch a train that would take us to the station in downtown Los Angeles. From there we'd take a Southern Pacific train to Chicago and thence get on the New York Central, which would carry us to New York City. From there we'd embark on the White Star Line's R.M.S. *Olympic,* which would take us to Southampton.

The *Olympic,* by the way, was one of three identical ships built by the White Star Line. They were the *Titanic,* which had hit an iceberg and sunk in 1912; and the *Britannic,* which had been torpedoed in 1916. To my mind, these facts augured poorly for our journey, but I didn't bother telling Harold or anyone else my thoughts on the matter. If the boat sank, I could be with Billy sooner, was the way I saw it. Providing, of course, the Methodist ministers I'd been listening to all my life were right, and I was going to heaven. Given my track record of fooling people for a living, I wasn't altogether sure I qualified. But that was too depressing to contemplate, and I already felt bum enough.

"Have a good time, sweetheart," said Pa, giving me a squeeze.

Aunt Vi thrust a little package at me and said, "Take care, Daisy. I'm sure this is exactly what you need."

Pudge Wilson, who looked like he might burst into tears, said, "I'll miss you, Miss Daisy." I think I've already mentioned that Pudge, the neighbors' boy, had been sweet on me for a long time.

"I'll miss you, too, Pudge," said I, trying not to cry.

"Oh, Daisy!" said my mother as she flung her arms around me.

I staggered slightly when she released me, and Sam took my arm. "Try to enjoy yourself and all the new experiences you'll be having." His voice was gruff. I opened my mouth to thank him when he suddenly turned to Harold. "Watch out for her. She gets into trouble at the drop of a hat."

"Sam!" I cried, any thought of thanking him for his good wishes vanishing in a pouf of ire. "I don't either!"

Before a fight could break out on our front porch, Mrs. Wilson and Mrs. Longnecker both took one hand each and squeezed.

"Have a wonderful trip, Daisy. I'll look in on your folks while you're away," said Mrs. Wilson.

"Me, too!" said Pudge.

"I'll miss seeing you walking that adorable dog of yours," said Mrs. Longnecker.

That did it for me. Spike, who was looking as hangdog as a dachshund could—which was awfully hangdog—reached out a paw and nudged me. My tears spilled over, and I squatted on the porch to give him a hug. "Take care of everyone for me, Spike."

He licked my chin.

"We'd better be going," said Harold. I knew he hated scenes.

Sam and the chauffeur had already packed my suitcases—there were three of them, stuffed to the gills—into the limo, and Harold took my arm and hauled me upright again. Although I was normally a crackerjack seamstress, I hadn't bothered to alter any of my dresses to suit my new size, mainly because I lacked any kind of motivation for anything in those days. If everyone was correct, I'd soon regain any weight I'd lost. Anyhow, there was less of me to haul than there used to be.

"I'll be sure she stays out of trouble, Detective Rotondo," said Harold, not even out of breath. "And I'll take good care of her, Mister and Missus Gumm. I'll miss your cooking, Missus Gumm."

"Get along with you, Mister Harold."

So I wasn't the only one she told to get along with himself or herself, eh? I guess it was some kind of—what do you call them? Colloquialisms?

Vi continued, "You'll be dining in wonderful restaurants run by expert chefs." Her own words must have sparked an idea, for she hurriedly said, "If you eat something particularly delicious, Daisy, try to find out how it's made. Will you do that for me?"

Oh, brother. Vi knew all about cooking and me, and how very much we didn't get along. Nevertheless, I said, "I'll do my best, Vi."

"Come along, Daisy," said Harold, his voice and hand on my arm both firm.

"I'll miss you all!" I said from the bottom of my heart, still fighting tears. Upon my last glance at Spike, I nearly broke down again.

Harold, who knew me well, said, "Yes, you'll miss your family and that dog. But you're going to be seeing and doing wonderful things, Daisy Majesty, so just don't you start crying again."

I sniffled my tears back and said in a shaky voice, "I'll try, Harold."

"Nuts to that. You either *try* or you *do*. I think you're the one who told me that once."

"I don't remember that." And I didn't, but the advice was good, and it got me to thinking, which was probably what Harold had intended.

"Did Mother give you your bonus?"

The mention of my "bonus" brought any thought of tears to a screeching halt. "My Lord, yes! Harold, do you have any idea how much money she gave me?"

"Whatever it was, it wasn't enough," said Harold, who'd been tormented by his sister all his life, while she'd only made my life miserable for several years.

"Well, it's a lot more money than I've ever seen before, and that's even after various bonuses paid to me by contented clients. Heck, even when that Russian duke or whatever he was gave me that bejeweled bracelet, I don't think it was worth as much as the amount of money your mother gave me."

He smiled. "Good. You deserve every penny."

I eyed him thoughtfully. "You really think so?"

"I really do."

Hmm. Maybe he was right. Perhaps the five thousand—five *thousand*—dollars Mrs. Pinkerton had insisted I take wasn't too much money for all the years I'd been at her beck and call.

Naw. It was way too much money, even if you figured Stacy into the equation. But I knew better than to argue with Harold, who'd had access to gobs of money his whole life. Anyhow, my family could use some of that five grand while I was away and not earning money for them.

At any rate, it didn't take long for the chauffeur to get us to the train station, which was on Fair Oaks Avenue and Del Mar Boulevard. When we got there, the chauffeur opened our doors (mine first), and I got out and looked around, not knowing what to do with myself.

Fortunately, Harold knew what to do with the both of us. He once again took my arm and began guiding me to the station. "Come along, Daisy. Folks will be out to get our luggage."

"Without you telling them where to put it?" I asked, feeling stupid, but curious anyway.

"They know. I booked all our plans in advance. Believe me, they're being well tipped to follow my instructions."

"Oh. That's right. Servants get tips, don't they?" Kind of like I got tips from my clients every now and then. Which made me on a par with a servant, I supposed. Well, heck, I already knew that. Some of my best friends were servants of one sort or another, waiting on people who were no better nor worse than they were, but had more money than we.

There went those bitter thoughts again. Shoot, if it weren't for the rich people in the world, how were the rest of us expected to survive? I should be grateful to them, not thinking snotty thoughts about them.

Nuts. At that moment, as we entered the Pasadena train station, I figured I'd never regain my good humor again.

But Harold had been absolutely correct about our plans working smoothly. I watched from the window as various people, from the chauffeur to uniformed train-station attendants, unloaded the limousine. Boy, until I saw how much luggage Harold had brought with him, I'd thought *I'd* packed heavily. But they unloaded five huge trunks full of Harold's stuff.

"Good Lord, Harold. How many sets of clothes did you bring?"

"Hundreds, darling," he said. I heard the grin in his voice.

"I didn't think men had to dress up in different clothes all the time like women do."

"We don't. Most of those trunks are filled with things I thought you might use." As I opened my mouth to protest, he held up a hand. "And don't start bellowing at me. I know you've never traveled, and most of the things I've brought along are from the studio and would never have been used again in this lifetime if I hadn't taken them. Better to give them a second chance to shine on you than to let them hang, neglected forever, on a back lot somewhere." He eyed me up and down, making me feel like squirming. "I brought along various sizes, since I aim to fatten you up."

I opened my mouth again, but nothing came out. There seemed to be nothing to say. If Harold wanted to lug five trunks' worth of ladies' clothing from one coast of the United States to the other, across the Atlantic Ocean and all over Europe and Egypt, what could I say? Anyhow—and I don't like to admit this—I'd worked on a moving-picture set recently and had been agog at the gorgeous clothes the women had worn. Mind you, that particular movie was set during the Civil War, but still and all, my folks and I—and Billy—had gone to enough pictures for me to have envied the stars their wardrobes.

Not that mine was anything to sneeze at. As I've said before probably too many times, I followed the fashion trends and made all of my family's clothes, mainly from bolt ends and sale-price merchandise from Maxime's Fabrics on Colorado Boulevard in Pasadena. The fact remained that I'd never spent more than a dollar and a quarter on any outfit I'd ever sewn for myself, not even the exquisite (if I do say so myself) evening ensembles I'd managed to patch together for my spiritualist business. I was nothing if not a skilled and thrifty seamstress. Which took a little of the sting out of not being able to cook anything more complicated than toast—but not much.

Speaking of dressing well, that day I wore a lovely, lightweight, dark-lavender traveling suit with a beige hat, shoes and bag. I'm not all that fond of purple as a color, and especially not on me, who's more or less a redhead. Still, the color was appropriate both for travel and for mourning, so I wore it.

A train shrieked into the station, a whistle nearly blew our heads off, and Harold and I moved from the window to the boarding platform. It wasn't long before the station attendant called, "All aboard for Los Angeles," we boarded the train and we were on our way.

Whether I wanted to be on my way or not.

In a little more than an hour, we were in Los Angeles. Boy, the LA train station is a bustling place! I thought it was quite lovely, too, although Harold told me it didn't hold a candle to Grand Central Station in New York City.

"But you'll see it for yourself in four days," he said complacently.

"You've been to New York a lot?"

"Oh, my, yes. Del and I like to take in the theater sometimes."

"In New *York?*" I gaped at him, agog that anyone would travel across an entire country to watch a play. I mean, I knew Harold and Del traveled together sometimes, but going all the way to New York to see a play seemed somehow excessive to me.

"Broadway is the heart of the American theater, darling. We'll catch a play or two in London, too. You'll enjoy that."

I would, would I? Well, maybe I would.

"Sure," I said. What else could I say?

We had a three-hour delay in Los Angeles before our train was to take off for Chicago, so Harold again took my arm and led me out into the hot August sunshine. "I'm taking you on a tour of downtown Los Angeles," he declared, hailing a taxicab with the ease of someone brought up to the action. Well, I guess he had been.

"Top of Angels Flight," Harold told the driver.

"Sure thing, mister." The cab sped off with a grinding of gears that made me wince.

"What's Angels Flight?" I asked Harold, holding on to my hat so it wouldn't fly off. The traffic was terrible, and the cabbie swung in and out of it as if he did it every day—which I guess he did. But it made for a bumpy ride.

"It's an adorable little railroad."

And it was. Only one block long, it was almost vertical and had been built because people didn't like to climb steep hills, I suppose, and that's all the two cars of Angels Flight did: go up and down that one block from Olive to Hill all day long. I thought taking a train for one measly block might be the least little bit self-indulgent, but I didn't dare say so to Harold.

After we rode Angels Flight, which I have to admit was fun, Harold took me to lunch at a place called Musso and Frank's Grill. It was quite lovely, and I think I noticed a couple of people I'd seen in the pictures, although I couldn't place them with names, having little interest in the flickers at the time. I managed to eat several bites of my chicken pie, Harold keeping an eagle-eyed stare on me the whole time. His close scrutiny became kind of annoying after a while.

"You know, Harold," I said at one point. "You can stare at me all you want, but I'm not going to eat more food than my stomach can hold."

He shook his head sadly. "You amaze me, Daisy."

"I do?"

"You've managed to lose a hundred pounds in a month without even trying, and I can't lose weight even when I live on celery and carrots for weeks at a time."

I gaped at him. "You actually *did* that? Eat celery and carrots, I mean."

"Yes. It was the most miserable experience of my life, and Del finally persuaded me that he loved me in spite of my avoirdupois."

"Del's a good man," I said. The thought crossed my mind that if Del died, Harold might understand what I was going through, both with food and my emotions, but the notion was so awful I didn't voice it.

"Yes," Harold said. "He is. And I know what you were just thinking, Daisy Majesty, so I promise not to badger you about eating more any longer." He shook his head. "If anything happened to Del, I don't think I could survive."

I stared at him for a second or two and finally said, "That's the problem, though, Harold. You probably would survive."

He sighed and said, "I suppose you're right."

We got back to the station in plenty of time to catch our train. My astonishment could hardly be measured when I found out that Harold had hired an entire railroad car for only the two of us!

CHAPTER TEN

"If anyone asks, just tell them you're my sister," Harold said as train employees bustled about us, tending to our luggage and our every need. "Not that people really care about such nonsense any longer, but still, it's better to lie than to be ostracized."

Boy, the thought that anyone might find it strange or objectionable that I, a woman, would be traveling with Harold, a man, and that we were neither husband and wife nor kin had never occurred to me. Sometimes I can be remarkably dim.

"Right. That's probably a good idea."

I scrutinized Harold, who was shortish, chubby, pink-cheeked and merry, with brown eyes and thinning brown hair, and compared him to me. I, too, was short, but I had dark-red hair and blue eyes. And I sure wasn't plump any longer, if I ever had been. A hundred pounds, my eye!

The last porter left after asking if we required anything and Harold said, "No, thank you"—he was invariably polite to the people who worked for him—and I took a good gander at the railroad carriage.

It was an impressive car. Red plush furnishings; polished wood. Don't ask me what kind of wood, because I don't know. Two bedrooms were curtained off, one at each end of the carriage, and there was a bathroom just for us off to the side. It was snazzy, all right. And for some inexplicable reason I felt extremely lonely, even with Harold there with me. Did being rich mean you had to be by yourself all the time? What if you wanted to mingle with other passengers and strike up acquaintances? I thought the point of all this traveling and so forth was that I was supposed to meet new people. Not that I felt much like being introduced to a bunch of strangers or anything, but still . . .

"Um, will we stay in this car all the way to Chicago and New York, Harold? I mean, will we leave it to eat in . . . what do they call it? The dining car?"

"We can do whatever you want to do, my dear. If you want to dine with the masses, so be it. If you want to isolate yourself, you can do that, too, although I wouldn't recommend it. What I think you need to do is get out and enjoy yourself." He must have seen me open my mouth to reply, because he hurried on. "Yes, I know you aren't in any condition to enjoy yourself at this point in your life. You've suffered a grievous loss. But if you meet new people and talk to them, you might begin to feel better eventually. Start small and work your way up, is my advice. Don't forget that there are millions of people in the world who have also suffered terrible losses, especially lately, since the war and the 'flu. It might help you to talk to some of them." In order to forestall any more protests from me, he added, "Or not. You choose. I'm not forcing you to do anything at all. This is your time to do with as you wish."

After pondering this mini-sermon for several silent moments, I had to admit it made sense, especially given my state of loneliness. "Thanks, Harold."

Harold rubbed his hands together. "So . . . what do you want to do first?"

"First?" I stared blankly at him.

"Sure. Here we are. What do you want to do first?"

"Um . . . I don't know. What is there to do?"

"To tell you the truth, not a whole lot. We're going to be

stuck on trains for four days. Once we get on the ship, there will be dancing and sunbathing and—"

"I can't sunbathe. I have to protect my pale complexion."

"Why?"

"Good heavens, Harold, do you think anybody would want to employ a spiritualist who looks like an athlete or a swimming instructor?"

"Good point. Forget sunbathing. But you can put on a big hat and go up on the deck and watch the dolphins frolic in the wake of the ship. Maybe we'll even spot a whale or a shark or something else interesting. You can read to your heart's content."

"Darn it!"

"What's the matter?"

"I forgot to bring any books! What a fool I am! About the only thing I'll be able to read are travel brochures."

"Not to worry. The ship will have a library, and there will be every magazine and newspaper known to man available to you. Hell, we can buy a whole library in New York City if you want to."

"That might be excessive, but really? The ship has books?" Hmm. That was nice to know. I might even pick up a book and see if I could concentrate on reading an entire novel while enjoying new experiences. And if I couldn't make my way through an entire book, I could try magazine articles.

"Absolutely. We're going first class all the way, my dear."

Another screech from the train's whistle told us we were about to take off for Chicago, so the first thing *I* did on my very first trip anywhere except to Massachusetts was rush to the window and watch as Los Angeles slowly began sliding past us. As the train picked up speed, the images outside seemed to move faster.

"Well, since all you want to do at the moment is stare out the window, have a chair."

Harold shoved a ladder-backed chair at the backs of my knees and I sat with a plop. "Thanks, Harold."

"Anytime, my dear."

He sounded a little sarcastic, but for me this was interesting. I don't know how long the train took to get out of the city proper, but soon we seemed to be flying past fields planted with all sorts of stuff. Again, don't ask me what, because I don't know. I was a true city kid, I guess, because it seldom occurred to me that farmers grew the food we ate at home. Well, we had a little kitchen garden, but we only grew tomatoes, carrots, onions and cucumbers there. But we sure never had a herd of cows in our backyard, and we passed tons of them on our way. And then there was the desert: miles and miles of what looked like absolutely nothing. Every now and then the train would pass through a tiny village somewhere, and a couple of times I actually saw a man leading a donkey.

"Oh, my," I said at one point. "Do you suppose that fellow is a miner? Are there mines out there?"

"Mines? I have no idea. Where are we?" Harold glanced out the window. "Hmm. Yes, probably he's a miner. I think we're about in San Bernardino County now, and there are lots of mines here."

"My goodness. I didn't know that."

"Good Lord, yes. I own interest in several boron mines around here. And haven't you ever heard of that old Wild West character, Wyatt Earp? He used to mine in this neck of the woods years ago."

"Good gracious." I felt something akin to awe. I'd read about Wyatt Earp in various periodicals, but all of those articles had concerned the gunfight at the OK Corral, Doc Holliday and that sort of thing. The fact that Wyatt Earp, the master gunfighter and lawman, had also been a miner had been totally overlooked by the writers of those pieces.

"Don't believe everything you read," Harold advised wryly. "Earp did more than shoot outlaws back in the day. In fact, I do believe he's still alive and living in San Berdoo."

"My goodness."

But I'm not going to describe our entire trip across the vast geography that is our great nation. Some of the scenery was fabulous; some of it was depressing. I guess trains don't generally run tracks through the fancy neighborhoods in big cities. They build the tracks where the people who live there are too poor to complain about the noise.

Darn. My attitude wasn't improving very fast, was it?

Well, never mind. The trip in the train was at times boring and at times interesting, and I found myself enjoying the luxury that Harold's money could buy. We did take dinners in the dining car, although I mainly stuck to soup and soda crackers while Harold frowned at me. I was more pleased than not when I discovered that we didn't get a table to ourselves, but had to share with other people, mainly because Harold couldn't scold me with other people around. Well, I suppose he could have, but he didn't, bless the man. Harold told me train travel was always that way—the sharing of tables in the dining car thing, I mean.

And I met new people. I didn't particularly take to most of them, especially a fat man who seemed to be a little too interested in me and who smoked smelly cigars. He followed Harold and me around all one evening, from the dining car to the smoking car (neither Harold nor I smoked, but that's one of the places where people gathered and spoke) to the lounge car. Finally Harold took him aside and chatted with him for a moment, the fat man took one last gander at me and then he left in a hurry.

"What did you say to him?" I asked Harold when he returned to sit beside me on a sofa.

"I told him that you, my beloved sister, had just lost her husband and that you found his attentions objectionable."

"Oh, my!" Gee, I didn't know you could be direct about stuff like that with people. I'd always been taught that one needed to pussyfoot around people's feelings and never say anything that might hurt them. "That was very brave of you, Harold."

"Why?"

"Telling him I found his attentions objectionable. I think that was brave of you."

Harold shrugged. "I only told him the truth." He eyed me keenly. "Didn't I?"

"Absolutely." After a pause, I said, "I guess it's the 'objectionable' part that floors me."

Thumping his chest, Harold said, "That's man-talk, Daisy."

For the first time in what seemed like forever, I laughed.

Chicago was a big city, but we didn't get to see much of it, which was all right with me. At that time, in the thick of Prohibition, you could read articles in all the newspapers about rival gangs trying to corner the illegal liquor markets in Chicago and New York, and Chicago seemed a particularly bloody place to be at the moment. We caught the New York Central from Chicago to New York City.

New York was interesting, but too big and bustling for me. Harold took me to see *Getting Gertie's Garter* and *Mr. Pim Passes By*. The latter, strangely enough, was by A.A. Milne, the same man who wrote *The Red House Mystery*. Both plays were comedies. I suspect Harold didn't think I was up to heavy drama, and I suspect he was right. I enjoyed both plays, particularly Mr. Milne's. Harold also took me to dine at what he said were fabulous New York restaurants, although I didn't enjoy them as much as the plays, because I still wasn't hungry.

And then we set sail on the *Olympic*, and I forgot all about plays, books, and everything else, because I was so horribly seasick for the first day or two. Harold was aghast at my plight, since he'd already freely admitted that his primary aim in taking me on this trip, besides making me feel better emotionally, was to fatten me up.

Didn't work.

By the time we eventually docked in Southampton, I was over my seasickness, but still neither cheery nor fat. Harold said he despaired of me. I told him it was his own fault.

Thank the good Lord Harold then loaded me onto what he called a boat train, where I recovered some of my cheer, if none of my fat.

And then there was the ferry to Marseilles. I absolutely dreaded that trip on another boat, but oddly enough, I didn't get sick on it.

"You're getting your sea legs at last," said Harold.

"Huh," said I, reminding myself of Sam Rotondo and bringing a huge wave of nostalgia to my heart. Now why, I ask you, should thinking of Sam Rotondo make me nostalgic? Probably because I always thought of Sam and Billy together, with my family. Ah, well. That part of my life was over forever. At least the Billy and Sam part.

In Paris we boarded the Orient Express. I was kind of excited about this leg of our journey, since I'd read about the Orient Express in books and magazines, and Billy had read an entire article from the *National Geographic* aloud regarding the Orient Express. It was a fabulous train, and we met more interesting people than we had on the trains to Chicago and New York City, including a countess from . . . somewhere. I don't remember. And a prince from some Baltic country who tried to pay me a lot of attention until Harold told him of my recently widowed status, and the prince backed off after offering me sympathy and kissing my hand. I don't think Harold told the prince I found his attentions objectionable; what I think was that the prince had better manners than the fat man with the cigar.

And then the train arrived at the station in Istanbul, which, as you must know by this time, used to be called Constantinople and still was by some folks. Oh, boy, I'd *never* expected to see sights like those we saw in Istanbul! Billy would have loved this. It was so . . . foreign. If you know what I mean. Sure, it wasn't foreign to the Turks who lived there, but I was simple Daisy Gumm Majesty from Pasadena, California, who'd never been anywhere or done anything before in my life, and Istanbul . . . Constantinople (oh, bother, choose either name for yourself!) . . . amazed and astonished me.

I was surprised that the costumes we saw on the people were so colorful. After hearing Billy read to me about Egypt, I'd expected everyone to be clad in black robes and to see veiled women everywhere. Then I recalled that Turkey had given women the vote in 1918, two years before we females were so honored in the United States, and decided that Turkey must be a pretty progressive place in spite of my preconceptions.

Harold and I dined in a restaurant where we ate an entire meal composed of stuff I'd never even heard of before, much less eaten. It was delicious, too, what's more, and I wondered if Aunt Vi would like a Turkish cookbook. Of course, nobody in the family could read Turkish, but still, it might be a nice conversation piece. I was sorry when Harold told me he doubted such a book existed and that he wouldn't know where to get one if it did.

And then there was another train from Constantinople to Cairo. This train wasn't as luxurious as the Orient Express, and not for the first time I doubted the wisdom to traveling to Egypt in the summertime.

"It's hot, Harold," I said, fanning myself with an exquisite fan I'd found in an Istanbul marketplace. Harold and I had promised each other we'd spend more time in Istanbul on our way home from Egypt because it looked like such a fascinating city.

"Yes," said Harold, fanning himself with his hand. "It is. I know people generally travel to Egypt in the winter, but I didn't think it would be quite this bad. Heck, it gets hot in Los Angeles during the summer."

I eyed the strange surroundings in which we were then chugging along. "Maybe it's because we're used to life in Southern California, and we aren't used to life here."

Harold, red-faced and perspiring, said, "Maybe."

"Um, maybe you should take off your jacket, Harold. There's no sense in wearing a jacket in this weather."

For only a moment, Harold appeared shocked at the suggestion. Then he said, "Good idea." He shucked his jacket, removed his tie, unbuttoned the top buttons of his shirt, and actually rolled up his sleeves. I don't think I'd ever seen Harold so casually attired before.

As for me, I wore a silver-gray sleeveless day dress made of lightweight cotton. I was still hot, but not as hot as Harold, I'd bet. And I'd also bet I wasn't as hot as the shrouded women we saw both on the train and in the towns we passed on our way to Cairo. They all wore long, shapeless black robes, had their heads covered and their faced veiled. I suppose the robes were comfortable, but all that black made me kind of feel sick.

"Do all women in Egypt wear those black robes and veils, Harold?"

"I believe so, Daisy. Egypt is a Moslem country, you know, and they like to keep their women under wraps."

"But Turkey is, too, isn't it? And the women in Constantinople at least wore colorful robes."

Harold shrugged. "I don't have any idea how the cultures of either country work."

"Golly, I'll feel sort of out of place in my lightweight clothes."

"No, you won't. There will be gobs of tourists to keep you company."

"In August?"

Harold frowned at me. "Very well, I guess August wasn't the most appropriate time to visit Egypt. Still, I want to see you on a camel. After we do that, we can go back to England early if it's too hot to carry on in Egypt."

"I don't want to spoil your trip, Harold." By that time I'd begun to feel guilty for bringing up the subject of heat. I was always feeling guilty about something or other in those days.

"You won't be spoiling my trip," Harold said upon a sigh. "If anything spoils my trip, it'll be the damned weather, and that's not your fault."

"Well, I hope it cools off a little. Maybe it will be cool on the Nile?"

"Maybe."

The notion of taking another boat, this one up the Nile, made my stomach feel queasy, but I didn't let on.

And then, at long last, we got to Cairo.

CHAPTER ELEVEN

Wow, talk about your teeming masses! I've never seen so many people as there were at that dingy little train station in Cairo. And hot? Merciful heaven, but it was hot in Cairo. I feared for the length of our stay there. Fortunately for us, one of the Cook's people was there to meet us and he swept us off to the grand and glorious (that's what Harold called it) Shepheards Hotel, which had been a haven for the wealthy tourist for decades. After we got there, I had to agree with his assessment of the place.

"The tour will begin the day after tomorrow," our Cook's guide told us, seemingly unaffected by the blistering heat, perhaps because his robe and turban were blindingly white. "Bright and early."

Harold checked us in to the hotel, and much to my surprise a bundle of letters awaited me. Naturally I'd been writing to my family practically every day from the moment our journey had begun, but I hadn't expected anyone to write back, mainly because I'd be on the move. I perked up considerably when I clutched the small stack of envelopes.

"Your family loves you, Daisy," said Harold. "I think it's grand that they all care so much."

But my attention had been diverted by the return address on one particular envelope. Why in the name of heaven would Sam Rotondo be writing me?

"Daisy? Are you still with me? Are you feeling faint from the heat?"

"What? Oh. I'm sorry, Harold. I was just . . . surprised by this letter. It's from Sam."

Harold's eyebrows rose and waggled, and he looked like a villain out of an old-time melodrama. "Aha. Is there dirty work afoot? Does he want you to solve a crime?"

I gave him a good frown. "Nuts. Sam's always made pains to keep me out of the investigations he's worked on."

"Not always," said Harold in a voice as dry as the weather.

"Well, yes, but that was only once." And both Harold and I had been arrested for our efforts. Oh, very well, to be completely honest, we'd been picked up in a raid on a speakeasy—where I had *not* gone to drink and carouse but rather to conduct a séance—and that's what had precipitated my involvement in the case in question.

"Let's go to our rooms. I'm sure they have fans in the rooms. We've got first-class accommodations, according to my travel agent."

"Good idea."

"I'll come to your door at fiveish, and we can take tea on the famous balcony of Shepheards, which overlooks the busy streets of Cairo. Maybe we can locate a fakir charming a cobra or something."

"I thought fakirs with cobras lived in India."

"They're got 'em here, too. Mother told me all about them."

"My goodness." My provincial mind could hardly make heads or tails of the sights I'd already seen, and I wasn't sure I was ready for more of them. Yet here I was, poised for further exotica whether I was ready or not. But first I wanted to read Sam's letter. And the rest of them, too, of course. It's only that I'd expected communications from my mother, father, aunt, sister, brother and nieces, friends, etc. I hadn't expected to hear from

Sam until I got home to Pasadena in another month or two. Or three.

The first thing I did once I'd been seen to my room and my things had been disposed of, not by me but by a servant, was arrange my letters. By the way, I don't think I'd ever get used to being waited on hand and foot. I'd make a lousy queen.

I had intended to read the letters from my family first, but discovered myself tearing open Sam's missive, my curiosity enormous. It read as follows:

Dear Daisy,

I hope you don't mind me writing to you. I keep remembering Billy telling me to keep an eye on you, and I can't do that now that you're thousands of miles away in Egypt. But I wanted you to know that you're in my thoughts, and I'm keeping an eye on the rest of your family while you're away.

Enjoy yourself. Please send me a postcard from Egypt.

Respectfully,
Sam (Rotondo)

Talk about your basic cases of astonishment! He hadn't written a single, solitary scolding word. To tell you the truth, I was touched, and I itched to take up pen and paper and write him back instantly. However, I read through the rest of the missives like the dutiful kinswoman and friend I was:

Ma was fine.

Pa was fine.

Aunt Vi was fine.

My sister Daphne, her husband Daniel, and their two little girls were fine.

My brother Walter and his wife Jeanette were fine.

Mrs. Pinkerton was fine, and gushed all over the paper about how wonderful I was. I'd have taken her words more to heart if I didn't know I was a fake who'd been falsely taking money from her for years and years. Not that she didn't want to be taken advantage of. But I think we've already covered the Pinkerton situation.

Even Johnny and Flossie Buckingham were fine.

So why didn't I have a mad desire to write all of them back, but only Sam?

Fortunately, before I could come up with a satisfactory answer to my question, Harold knocked on my door. "Time for tea, Daisy!" he called out cheerily.

"On my way," said I, wondering if I should have changed my clothes. The dress I wore, the same sleeveless gray one I'd worn on the train, was kind of rumpled. Maybe Shepheards frowned upon rumpled people. Oh, well.

I opened the door and asked, "Do I have to change clothes to take tea on the balcony?"

Eyeing me up and down with no particular relish, Harold said, "It wouldn't have hurt you to have changed into something a little less dismal, but I know you're determined to carry out this mourning thing until you've wrung the last of its discomfort from it."

"Harold!"

"Sorry, Daisy. It's just that I prefer you in brighter colors."

"Yeah, well, let something happen to Del and then tell me how bright you feel and for how long, Harold Kincaid."

"You have my profound apologies, Daisy. Would you like me to grovel at your feet?"

I smacked him on the arm and said, "Let's go get some of this tea about which you speak and see if we can find ourselves a fakir. Other than me, of course, but I'm another kind of faker." I grabbed a straw hat on my way out, in case hats were *de rigueur* at Shepheards.

And, boy, did we! Find fakirs, I mean. There were also dozens, if not hundreds, of dirty little children begging for money—or *"baksheesh,"* as it's called there—and innumerable Egyptian guides everywhere, eager to rent rides to tourists on donkeys or camels. I eyed the camels with speculation. They were the dromedary variety. I remembered that from a lecture Billy had given us at the dinner table once, in which he'd explained the differences between dromedary and Bactrian camels. I never thought I'd get to ride on either type, and I still wasn't altogether sure I wanted to. Those things were tall and, from what Billy had read in the *National Geographic,* they weren't the best-tempered of beasts.

"I love the blankets they have on the camels, Harold," I said as a very proper waiter whose dark skin proclaimed him some type of native specimen pulled out my chair for me. "Look at how beautifully they're woven and in such intricate patterns, too. The colors are gorgeous."

"They probably all smell like camel," said Harold, destroying any romantic thoughts I'd begun to harbor for camels, which, granted, were few at that point.

Although it was only five or so in the afternoon, the heat still bore down on us in waves, making me glad for the umbrella on our table and for the straw hat whose ribbons I had tied under my chin. Harold sported a pith helmet. I didn't tell him so, but he looked kind of silly in his "tourist" uniform, which consisted of a tailored white linen suit and that pith helmet. As soon as we sat and were under the shade of the umbrella, he shucked the helmet, probably because it had made his head sweat. I could tell, because his thin hair was plastered to his head.

"I don't know how much of this heat I can take, Daisy," he said. "I'm sorry I dragged you all the way out here."

Shrugging, I said, "It gets this hot in Pasadena. Sometimes."

"Not very bloody often."

"True, but as long as we're here, we might as well take in a pyramid and the sphinx and stuff like that." I hoped I wouldn't cry when I looked at all the amazing Egyptian monuments Billy had told me about. He'd been fascinated by Egypt, probably because so many astounding things were being discovered there around that time.

"I suppose you're right," said Howard, wiping his face with his handkerchief.

A waiter came over, and I let Harold order for the both of us, since he was accustomed to giving orders to waiters and I wasn't. When the "tea" arrived, I was amazed that, along with the beverage, a platter containing about a thousand little tiny sandwiches and cakes accompanied it.

"Egypt is still a British protectorate," Harold explained. "So I asked for a proper English tea."

"English people eat all this for tea? What do they have for dinner and how do they fit it in on top of this?"

Pouring out a cup of steaming tea for me—I'd have preferred cold lemonade, but I didn't want to make a fuss—he said, "This meal would be considered dinner for the lower orders of the British Empire, my dear."

"You mean people like me?"

He nodded. "Indeed. It's only the very wealthy who can afford to have this kind of tea in the afternoon. Then they go to their theaters, balls and parties and eat supper at midnight or so."

"Good Lord, really?"

"Well, to tell the truth, I think the custom is fading out, but yes. That's the way it used to be."

"So the people who do all the work have sandwiches and cakes and tea for dinner?"

"Not exactly. They eat their final meal of the day then, but they still call it having tea."

"How long are we going to stay in England on our way back home? Maybe I'd better study up on the language and culture.

It sounds more complicated than Egypt."

With a laugh, Harold urged me to try one of the tiny sandwiches, all of which had their crusts removed, naturally. "Try one of the cucumber sandwiches. They're good."

"If you say so." I peered at the tray Harold held out to me, trying to find myself a cucumber sandwich. I wasn't hungry, but I did want to please Harold, who had gone to a whole lot of trouble for me. At the risk of being rude, I pointed at a sandwich. "Is that a cucumber sandwich?"

"How the devil should I know? Take a bite out of it and you tell me."

So I did. And it was. A cucumber sandwich, I mean. It wasn't bad, and it wasn't heavy, and I appreciated that aspect of it particularly.

"Oh, look," said Harold. "There are tomato sandwiches, too."

"Don't they put anything on them but tomatoes? Heck, Aunt Vi would combine the ingredients and give us tuna fish with cucumbers and tomatoes both on the bread."

"Different cuisines, sweetie."

"I guess so."

After tea, which didn't last very long, since I couldn't eat more than a bite of two of the sandwiches and didn't want any of the cakes, Harold and I decided to stroll across the street to see the gardens. Billy had told me about the gardens, too, and my heart hurt when I thought I should be with him on this trip and not Harold. But if Billy had lived, we never could have afforded to visit Egypt, and even if we'd come into a pile of money, Billy's health wouldn't have allowed him to take the trip, so it didn't make much difference. Why was life so difficult? You needn't attempt to answer that question. It was rhetorical.

The aroma of the roses and other flowers was very pleasant, and I again wished Billy could have been with me. Stupid thing to wish for, but there you go. After we'd wandered about a bit, Harold said, "Well, it's a nice garden, but it's too damned hot out here. I say we head for the hotel and rest until dinnertime."

"Good idea. I have some letters to answer. When's dinnertime?"

"I'll come to your room at eight. Will that be all right with you?"

"Perfect." It didn't matter to me what time we ate—or didn't eat. Maybe by eight the two bites of sandwich I'd taken at tea would have disappeared and I'd be hungry.

The first letter I answered was Sam's. Don't ask me why.

Dear Sam,
  Thank you for your letter. I truly appreciate it.
  The trip, so far, has been interesting. I was kind of seasick on the voyage over on the ship, but the trains have taken us through some fascinating country. I really liked Constantinople, which people are now calling Istanbul.

I contemplated that last sentence. Had I liked Istanbul? Well, I'd found it interesting, but you couldn't use the word "interesting" in every sentence because that would get boring. Nuts. I tried again.

The people both in Istanbul and Cairo are, for the most part, Moslem. You probably know that already, just as you probably know the Egyptians keep their women clad in black from head to foot, and they only have little slits for eyeholes so they can see where they're going when they're out and about. The robes themselves (I'm sure there's an Arabic word for them, but I don't know what it is) look comfy, but I sure wouldn't want to be covered from head to toe in this ghastly heat. I think August is definitely the wrong time to see Egypt. Anyhow, women in Turkey are given more scope in their choice of dress, and while I saw a lot of head scarves and things, I didn't see any women muffled from head to toe in fabric. On the other hand, we were only there for a short while.

Still and all, tomorrow Harold and I are going to visit the pyramids at Giza and maybe ride on a camel. Billy always wanted to do that. There's a train that takes passengers to the pyramids. Somebody on the train from Istanbul to Cairo told me that people used to have to ride donkeys from the hotel to the pyramids. I'm glad we no longer have to do that.

I sat still, chewing the end of my pen and wondering what else to write. Was I being too chatty? Not chatty enough? I reminded myself that Sam had been Billy's best friend, that my folks liked him, and that he'd helped me out of a jam or two. I dipped the pen in the ink bottle once more.

Well, I have to write return letters to my family now, so I'd better sign off for the time being. Thanks again for your letter, and please keep in touch. I'll tell you all about the pyramids when I write again.

Contemplating my last paragraph, I wondered what had prompted me to write it. When Sam read it, he'd know I'd written to him first. Did I want him to know that?

"Aw, nuts," I muttered as I lay down my pen, folded the letter, stuck it in the envelope—both paper and envelopes, by the way, were thoughtfully provided by the hotel itself—licked the gummed flap and closed the stupid thing. So what if Sam knew I'd written to him before I'd written to my parents? And did I really want him to keep in touch?

"Who cares?" I growled at the room.

Then I wrote basically the same letter to Ma, Pa and Aunt Vi and my brother and sister; penned a more effusive, but much shorter, letter to Mrs. Pinkerton in which I said I could feel the spirits of the pharaohs all around me. That, of course, was pure bunkum, but she expected stuff like that. If I could really sense spirits, I'd probably be overwhelmed by those of the however billion common folk who'd lived and died in Egypt during the last several thousand years, the ratio of pharaohs to common folk being what it was.

I decided to drop a note to Johnny and Flossie, too, but thought I'd get them one of those pretty postcards with scenes of Egypt I'd noticed at the front desk. And I probably should get a funny card for Pudge Wilson. Thinking I might as well do that now, since eight o'clock was still an hour and a half away, I slipped out of my room and walked to the elevator—or "lift," as they called it there.

While searching through the rack of postcards, I heard a voice close by. The voice addressed me.

"First trip to Egypt?" the voice asked in a pleasant, clipped British accent. I looked up to see a tallish man, very blond and handsome and impeccably dressed in the same sort of white costume Harold had chosen to wear at tea only without the pith helmet, reaching for a postcard of his own.

I wasn't accustomed to being accosted by strange gentlemen in strange places—or heck, even in Pasadena—and at first thought maybe I shouldn't answer him. Then I figured *what the heck,* and said, "Yes. You?"

"Oh, no. I come here often on business. Egypt is one of my favorite places on earth."

Somewhat surprised, I asked, "Even in August?" Then I felt stupid.

But the fellow only offered me a gentle laugh and said, "It's hot in August, all right, but it's always fairly hot here. Egypt gets into the blood, though, if you study it enough."

"It does?"

"It does." He tilted his head and studied me. "Do I detect an

American accent?"

He must have seen me stiffen slightly—I mean, who the heck was he to be quizzing me over a stack of postcards, for Pete's sake?—because he said, "I beg your pardon. I don't generally address young women whom I don't know. Please allow me to introduce myself. Wallingford Stackville, at your service."

"Daisy Majesty," I said in a neutral voice, "and I don't believe I need your service, but thank you."

"Oh, dear, I've upset you. I beg your pardon again."

"Think nothing of it," I said, and went back to studying postcards. After a good deal of thumbing through cards, I purchased one of a colorful caravan of camels and white-clad men traveling across the Sahara desert, one of the pyramids at Giza, one of a boat traveling on the Nile and a funny one of the face of a camel showing all his (or her—I couldn't tell its gender) crooked teeth. Then, without giving my unwanted companion another thought, I went back up to my room and wrote a note on the caravan postcard and addressed it to Johnny and Flossie. I addressed the boat-on-the-Nile postcard to my nieces and the one with the pyramids to Edie and Quincy Applewood. And Pudge Wilson got the snaggle-toothed camel. He'd love it.

CHAPTER TWELVE

After I'd taken all my letters and the postcards down to the front desk, where they had a mail service, I went back up to my room yet once more, stripped my overused gray dress off over my head, flung it aside and plopped on the bed, thinking to rest up for twenty minutes or so.

I awoke with a start when I heard a knock at the door. Glancing at the clock on the bedside table, I noticed with horror that it was eight o'clock already! The heat must have a soporific effect on a body, because I very seldom napped in the afternoon. Scrambling up off the bed, I darted to the closet, praying whoever had unpacked for me had hung my robe on the door. S/he had. Thank God. I fumbled into the robe and walked to the door, feeling guilty. Again.

Harold took one look at me and said, "Good Lord, Daisy. You can't go down to dinner looking like that!"

"I'm sorry, Harold. I lay down, thinking to take a little nap, and just woke up when you knocked at the door. I'll change quickly and join you downstairs in a few minutes. Is that all right?"

With an expression of sympathy I knew I didn't deserve, Harold said, "Of course you may, Daisy. Take your time. You needn't hurry. I'll have a drink in the bar, and you can join me there."

At first his words shocked me because I'd become so accustomed to life in the USA, where Prohibition was supposed to be in effect, although it was honored more by word than deed from what I'd seen and read. I guess it had slipped my mind that people in other parts of the world could still take a sip of something alcoholic when they wanted one, without fear of arrest. "Thanks, Harold. I'm really sorry."

"No need to be. You need your rest." He gave me another searching glance, and I knew what was coming next. "And some food."

I regret to say I borrowed a gesture from Sam Rotondo and rolled my eyes at Harold, who held up a hand. "I'm sorry. I'll stop pestering you about your weight."

"That's okay," I told him. "But you know I eat as much as I can. It's just that right now . . ."

"Yes, yes. I know." He turned and hurried off, and then I felt guilty for making him feel guilty. How stupid life could be sometimes! Or maybe it was just I who was stupid. I didn't want to think about it.

I selected my evening costume with care, wanting to placate Harold, who was such a good friend to me, even though he tended to fuss. Because he was tired of seeing me in black and gray, and because we Americans really didn't follow the wearing-of-black custom as much as we used to do, I decided I'd wear a blue silk frock at dinner. It was very comfortable and light of weight, which aided my selection, since the weather, in spite of electrical fans in the room, was still quite warm.

The frock had an unfitted hip-length, tubular-shaped bodice. It actually looked tubular on me, too, which came as something of a shock. I knew I'd lost some weight, but hadn't realized exactly how much. Maybe everyone was right, and I should try to eat more. On the other hand, the thin, boyish figure was "in" then, so nuts to that; I'd eat when I darned well felt like it. Anyway, the bodice had a scooped neckline and short sleeves, with a silver lace overbodice. The tiered skirt came to mid-calf, and the whole ensemble was pulled together by a little rosette of pink looped ribbons and two streamers where the overbodice met in the middle. When I'd made the thing, I'd thought about putting little rosettes on each of the tiers, but had decided that would look funny and overdone, so I didn't.

Anyhow, I thought Harold would be pleased. I wore silver cross-strapped evening slippers I'd purchased at Nash's on sale. Actually, this had been one of my more expensive outfits if you count the shoes. The lace overbodice I'd made using leftover fabric from something Mrs. Pinkerton's seamstress had sewn for her. My friend Edie Applewood, who worked as Mrs. Pinkerton's lady's maid, gave it to me after Mrs. Pinkerton gave it to her, since Edie didn't sew. But the shoes had cost a dollar and a half, which is where the expense came in.

There was no need to wear a hat at dinner, so I just donned some flesh-colored stockings and slipped into my shoes. Then I tackled my hair, which had gone kind of flat on one side. But I have thick hair that's easy to manage, and not much more than twenty minutes had slipped away before I grabbed a feathery-light shawl, left my room and headed downstairs to the bar. The bar. Imagine that!

Another surprise awaited me at the bar. Harold sat on a stool in animated conversation with the same gentleman who'd accosted me at the postcard rack.

I hesitated at the door of the bar, wondering if I should simply walk boldly in and interrupt their discussion or wait a bit. Harold solved the problem for me when he spotted me in the doorway and waved me over.

"Daisy! I was just chatting with this gentleman, and when I told him my sister was traveling with me, he asked if that sister was you." He winked to let me know I should keep up the deception.

That was all right with me. What's more, I hoped Harold had

mentioned that I was his recently widowed sister who was suffering agonies of bereavement over her late husband. For some reason, this blond guy didn't seem quite right to me, although I couldn't come up with a reason for that to be so, unless it was because he'd spoken to me before we'd been introduced. But that was silly. It was 1922, for heaven's sake, and the old, formal ways had bitten the dust a long time ago.

Both Harold and the other man, whose name I'd forgotten, rose from their stools. "How nice to meet you again, Missus Majesty. Please accept my deepest condolences on the loss of your husband."

"Thank you." I turned to Harold. "I fear this gentleman and I weren't properly introduced, Harold, and I can't remember his name."

I got the feeling Harold was taken aback by the frigidity of my manner—although, God knows, any sort of refrigeration would have been welcome at that point—because he said, "Oh. Well, please allow me to introduce you to Mister Wallingford Stackville. Mister Stackville, my sister, Daisy Majesty. Daisy, by the way, is short for Desdemona."

Darn, I wish he hadn't said that! I'd never live down that "Desdemona" name I'd saddled myself with when I was ten. Oh, well. I held out my hand for him to shake. "How do you do?"

"Fine, thank you. It's good to see you again."

"Thank you." I probably should have said something else, but I couldn't think of anything else to say. I certainly wasn't happy to see him again, although I couldn't have given you a reason for my aversion to the chap.

"Would you like a drink, Daisy?" asked Harold. "I think sherry is generally taken by ladies before the evening meal."

If there was anything I wanted less than an alcoholic beverage at that moment in time, I didn't know what it was. Unless it was to get rid of Stackville. "No, thank you, Harold. I don't care for anything right now."

"Very well. Would you like another, Stackville?"

"I don't think so, thanks." He turned to me. "I was just saying to Harold that since I'm traveling alone in Egypt, it would be my pleasure to take my new friends to dinner at the hotel," said the suave Mr. Stackville.

I didn't like that idea. Mind you, I'd come to the conclusion that I really ought to make an effort to meet more people and get back into some sort of social life again, but I was thinking more along the lines of meeting other women. Women who could become friends and to whom I could write about this and that when we got back to our real lives.

"And I told him I thought that was a swell offer," said Harold, dashing my hopes of getting rid of the man.

Then I decided I was being too hard on him. After all, I'd only just met him. So I said, "Thank you, Mister Stackville."

"It will be my pleasure, believe me, Missus Majesty."

That's when I figured out why this fellow put me off. He acted toward me as the fat man with the cigar had acted. The fact that Mr. Stackville was tall, blond and handsome didn't make his attentions any more welcome to yours truly. But perhaps I was doing the man an injustice. Time, as people always say, would tell. Anyhow, there was no getting away from dining with him this evening, since Harold had already accepted his invitation.

The meal was delicious, I suppose. I couldn't eat much of it, and waiters kept coming with various courses until I stopped counting. I sipped some lentil soup and discovered I wasn't a great fan of lentils. The fish was good, so I ate a bite or two of it. The lamb was spiced in an odd way—odd to me, I mean, who was accustomed to good old American food—and I wondered what seasonings were used, because it was quite delectable. I actually ate four or five bites of that before I had to push it away.

I noticed Harold eyeing me through the meal, which only lessened my already enfeebled appetite, but I tried not to let his scrutiny bother me unduly. It wouldn't do to make a scene in public, after all.

Mr. Stackville produced a glib spate of tidbits about Egypt throughout the meal. I suspected he was trying to impress us, although he didn't seem to be bragging, only telling us things he thought we might find interesting.

"You're both visiting the pyramids at Giza tomorrow, I understand, Missus Majesty."

"Yes."

"Be glad you're going nowadays instead of back in the nineties. They actually have railcars to take you out there today, but when I first began visiting Egypt—I was only a lad then, of course—"

Of course, I thought nastily.

"—we had to ride donkeys."

"Yes, I've heard that," I murmured as the waiter took away my lamb and plunked a salad down in front of me.

"You can still ride donkeys if you want to."

I blinked at him. "Why would we want to do that?"

He apparently thought that was extremely funny, because he threw his head back and laughed. When he'd recovered, he said, "No reason. In fact, if this is your first trip to Egypt, I expect you'd rather have a camel ride. Camels are rude brutes, but they're useful."

"Yes. So I've heard," I mumbled.

"Daisy's husband studied a great deal about Egypt before his death," said Harold. I think he sensed my uneasiness about Mr. Stackville. "So Daisy has been filling me in on a lot of stuff about the country. My mother and stepfather visited here last winter."

"Winter is the best time to visit," agreed Stackville. He eyed me with more interest than I cared for. "So you've been told a lot about Egypt, have you?"

"Only what Mister Majesty used to read in the newspapers and *National Geographic,*" I said, wishing the guy would shut up and go away.

"There are new discoveries being made every day, and they're being reported all over the place, although you can't really get a feel for the place until you see it for yourself. So you're taking a Cook's steamer up the Nile?"

I looked at Harold, who was still munching lamb, so I answered the man. "Yes. And a Cook's guide is taking us to the pyramids tomorrow."

"They call those fellows *dragomen* here," said Stackville. As if I cared. "And don't believe everything they tell you. They're mainly entertainers, and they take pride in giving the customer what he—or in your case, Missus Majesty, she—wants, which they think is a good time and good stories."

What I wanted at that moment was to be back home again. I didn't say so. "I see."

"But you can browse bookstalls in the marketplace—they call it a *souk* here—and perhaps find a book that will give you the unedited, educated version of events and places."

"I'll keep that in mind."

"If you ever need me for anything, I'll be up on the third floor. The *dragoman* can find me."

Whatever would we need you *for?* thought I, and decided I was still in a grumpy mood. After all, the man was only trying to be pleasant. So I said, "Thank you."

"We're on the fourth floor. I got us a couple of the better suites," said Harold. With a laugh, he added, "God knows we're not used to roughing it. This trip was my idea, in order to get Daisy out and about a bit after her terrible loss, and it came about rather suddenly."

"I see," said Mr. Stackville, stroking his mustache. "Yes, I can see why it might have been a sudden decision, given the weather in August as compared to the weather in, say, December."

His comment irked me, and I snapped, "It just happened that my husband passed away in June, Mister Stackville. Harold is doing me a great kindness, and he didn't think it would be wise to wait until December. I . . ." Oh, good Lord, I felt tears spring to my eyes. How embarrassing! Swallowing them with determination and anger at this insinuating specimen, I said, "Harold wanted to get me out and about now. He didn't feel it wise to wait until December."

"Of course. I meant no criticism, Missus Majesty." Turning to Harold, he said, "I hope you understood that, old man. No criticism at all."

Harold waved his hand, which held a buttery knife. "I understand completely, Stackville. Daisy's a bit . . . touchy these days." Then he looked at me to see if I was going to pounce on him and beat him to a pulp with a dinner plate.

Naturally, I'd never do such a thing to Harold, who was one of my closest friends, even if he was calling me touchy, which I resented like fire. Although he was right. My shoulders slumped slightly when I realized the truth. I was not merely touchy and short-tempered, but sometimes I felt as though my skin was so sensitive, if anyone even touched me I'd jump a foot in the air and scream. Maybe someday somebody will invent a pill that will help people who were in the state I was in back then.

"Yes. I have to admit to being somewhat . . . out of sorts lately," I said softly, hoping both men would forgive me, although I wasn't sure for what I needed to be forgiven.

"Of course, you are," said Stackville, oozing sympathy. "I'm sorry if anything I've said has annoyed or offended you, Missus Majesty. That's the very last thing I intended to do."

I didn't believe him. I told myself to stop being ridiculous. Perhaps this man was lonely and only seeking some English-speaking company. God knew I'd heard languages from places all over the world since we entered Shepheards Hotel, and that was only earlier in the day.

"Think nothing of it," I said to him.

A waiter came and whisked our dishes away. He gave me an uneasy glance as if to ask me why I wasn't eating anything and if I found the food distasteful. Great. Now even waiters were getting into the "force Daisy to eat more" mode. I smiled at him to let him know I thought the salad had been delicious. He smiled back and took our plates back to the kitchen.

There followed what Harold assured me was a typical English trifle. It tasted funny to me, but I didn't say so.

Harold noticed anyway, since I wasn't eating much of it. "What's the matter, Daisy? This is one of the best trifles I've ever tasted."

"I'm sure it's wonderful. I'm just . . . not very hungry." I braced myself for a lecture, but Harold didn't give me one.

Rather, he squinted from the trifle to me and back again. "I know what it is!" He declared triumphantly. "The trifle has liquor in it. This time it's . . ." He paused to savor another bite. "I believe I detect the taste of sherry."

"Right," said Mr. Know-It-All Stackville. He gave me what seemed to me to be a patronizing smile. "You're American, and I'm sure you aren't accustomed to the flavor of sherry in your desserts."

"You're right about that," I said, trying not to sound cold and failing. To make up for it, I said, "The fruit is good, though." And when I got home, I decided, I'd ask Aunt Vi to make the family an English trifle *sans* alcohol. It would taste pretty good

123

if it weren't for the stupid sherry. And then I recalled Aunt Vi telling me once about how she used to make something called "tipsy pudding," and I wondered if it was anything like an English trifle. I decided to ask her in my next letter home.

The two men dug into their trifles while I sported with a strawberry or two from my own dish, wishing the interminable meal would end. When it finally did, Mr. Stackville asked, "Would the two of you care to accompany me to the saloon, where dancing will take place shortly? Shepheards has a wonderful band."

I couldn't offhand think of anything I'd like less, so I said, "I'm sorry, but I'm really awfully tired from the long trip." Speaking directly to Harold, I said, "Would you mind if I begged off this time, Harold?"

"Not at all, Daisy. But I think I'll take Mister Stackville up on his invitation. Might as well have a little fun while we're here."

"Excellent," declared Mr. Stackville. "Why don't we escort Missus Majesty to her room, Kincaid, and then we can return to the saloon."

"Sounds like an idea to me," said Harold as alarm bells went off in my head. Mr. Stackville didn't strike me as a person of Harold and Del's stripe, but if he was, was Harold being untrue to Del by hanging out in a saloon with him?

And was it any of my business if he was?

Yes, darn it! I was Harold's friend. And Del's, too. I'd never, ever help a person I liked commit a sin against a marital commitment. Or even a non-marital commitment.

But Harold was behind me, pulling out my chair, and I'd already sealed the evening's doings by refusing to accompany the two men. Bah. It occurred to me to change my mind, but the notion of lingering in the saloon, where people would undoubtedly be smoking and drinking and where the music would be loud, made my head ache, so I silently commended Harold and Del to God. I didn't go so far as to commend Mr. Stackville to the devil, but I felt like it.

CHAPTER THIRTEEN

Although I didn't think I'd sleep much that night because I'd slept away the entire afternoon, I was wrong. I slept like the proverbial baby—not like a real one who, according to friends of mine who knew about such things, cried, screeched and fussed all night long.

I was dressed and ready to go when Harold knocked at my door at eight A.M. Since this was to be, I hoped, the day during which I'd actually get to ride a camel and climb a pyramid, I'd worn jodhpurs. And what, you might be asking, would a middle-class city kid like Daisy Gumm Majesty be doing with jodhpurs? Well, I'll tell you. I made them for a class play when I was a senior in high school, and they now fitted me again. It was kind of nice to be able to fit into clothes that I hadn't been able to wear for a long time, but I'd rather have had Billy back.

However, I did my best to suppress all unhappy thoughts and vowed to myself that I'd enjoy the day whether I wanted to or not. I opened the door to Harold, who'd had the same brilliant idea as I, and who also wore jodhpurs. I grabbed a jacket that went well enough with my puffy pants so as not to look odd, and Harold and I headed to the dining room. Before we got there, I'd used up my quota of conversational tidbits for the morning by asking him if he'd had a good time the night before. He said he had, that Shepheards' band was quite good, that he'd danced a bit, and that was that.

An obsequious waiter led us to a table. I ordered toast and

tea. Harold had a full English breakfast, which consisted of . . .
Lord, just about every type of foodstuff you can imagine, and
even some I never knew existed.

"What did you say that stuff was?" I asked, nodding at a pile
of a rice-based concoction on his plate.

"Kedgeree. Have a bite. It's delicious."

"What's in it?"

"Smoked fish, eggs, rice, mushrooms." He squinted at the
forkful of the mélange he'd lifted toward his mouth. "I don't
know what else, but it's really good. It has an East Indian flavor
to it. I guess the British stole the idea from India—kind of like
they stole India from the Indians. Have a bite," he repeated.

"Um, thanks, but I don't think so."

And here I used to think I was up to anything. That morning
the mere thought of kedgeree conquered me. I lifted a piece of
my toast and spread a little marmalade on it. We didn't get
marmalade much in Pasadena, although I don't know why.
After all, we had two orange trees in our very yard, a navel and
a Valencia, giving us oranges darned near year-round, and Aunt
Vi made all sorts of other kinds of jams and jellies. Although it
was a little bitter, I liked the taste of marmalade. Perhaps I
wasn't a total coward when it came to food. Not that it matters.

Before we were through with our meals—well, before Harold
was through with his, anyhow, I was finished practically before I
started—who should walk up to our table but Mr. Wallingford
Stackville. He pretended to be surprised to see us.

"Well, my goodness, look who's here!" he said in a jovial
voice.

Harold waved to an empty chair at our table. "Have a seat.
We're nearly through with our meal, but it's nice to have
company."

I didn't think it was nice at all, but I managed a weak smile
for Mr. Stackville.

"Don't mind if I do," said he, and he pulled out a chair and sat. He eyed my plate. "You certainly don't eat much, Missus Majesty. That's probably how you manage to keep your figure so trim."

I'd have slapped his face if we'd been at home, but I presumed this person, who seemed to have been everywhere and done everything, didn't find personal comments of such a nature in the manner of an insult. Nevertheless, while I didn't answer him, I gave him a frown for his efforts.

He grinned. "Oh, dear. I see I've stepped in a mess again. Please forgive me, Missus Majesty. I've been away from home for so long, I seem to have forgot my company manners."

I sipped some tea so I wouldn't have to speak to him.

Thank the good Lord, Stackville turned his attention to Harold. "So what's on the agenda first, old man?"

"We're going to see the pyramids first. Then I want to get Daisy on a camel."

Mr. Stackville laughed. "I'd love to see that. There are camel drivers near the pyramids who can accommodate you. Do you have a Kodak?"

Harold patted a big satchel he'd deposited on the fourth chair at our table. "Sure do. Bought it especially for this trip. I want Daisy to have mementoes of all the places we've been when we get back home again."

"To Pasadena?"

"Right. Good old Pasadena."

"And then you're taking the Nile cruise?"

"Right again."

"But you'll be stopping in London for a day or so before you head home, won't you?"

Why in the name of Glory was he quizzing Harold about our itinerary? I decided to ask him, thereby risking being told once more that I was touchy. "You seem quite interested in our travel plans, Mister Stackville." I tried to keep my tone neutral, but I sounded relatively icy to my own ears.

"Oh, my, just curious, my dear Missus Majesty. I see so few people from home in Egypt this time of year."

"Home? I thought you were British."

"Well, yes, I am. But I've been to the United States so often, I almost feel like an American. I beg your pardon if my question seemed forward."

Hmm. Flummoxed again.

Oh, stop it, Daisy Majesty. He's probably only an innocent tourist like we are. That's what I told myself. After considering the matter for a moment or two, myself didn't believe it.

I gave him a glacial smile. "Think nothing of it. Ask all the prying questions you want to."

"Daisy!" Harold gaped at me.

Mr. Stackville gulped.

To heck with the both of them. "Harold, I'm going back to my room to freshen up. I'll meet you downstairs in half an hour. Will that give us time enough to catch the train to the pyramids?"

"Plenty of time."

He and Stackville rose as I got up from my chair and exited the dining room, feeling like an idiot, which I probably was. Ah, well. Wouldn't be the first time. And I had no idea why Mr. Stackville's persistent presence irked me so much. Perhaps if we'd met a single woman—say, a middle-aged lady who was traveling with a companion after her husband's death or something like that—I wouldn't have been so bristly.

Fortunately for Harold, Mr. Stackville and me, Stackville was nowhere to be seen when I met Harold downstairs. There, we were loaded into an automobile and driven to the station, where we boarded the train for Giza. The group we joined had an Egyptian guide at our beck and call, a fellow whose name was

Mohammed. I think all Egyptian men are named Mohammed, actually, although I'm not sure why.

It seemed that Harold intended to keep the peace, because he didn't mention Stackville once during the train ride or our subsequent activities that day. I appreciated his consideration.

We did meet some other people in our group, by the way, and it was kind of fun to exchange oohs and aahs with folks from England, France and even Canada. I particularly enjoyed the company of the Canadians, who were three college friends whose parents had financed a trip around the world for them before they began working at more mundane jobs. As I'd thought a million times before—actually, probably more times than that—it must be nice to be born into money. Still, they were very nice, courteous young gentlemen, and two of them helped me climb the Great Pyramid.

To look at a picture of the Great Pyramid, you'd think it was straight up and pointy on top, or just barely squared off, but it's not. Even though Billy had read me everything he could find on the pyramids, I hadn't anticipated their size. The Great Pyramid's base took up over thirteen acres of land, for Pete's sake! And tall? My goodness, I've never seen so tall a structure. Not only that, but the sides of it weren't smooth at all. They were built sort of like stairs, only out of huge, square blocks of limestone, and must each have been three feet on all sides.

In fact, before we were halfway to the summit, I'd begun to wish I'd stayed below and bought a postcard instead of attempting the climb. But such was not to be, and I have to admit that once we reached the top of the thing, the view was spectacular. If you're fond of deserts. I'm not particularly, but knowing something of the history of these magnificent monuments made the view worthwhile even so.

"Oh, my," I said to one of the young men who'd helped me and whose name was Nathaniel Gentry, "I'm so out of breath. I should start doing Swedish exercises when I get home, I reckon."

He laughed, as did the other fellow who'd helped me achieve the summit and whose name was George Washington (I'm not joking about that, although George himself had a ready supply of jokes about his name at his disposal). Nathaniel said, "It's a steep climb, and it's hotter than Hades, too. I think you did very well."

Wiping my perspiring brow with one of the several hankies I'd secreted on my person, having anticipated the weather, I said, "It sure is. But, my goodness, it's hard to imagine people without our modern-day tools building these monster monuments."

"I agree," said George, who was similarly occupied in mopping sweat from various parts of his body.

"God, Daisy, I damned near gave up before we were halfway to the top." This gem was dropped by Harold, who staggered toward our little group with the last Canadian (whose name was Brian Brandt) in tow. With them came a couple of the ever-present Egyptians who expected *baksheesh* for helping hapless tourists up the pyramid. Harold handed them a bunch of coins. From the looks of ecstasy on their faces, he'd grossly overpaid them.

"You probably shouldn't have done that," said Nathaniel. "You're going to be haunted by little Egyptian kids begging for *baksheesh* when word gets out that you're so generous."

"I don't even care." Harold plunked himself down on the dusty ground, the limestone blocks having been gathering dust for millennia. I had a feeling that, what with the dust and the perspiration, Harold and I were both going to be muddy messes by the time we got back to Shepheards.

"It's an amazing sight," said Nathaniel, awe clear to hear in his voice.

"It sure is," agreed George. "Too bad we couldn't have come

in January instead of August."

"You've got *that* right," said Brian.

All of us had sweated through our garments, and I took off my jacket. I had meant to pay due deference to the sensibilities of the Egyptian people and cover up as much of myself as I could, but common sense took hold of me at last and I couldn't get the stupid jacket off fast enough. As it was, my white shirt was soaked through, and I hoped nobody was shocked at the sight. They didn't seem to be.

Although we all could have used a good long rest after our arduous climb, it was too darned hot to linger at the top of the Great Pyramid, so as soon as Harold had caught his breath and taken gobs of pictures with his Kodak, several of which included our Canadian friends, we started down again. Going down was no more fun than going up had been, but we finally made it to the dusty earth. You know, whenever I think about that trip to Egypt, the first thing about it that pops to mind is the dust. I don't think that's being fair to Egypt, but I can't help it.

And then I rode a camel. The beast stank to high heaven. And the ride was hideously uncomfortable, in spite of the little saddle-like thing perched on top of the beautiful saddle blanket. The gait of a camel isn't, say, like riding in a car over a bumpy road. It's more like sitting on something that joggles you on purpose every third second or so and threatens to send you top-pling. Fortunately for yours truly, the camel was led by one of those universal *dragomen,* who only smiled up at me with his brownish teeth showing and who said every now and then, "Good, good. You ride good."

If he said so.

By the time my camel ride was over, my legs were so tired and I had such a fierce headache from heat and exertion, I could barely walk. Fortunately for me, the train was there to take us back to Cairo. I don't think I'd ever been so exhausted in my entire life.

"But I got several shots of you on the camel and on top of the pyramid, Daisy. Once you recover from your ordeal, you'll enjoy looking at them and showing them to your family," said Harold as we chugged back to Cairo.

"I'm sure you're right, Harold."

This train wasn't anything like the Orient Express. One couldn't, for example, go to the dining car and get a glass of water or some bicarbonate of soda or some salicylic powders to cure one's headaches and other assorted aches and pains. So I sat there and suffered and wished I was dead. Or back home. Either option would have done at that moment. I was so happy when we finally returned to Shepheards, I could have cried, but I didn't.

As soon as we got inside, Harold went to the bar, claiming he needed liquid refreshment. I headed straight for the elevator, but the man behind the desk called my name. "Missus Majesty?" Don't ask me how he remembered people's names, but I'd heard him call out like that to other people before that time.

Although I didn't want to, I turned and smiled at him. To my surprise, I saw he was holding up an envelope. I stood at the elevator like a dope, staring at the envelope, until he said, "A letter was delivered for you while you were out."

"Oh. Oh, yes. Of course." My head throbbing a jungle beat, I walked to the desk and took the envelope. "Thank you."

"Of course," said the excruciatingly polite man. I guess Shepheards only hired the best.

So I took the letter on the elevator with me and on the way up to the fourth floor, I perused its envelope. Sam. Sam had written me another letter. How very strange. My heart twinged as I considered the letter might contain bad news about Pa or something.

But that was silly. If anything had happened to Pa, Ma would have sent a telegraph wire.

As soon as I reached my room, I plowed through my little bag of toiletries—Harold had told me that English folks call these bags sponge bags, God knows why—and dug out my bottle of aspirin. I took three of them with a tall glass of water, refilled the glass from the pitcher of boiled water the hotel supplied to each room, sat on my bed and carefully opened Sam's letter. I began reading.

Dear Daisy,

You will probably laugh at this, but I miss you. I know you don't care for me and that we've had an adversarial relationship a time or two, but I have to say that I do miss you when you're gone. So, naturally, do your mother, father and aunt. But I thought you might at least get a laugh out of my feeling lonely with you away.

The aspirin hadn't begun working yet, my head throbbed like mad, and I wondered if I'd misread Sam's words, which seemed . . . so unlike him, I guess. Blinking several times to make sure my vision was clear, I went back to his letter.

But enough of the maudlin stuff. I just want you to know that your father is doing well. He and I take Spike for a walk most evenings. Spike is pining, missing both you and Billy, I suspect, but we're doing our best to keep his spirits up.

"Oh, poor Spike," I murmured into the warm air, which was being stirred by an electrical fan, which felt wonderful. "I shouldn't have left him to go on this harebrained trip." Feeling terrible about abandoning Spike, not to mention the rest of my family, I read further.

I know you think I spend more time at your house than my

own, and you're probably right. But the truth is, I'm a lonely man. Ever since Margaret passed away, I've felt as though I have a hole in my heart. You probably don't want to hear this, but I feel as though your family, and especially Billy, more or less adopted me. You're fortunate to have such kind and generous relations, Daisy. But it seems to me as though you're the glue that holds the family together. Without you, everyone seems sort of at loose ends.

Please don't think I'm trying to make you feel guilty . . .

He could have fooled me, blast the man. Nevertheless, I read on.

. . . because I'm not. Your entire family believes you're doing the right thing in going on this trip with Mr. Kincaid. Sometimes it's good to get away from what we coppers call "the scene of the crime." Not that Billy's death was a crime, unless you count the late war as a crime against humanity, but I'm sure you see what I mean.

Anyhow, I don't want to bother you, but I do want you to know that everyone here at home in Pasadena thinks of you daily, and we all send our best wishes. I'm not a very good hand at letter-writing, but, well, writing to you seems to be helping me feel better, so I'm going to keep doing it. If you want to, you can throw my letters away. Just writing them is something like what the alienists call a "catharsis." At least I think that's the word.

I look forward to seeing a photograph of you on a camel.

Sincerely,
Sam (Rotondo)

By the time I'd finished Sam's letter, tears stung my eyes. I chalked them up to heat exhaustion. Then I peeled my clothes off and headed to the bathroom to take a cool bath. By the time

I'd finished my bath, taken a nap and changed into a very cool sleeveless dress in which I aimed to pass the remainder of the evening, I thought I might be able to write Sam a letter without crying all over it.

So I did.

Chapter Fourteen

Dear Sam,
Thank you very much for your letter. I enjoy reading news
from home.

"What a stupid way to begin a letter," said I to myself.
Nevertheless, the truth was the truth, so I allowed the words to
remain on the paper and the paper to remain on the desk, and I
didn't throw it into the wastepaper basket.

The heat here is truly awful. Harold and I climbed the Great
Pyramid at Giza today, I rode a camel afterward, and I can
now tell you from experience that camels are stinky, hateful
beasts. I think I got too much sun, because I had a roaring
headache when we returned to the hotel.
We've been meeting people here and there on our trip, but so
far I haven't felt up to socializing much. Please tell Ma and
Aunt Vi that I'm eating as much as I can, although that's not
very much. And I truly appreciate you and Pa taking care of
Spike, who must be really confused about the changes in his
family.

I tapped the end of the pen on the writing table and wondered
what I should write next. Should I tell Sam what was in my
heart, or should I keep the letter light and skirt the important
stuff?
"Oh, to heck with it."

Your letters mean a lot to me, Sam, perhaps because you have suffered the loss of a beloved spouse, as I've done. I know we got off on the wrong foot together, but I do appreciate that you're continuing to spend time with my family. Please tell them I'm doing as well as can be expected, but I sure do miss them and home and Pasadena.

Since I didn't want to descend into the maudlin, I decided to try to make the man laugh. Making Sam laugh was no easy task, as I knew from experience.

I must say, though, that it's nice to get away from constant calls from Mrs. Pinkerton, wailing at me about Stacy. I hope Stacy is sticking to the straight and narrow. Well, I don't suppose she can help it since she's still locked up, but when she gets out, I hope she goes back to the Salvation Army as she's promised to do.

A knock came at the door at that juncture, and a glance at the clock next to the bed told me it was probably Harold, come to fetch me for dinner. I actually felt a smallish pang of hunger, believe it or not, and that brightened my mood. Unless it was Sam's letter that had done the brightening. But I didn't want to think about that.

Well, Harold is here to fetch me so that we can go down to dinner. Thank you again for writing. Please give my love to everyone.

Fondly,
Daisy

After I let Harold in, stuffed the letter into an envelope, addressed it and picked up my filmy shawl, I contemplated that "fondly" all the way down to the magnificent dining room, with a detour to the desk, where I handed the letter to the clerk. One moment I regretted the word; the next moment I figured I actually meant it, so why not write it? At any rate, I continued distracted as I read the menu.

"So what did you do with your afternoon, Harold?" I asked as I tried to imagine what sirloin of beef Châtelaine was. I suspected it was roast beef dressed up. It sounded okay to me.

"Chatted with our friend Stackville."

I glanced at Harold over my menu. "He's no friend of mine. I think he's sneaky."

"I think your imagination is working overtime, Daisy."

"Maybe. But he always seems to be there. If you know what I mean. You show up somewhere, and there he is. I show up somewhere, and there he is."

With a shrug, Harold said, "Maybe he finds us good company." He glanced around the dining room. "Most of the rest of the guests here look as though they're nearing ninety, at least."

I perused the room, too. "Well . . . I guess you're right."

Harold put his menu down. "Listen, Daisy, I'm rethinking this Nile cruise thing. I damned near dropped dead from heatstroke today, and I know you were suffering, too."

"You've got *that* right," I told him with fervor. "I had such a ghastly headache, it isn't all gone yet, and I took three aspirin tablets."

"It's occurred to me that perhaps we should go back to England. It won't be nearly as miserable there, and we can see the sights in London. Mind you, if you want to continue up the Nile, I'm game, but everyone who's told me August is the wrong time to visit Egypt has been absolutely right so far."

I could have kissed him. Not that I wouldn't love to see the sights of Egypt someday. But if I had my druthers, it would be a day approximately forty degrees cooler than the one in which we now existed. "Oh, Harold, I'd *love* to go back to England! Egypt was Billy's dream, and I'll carry on for his sake, but if you don't want to take the tour up the Nile, either, then let's not."

"Thank God. I was afraid you'd think you failed Billy somehow if we backed out now."

"Failed Billy?" I shook my head. "Billy's dead, Harold. I might have failed him in life, but there's no way I can fail him now."

"And you call yourself a spiritualist," said Harold with a chuckle.

"Not on this trip, I don't."

"What's this about a spiritualist?" came a voice at my back. Stackville. Since he couldn't see me do it, I made a face at Harold.

"Good evening, Stackville," said Harold, ignoring the spiritualist business, thank God. "Care to join us? We haven't ordered yet."

After making another, even more horrible face at Harold, I turned my head and forced a smile. "Good evening, Mister Stackville." I didn't repeat Harold's invitation.

"Good evening, Missus Majesty. Thanks, Kincaid, but I'm dining with some other friends tonight. Please allow me to introduce them."

Harold stood. I didn't, although I did turn farther in my chair to see what Mr. Stackville's friends looked like. They looked like a couple of male human beings dressed for dining in a nice hotel restaurant. If I were really what people think I am, I could probably have penetrated the outer facades they presented to the world and figured out if they were good, bad or normal like the rest of us, but I'm not. Heck, for all I knew, Mr. Stackville wasn't really a pushy sneak but a hardworking gentleman of means. The two men presently standing beside him didn't look as though they were hurting for money, either, to judge by their clothes.

As a gentleman should, Stackville said, "Missus Majesty and Mister Kincaid, please allow me to introduce you to Mister Gaylord Bartholomew and Mister Pierre Futrelle."

"Pleased to meet you," I said to both men, although I didn't mean it. Not that I had anything against either of them, but I still didn't like the way Stackville seemed to show up wherever Harold and I were. But perhaps I was being illogical. Heck, if he was staying at Shepheards, why shouldn't he show up in Shepheards' dining room? For a fleeting moment, I had the melancholy notion that the bad mood I'd nursed since Billy's death was taking over my entire life, and the idea didn't appeal to me one bit. Therefore, I tried to make my smile appear a trifle more genuine.

"Yes, indeed," said Harold, bowing slightly to the two men and holding out his hand to be shaken.

To my astonishment, Mr. Futrelle executed a bow that might have looked normal in King Louis the Fourteenth's ballroom, but the likes of which I'd never seen before anywhere. Then he took my hand, although I hadn't extended it, kissed it, and said, "*Bonjour,* madam. The pleasure is all mine," in an accent so thick I could scarcely make out the words.

Then Futrelle executed another bow in Harold's direction. Thank the good Lord, he didn't kiss Harold's hand, but merely shook it.

"Don't mind Pierre," said the other man, Mr. Bartholomew, with a smile and as precise an English accent as Stackville's. I could tell he and Stackville were British because of the two days Harold and I had spent in London. "His old-world manners are a bit on the heavy side." He bowed less extravagantly than his friend had, and then shook Harold's hand.

"Messrs. Bartholomew and Futrelle and I are in business

141

together," explained Stackville. "Believe it or not, we're about to discuss that business over dinner this evening."

Why wouldn't we believe it? I didn't ask, although I thought the comment was kind of odd.

"Well," said I, hoping to speed the men on their way, "have a productive meeting."

"Yes," said Harold. "Perhaps we'll see each other again this evening in the saloon."

"Perhaps," said Stackville.

Mr. Futrelle, who was tall and dark-haired and who looked like a Frenchman about to gamble away the family fortune—in other words, kind of rascally, although who was I to judge?—actually twirled his black mustache. I'd never seen anybody do that in person, even though the gesture had shown up in a couple of the flickers I'd watched.

Mr. Bartholomew, shorter, plumper and far less flamboyant than his friend, merely smiled, nodded, and made as if to leave. Stackville hesitated an instant beside our table, then gave us a nod and joined his friends at the table toward which a waiter had been leading him before he halted for introductions.

When the men were too far away to hear anything I said, I told Harold, "I'm glad they didn't join us."

"I know you are. Sorry I didn't consult with you first. I realized right after I made the offer that you probably wouldn't appreciate it."

"It's just that I don't much care for Stackville." I shot a glance at the back of Mr. Futrelle. "And that French guy gives me the willies."

Harold laughed, but he didn't scold me for making snap judgments. He didn't have to; I was already smacking myself upside the head for my lousy attitude.

Our dinner was delectable, and I managed to get down a good deal of it, which heartened Harold considerably and did much to restore my humor after the Stackville incident. By the way, sirloin of beef Châtelaine is roast beef, just as I'd figured it would be. I guess maybe they cook it a certain way or use a special sauce or something. It was delicious, however it was prepared. I also learned that *haricots verts* are skinny green beans. I wrote down that nifty tidbit to tell Aunt Vi. I'd never let on to the folks at Shepheards, but Aunt Vi's Yorkshire pudding is better than theirs. Still and all, the entire meal was wonderful, and I felt rather like a stuffed sausage when it was over.

"Would you like to stroll in the gardens for a while, Daisy?" Harold offered after we polished off the last of our dessert, which was some kind of raspberry confection. I tried to figure out what was in it but had no luck, not being culinarily inclined. Which was a shame, since I'd bet Aunt Vi would love to make it. Oh, well.

Did I want to stroll in the gardens? Not really. However, Harold was being so very kind to me in giving me this extraordinary trip to exotic ports and climes that I couldn't refuse him. "Sure, Harold. You might have to drag me part of the way since I ate so much."

"Huh. You didn't eat *so much*, Daisy Majesty. You consumed approximately a quarter of your entire meal."

"It was more than that!" I protested. "At least it feels like it now."

"That's only because you've become accustomed to starving yourself."

"Maybe, but I feel kind of like I ate an entire elephant."

"Good. Let's walk off some of that pachyderm in the gardens. They smell really wonderful in the evening."

As I've mentioned before, the gardens across the street from Shepheards are truly a marvel. To get there, one had to wade through a herd of impoverished Egyptians, both children and adults, begging *baksheesh*. This was more sad than annoying, at least for me. Sometimes I forget that I live in the good old USA, and that, even though my family is far from wealthy, we lived a whole lot better than these poor folks. I was tempted to throw a few coins at them but had been sternly lectured by our tour guide and several other people not to do so, or we'd be swarmed by the wretched people. Nevertheless, I couldn't help but compare their lot to that of the folks who could afford to stop at Shepheards Hotel and to wonder why the people in charge of things in Egypt didn't do something to help the poor.

But there you go. Billy used to say I had a bleeding heart when it came to lots of things, including poor folks, and I guess he was right. Still and all, I doubt that all of those wretched beggars were indolent sluggards, as rich people like to pretend all poor people are. I'd bet anything, if I did stuff like that, that they were merely born in the wrong place at the wrong time. One more reason to be glad I was an American, I reckon. Not that America didn't have its share of poor folks.

Oh, never mind. The poverty problem is too large a one for so small a person as I to solve, even in my thoughts.

The warm night air negated its purpose, but I took along the filmy wrap that went with my sleeveless evening dress because I thought I ought to. It didn't do to offend the natives, who covered themselves from head to toe, or even potential clients, who dressed to the nines even during the month of August in Egypt. I'd noticed several elegant couples in the dining room. Mind you, I didn't expect to meet them again in Pasadena, but one never knew what the fates had in store for one. If you don't believe me, ask Billy. Oh. That's right. You can't, can you?

See what I mean?

"I wonder how Victorian ladies survived trips to Egypt," I murmured as I inhaled the heavenly scent of honeysuckle and roses as we ambled along the main path of the garden. "Can you imagine wearing a corset, a dozen petticoats, and those horrid, heavy tight-waisted gowns in some thick fabric like bombazine? I'm glad I live in nineteen twenty-two. At least I don't have to suffocate for the sake of fashion."

"True. You look lovely this evening, by the way, Daisy. Of course, you always dress impeccably."

"Thank you, Harold." I took his arm. "I appreciate your kind words."

"You know I'm right."

"Well . . . yes, I do. I'm careful about my clothing for the sake of my job. Nobody wants to hire a shabby spiritualist, don't you know."

He chuckled.

We didn't walk for long, primarily because, even though I'd taken a nap that afternoon, the remnants of my headache were still hovering at the edges of my brain, and I wanted to take another couple of aspirin and go to bed.

"Are you sure you don't want to sit in the saloon for a bit, Daisy? My primary aim in getting you out of Pasadena and into the big, wide world was to introduce you to new people and experiences. You can't do that if you insist on staying in your room all the time."

"Harold. You're one of my very best friends in the entire world, and I love you like a brother. In fact, as much as I love Walter, I'd sooner hang out with you than him because you have my kind of sense of humor. And I can't tell you how much I appreciate you taking me on this magnificent trip. But if you don't mind, I'd really like to go back to the hotel and hit the sack. My headache is coming back, and I'm afraid I'm not interested in Mister Stackville and his business associates, whom I fear would attempt to monopolize the two of us if we returned to the saloon together."

"Boy, you really don't like that guy, do you?"

"No, I don't."

"How come?"

I shook my head. "Darned if I know. He just rubs me the wrong way I guess. I can't point to anything specific and tell you 'this is why I don't like this man.' I suppose that sounds stupid."

"Actually, it doesn't. I've had reactions like that to certain people. Very well, it's back to the hotel for us, and I'll deposit you at your room before heading saloon-wards." He paused for a moment, and I saw him frown. "I have to admit that we haven't met too many people so far on our journey with whom I'd care to spend a lot of time. Maybe we should do this again in January or something."

I laughed out loud for perhaps the second time since Billy died. "Harold! You're the most generous person I've ever met in my life, but I'm not going to allow you to spend another fortune on cheering me up come January. If I don't feel better by the first of nineteen twenty-three, I suspect I'm going to be a grumpy Gus forever."

With a sigh, Harold said, "That would be a true shame, Daisy. What's more, I'm sure Billy wouldn't want you to act like Queen Victoria after her beloved Albert passed. He'd want you to get on with your life and be as happy as you can be."

"You're right, Harold. But I am getting on with my life. I know I won't feel this awful forever, mainly because that's impossible." And because Sam Rotondo had told me so, and he should know. I didn't say that part to Harold. "Still, it's going to take time for me to get used to Billy not being in my life. This trip was probably a good idea because everywhere we've been and are going to be is so different from home, I don't *expect* Billy to be there. If that makes any sense."

"It does, sweetie."

So we plowed our way through all the street beggars one more time, passed the white-clad and stern-looking *dragomen* stationed at the foot of Shepheards' stairs in order to keep the riffraff out, and Harold escorted me to my room.

As soon as I opened the door, I could tell someone else had been there before us. I told Harold so.

"Are you sure?" Harold stood in the doorway, casting his glance this way and that, attempting to see what I saw. Which he did, but he couldn't know what I knew, which was that things weren't the same as I'd left them.

"Yes, I'm sure!"

Harold walked into the middle of the sitting room of the suite and looked around. "Maybe it was a maid who came in to clean while you were out."

I frowned. "Maybe." But I opened the door and beckoned to the floor man, called a *suffragi*, according to Mr. Stackville, who, as much as I didn't like him, seemed to know his way around Egypt and its language. He came trotting up, his brown teeth gleaming. I guess nobody in Egypt brushed their teeth.

Smiling at him to let him know I wasn't accusing him of anything, I asked, "Did you happen to see someone enter my room while I was away this evening?"

"Enter your room? No, ma'am. No one enter."

"Not even a maid or a cleaning person?"

He shook his turbaned head. "No, ma'am. No clean."

"Thank you." I handed him a coin, he ducked his head in a kind of bow, and went back to his chair in the hall, which was approximately midway along the row of rooms.

"There. You see?" said Harold. "Nobody's been here, Daisy. You're imagining things."

"Am not. Besides, that guy's been asleep pretty much every time I've passed him in the hall, and I doubt that he changed his ways just because we went to dinner."

"Well, what do you want to do? Call the police?"

"Don't be silly. But I do aim to look around and see if

anything's been taken. Although what anyone would want to take is beyond me. I don't own any precious gems—well, except for the ugly bracelet that Russian count gave me a year or so ago, but that's in a safe-deposit box at the bank in Pasadena."

"I think you're imagining things," Harold said flatly. "Or you've been reading too many spy novels."

"Have not. I read mysteries, not spy novels. Well, except for John Buchan, but . . . oh, never mind."

With a sigh, Harold said, "Want me to search with you?"

"No, thank you. Go on down to the saloon. I'll check around and see if I can figure out whether or not anything's gone missing. Have a good evening, Harold."

He gave me a quick peck on the cheek. "You, too, Daisy." He headed for the door but stopped before he reached it and turned around. "You know, I don't like the idea of leaving you here when you suspect someone's been snooping. If you're right about that, whoever it was might still be here."

Oh, wonderful. I hadn't thought of that possibility until Harold brought it up. Now I was scared as well as baffled. "Really, Harold, I'm sure I'll be fine."

"No, sir. I'm going to look through every room in this suite and make sure you're in no danger before I leave you alone here. And be sure to lock your door after I leave."

I appreciated his valor, although I seriously doubted that Harold would be able to overcome a lurking thug if we found one. Nevertheless, his suggestion was a good one, so I went with him to the bedroom, and together we looked through closets and under the bed. Then we went through the bathroom. Results from all three rooms were negative. If someone had been in my suite—and I could almost swear someone had been—he or she was long gone now.

Therefore, I said, "Thanks, Harold. You go on down to the saloon now, and I'll just take a peek through my things to see if anything's been taken."

"Good idea."

"You might want to check your suite, too, since you have considerably more items of value than I have."

"I have all the expensive stuff locked in the hotel's safe," he said.

"Well . . ."

"Don't worry, Daisy. I'll make sure my room is unoccupied before I retire for the evening."

My opinion of Harold's ability to protect himself against an armed bully remained the same as it had been before, but I decided I'd better not say so. "Very well. Thanks, Harold. See you tomorrow."

"Indeed. Tomorrow we invade the *souks* and find gifts to take home to everyone."

"I'm looking forward to that." We'd decided on that course of action while eating our raspberry desserts. Since we'd opted out of the Nile cruise, we had one last day in Egypt to explore the mysteries of Cairo.

I looked through my luggage, the dressers, the closet, and everything else that might have had anything taken from it; I discovered nothing amiss. Then I took an extra aspirin for the *souk*'s sake—I was no more interested in walking around in the heat in a marketplace than I was in sailing in it, although I was looking forward to shopping. But Harold was right: we had to procure gifts for our families and friends back home, and it might be fun to find just the right souvenir for everyone.

Then I doffed my evening dress, climbed into my lightweight lawn nightgown, and crawled into bed, exhausted. I don't think I'd ever felt so utterly enervated. I chalked my state of fatigue up to the heat, the Great Pyramid and that smelly camel.

CHAPTER FIFTEEN

Except for being swarmed by indigent Egyptians of all ages and sexes as we wandered the streets of the various *souks,* and in spite of the crushing heat, I managed to find gifts for everyone in my family, Flossie and Johnny, Edie and Quincy Applewood (as I think I've mentioned before, Edie was Mrs. Pinkerton's lady's maid, and Quincy looked after Mr. Pinkerton's horses), Pudge Wilson next door and a few other neighbors. I even bought a pottery sphinx for Sam. I was pretty sure Pudge was going to love his turquoise scarab. The thing was so cheap that I doubted it was made of real turquoise, but I didn't think Pudge would mind. He liked bugs and stuff like that.

Fortunately for me, Harold had thought to hire a man to carry our many packages, one of the non-guardsman *dragomen* who haunted the street around the hotel. I felt sorry for the man, although he seemed quite cheerful about his burdensome occupation, probably because Harold was lavish with his *baksheesh.* This was a smart move on Harold's part because the fellow, named Mohammed of course, was adept at bargaining with the various *souk* keepers, a form of exchange at which I would have been lousy, not being inclined to argue with anyone at all, much less with a native in a land where I was every inch an outsider.

Harold bought I don't know how many sphinxes, scarabs and pieces of pottery, all of which were lovely to look at but incredibly bulky, not to mention expensive.

During one bargaining session—Harold wanted to purchase a perfectly gorgeous golden urn, which the *souk* proprietor said had been discovered in a pharaoh's tomb—Harold whispered to me, "I'm sure he's lying through his teeth. Somebody probably made it the day before yesterday."

Shocked, I whispered back, "Good Lord, Harold. Do you mean that?"

"Sure. Making fakes with which to fool tourists is the national industry in this part of Egypt."

"But . . . but that urn is positively beautiful, Harold. What a shame if the merchant is lying about it."

With a shrug, Harold said, "Honestly, Daisy, I'm not a collector of Egyptian artifacts. I don't care if the thing is brand-new or three thousand years old. I just think it's pretty, and I want to get it for Del. Thanks to our guide there, maybe I'll get a deal on it."

"Oh." And since I couldn't think of anything more cogent to say, I remained silent as the *dragoman* and the shop's proprietor argued and argued.

As they argued, I gazed at the item in question. It really was quite charming in all its gleaming goldness. Figures of ancient Egyptians had been engraved or carved or etched—or whatever the proper artistic term for the process is—on the sides of it, and it contained one panel that looked as if someone had pasted tons of tiny tiles together and then had it inlaid into the gold. The top of the thing featured the head of a cat, I presume the god Bastet of Egyptian lore. Not for nothing had I listened to Billy read all those articles about Egyptian discoveries in the *National Geographic*. Although, come to think of it, I think Bastet was a goddess. Well, whatever s/he was, the urn thing was fabulous, and I was pleased that Harold had found it.

Finally our guide turned to Harold, gave him a shrug and threw up his arms as if he couldn't stand to continue bandying words and prices one second longer.

"I guess that's the best price I'm going to get?" Harold asked, interpreting the shrug.

The man nodded. So Harold bought the lovely urn and, as both the shop owner and our guide appeared quite pleased, I assumed the guide was going to get a percentage of the purchase price for himself. It seemed to me that this was a very queer way of doing business, but Harold assured me on our further perusals of various shops, that barter is the way most of the rest of the world worked. While I thought that was a most interesting point, I was once again glad I lived in the USA, where you paid whatever was stamped on the label and went away with your purchase. I suppose a person can get used to bartering, but I imagine the people who are really good at it generally start when they're babies. If you see what I mean.

As for me, I almost certainly went a little overboard when we found a little shop that sold fabrics. But what the heck. Mrs. Pinkerton had given me all that money to spend, and I aimed to use at least some of it while I was in Egypt. I spent nowhere near five thousand dollars, however, and I aimed to use the fabrics for clothing for the entire family and not just me. My own personal biggest purchase was a rug that I thought would look great in our dining room back home. Besides—my heart twanged painfully as the notion hit me—Billy would have loved it.

What a crime that it was I, and not Billy, who was seeing the world. He'd been the avid reader of travel stories, the *National Geographic,* and so forth. But he'd only got as far as France before he'd been shot and gassed and had to come home again. The Lord works in mysterious ways, all right, and I didn't approve of a good many of them. Not that the Lord cares, I'm sure.

After the rug seller and our guide came to an agreement

about the price of the thing, and Harold turned over an edge of the rug and squinted hard at it for several seconds, I refrained from fainting from shock when the proprietor named his final sum, but merely handed over the dough. But . . . oh, boy. I'd never spent that much money on one thing in my entire life. Well, except for our Chevrolet.

Harold patted me on the back. "Don't worry, Daisy. That's a darned good price for that rug. Del's the rug expert, but he's taught me a lot, and I think that's the genuine article."

"What kind of genuine article?" I asked, puzzled.

"A genuine, authentic Egyptian rug made here and by Egyptians by their own hands. And from the looks of it, it was made a good many years ago."

"Well . . . why wouldn't it be?"

Harold chuckled. "I just mean that you got a bargain, sweetie. I turned it over to make sure it was woven by real people and not by any old rug-making machine."

"I didn't even know there were such things as rug-making machines."

"Good Lord, yes."

Shows how much I knew about anything.

We'd left the hotel early, and by about one o'clock in the afternoon, not only was our guide about to drop from all the souvenirs we'd loaded upon him, but I was about to expire from the heat.

"We'll go back to the hotel and clean up a bit. Then we can have lunch there," said Harold. "That all right with you?"

"Perfect," I panted.

So we hoofed it back to the hotel. Our guide and Harold made arrangements with one of the hotel staff to get our purchases safely transported to our suites, and I, on a whim, staggered over to the reception desk, just to see if any letters had arrived for me since yesterday. To my utter astonishment, a letter awaited me.

It was from Sam. How very odd.

Harold joined me at the desk, and the reception person handed him a couple of letters, too. "All set. I'm having everything carted to my room." He squinted at me. "Do you need something to drink, Daisy? Your face is flushed and you're glowing with perspiration."

Although I wanted to rip open my letter, Harold was correct. My mouth was as dry as the Sahara, which was almost appropriate; and I was sweating like a pig, which wasn't, since Egyptians didn't eat pork. I gathered all the spit left in me and said, "Yes, thanks."

So we went to the bar, where Harold ordered some concoction with alcohol in it for himself and I asked for lemonade. Harold also ordered some sandwiches to be served with our drinks.

Fanning himself with his straw hat—he'd eschewed the pith helmet as being too hot almost as soon as we'd arrived in the country of Egypt—Harold said, "Phew. I'm glad we're leaving tomorrow."

I'd already polished off my first glass of lemonade and was working on my second when I said, "Me, too. I'm sure Pasadena gets this hot sometimes, but there's something about the heat here . . . I don't know. Maybe it's all the dust and poverty that makes this heat seem worse here than in Pasadena somehow."

"I suspect you're right."

I ate about a half of a cucumber sandwich, but that was it for me. Harold didn't seem to mind, as he finished the rest of the sandwiches on the platter. At least he didn't scold me for not eating more.

"Small wonder everyone takes a nap in the afternoon here. In fact, I think I'm going to do that very thing."

"Sounds good to me. After I finish the last of the sandwiches, maybe I'll toddle upstairs and take a nap, too."

By the time I'd finished my third glass of lemonade and eaten that half of a sandwich, I felt rested enough to make it to my room, where I flopped on the bed fully clothed and slept like the dead for a couple of hours.

I could hardly wait to get back home again.

I'd forgotten all about the letter from Sam until I awoke at about four that afternoon, rolled over, and felt the envelope crinkle underneath me. Then I sat up quickly, removed the envelope which, I regret to say, was rather damp from my having perspired all over it, and carefully opened it.

Dear Daisy,

You probably think I'm crazy to be writing you all these letters, but I'm very concerned about something I've learned recently.

I straightened from my slump, shocked. Good heavens, was another flu pandemic abroad in the world, and was it particularly virulent in Egypt? I read on:

Your safety might be at risk. According to the bulletins we've been getting, white slavers are still at work in Egypt and other Middle-Eastern and African countries. These people don't act like villains, you know, but are probably quite personable until they snatch you.

Oh, for Pete's sake. Did Sam Rotondo take me for an absolute ninny? White slavers, my foot. This was 1922, for goodness' sake! Bristling, I continued to read his missive:

I know you think you can take care of yourself, and you

probably think that since you're a fraud, you'll be able to spot another one at ten yards, but these people are smart and cruel and can be vicious.

My mouth had dropped open at the word "fraud." Blast Sam Rotondo to perdition, anyway! I was *not* a fraud! Maybe I couldn't actually raise spirits from the grave to chat with their living friends, but I always strived to help people with my work, and I resented being called a fraud. Well . . . oh, very well, maybe I was a fraud, but I was neither cruel nor vicious, and Sam knew that!

Please be on your guard. I'm sure Harold is a good friend and will try to look out after you, but he's every bit as naive as you are. Look out for people who seem too friendly upon first meeting and who attempt to get chummy whether you want them to or not.

I'm not trying to scare you, but I've been reading the police bulletins, and I know what I'm talking about. Please be careful. You tend toward rash actions, and if you act impulsively around these organized criminal gangs, rashness might just get you kidnapped or killed. You may not be thinking clearly these days, what with the grievous—

My eyes got stuck on the word *grievous.* I'd known ever since I'd met him that Sam was no dummy, but I'd never have suspected him of having a vocabulary large enough to include the word *grievous.* Although I felt like crumpling his darned letter up and heaving it at the wastepaper basket next to the desk, I restrained myself and kept reading. I also tried to keep in mind that Sam was trying to help me out. The fact that he clearly believed me to be an idiot shouldn't negate his good intentions on my behalf.

Only they did. Nevertheless, I kept reading.

*—what with the grievous loss you've recently suffered, but
keep your eyes open and your wits about you. You've got wits. I
know that. It just seems to me that you don't use them quite as
often as you should. I hope you won't take my words amiss.*

As if! I didn't use my wits, my foot! If Sam Rotondo were
standing in front of me, I'd stomp on his big, fat policeman's
shoes. Or, better yet, I'd have Spike piddle on one of them. He
did that once when he was a puppy, and I've loved him all the
more for it ever since then.

*You're probably steaming mad at me right now, but I honestly
only wanted to warn you about the gangs that may be operat-
ing in Egypt while you're there. You don't want to get entangled
with the police in Egypt, I'm sure. I hear they're a good deal
harder on their prisoners than we here in Pasadena are.*

> Sincerely,
> Sam

Offhand, I couldn't recall a single other person who could
aggravate me the way Sam Rotondo could. Well, Harold's father
had been an ugly specimen, but when he was around he didn't
shove himself into my life the way Sam did. Furious, I slammed
the letter on the desk and retired to the bathroom to take a cool
bath and wash my hair, which felt as though it had acquired
pounds of sand and dust during our perusal of the *souks*.

I was still steaming internally when I joined Harold for dinner that night, although my outsides were much cooler than
they'd been when I'd come home from shopping that afternoon.
And I didn't intend to answer Sam's latest letter, either. So
there.

Very well, I know my reaction was childish, but it was still my
reaction. I wasn't about to allow Sam Rotondo, of all people, to
spoil the remainder of my visit to Egypt. Not that I'd been

enjoying it a whole lot before his letter arrived. Still . . .

"You look a little flushed, Daisy. Are you feeling all right?"

I glanced at Harold over my menu. "I'm fine, thanks."

"Hmmm. Your cheeks are very pink. Maybe you got a touch too much sun today."

"Probably." Drat it! If there was anything I didn't want, it was healthy-looking pink cheeks! No self-respecting spiritualist would run around with pink cheeks. Fortunately, I knew from whence the color in my cheeks had come, and it wasn't from the pernicious sun. It was from the pernicious Sam Rotondo. Because I didn't want to worry Harold, I didn't tell him about Sam's fairy story about criminal gangs of white slavers.

I considered it fortunate that Mr. Stackville didn't show up during our meal to spoil our last evening in Egypt.

We made an early night of it, and I was in bed and asleep by ten o'clock. The next morning, I dressed in a pretty blue lightweight traveling costume and wore white sandals and a white straw hat along with it. I felt far from cool in my costume, but at least I wasn't as hot as poor Harold, who had to wear one of his white linen suits or be considered by fellow tourists as totally beyond the pale. Stupid traditions. I think everyone who visits Egypt in August should be assigned loose white robes to wear, but nobody asked me.

Our luggage was loaded and we were just about to step into the motor that would take us to the train station when Mr. Stackville hurried up to us. He looked perturbed. I didn't care about his state of perturbation. I wanted to get out of there and didn't appreciate this interruption of our plans on his part.

"Missus Majesty! Mister Kincaid! Please wait up a minute."

I didn't wait. I climbed into the automobile. Harold, much more polite than I, hesitated and turned to greet Mr. Stackville with a smile that appeared genuine to me. Clearly, Harold didn't share my opinion of the pushy Mr. Stackville. "Oh, good. Glad you're here, old man." He stuck out his hand. "Daisy and I can't take this heat, so we're departing for cooler climes today."

"You're *leaving?*" Stackville said, as if thunderstruck.

His reaction seemed peculiarly odd to me, and I stared at him through the window of the automobile, trying to discern the motive of what seemed to me to be exaggerated surprise. Not being a mind reader, no matter what Sam Rotondo accuses me of, I couldn't do it.

Evidently Harold was taken aback by Stackville's alarm, too. "Why, yes. It's just too damned hot here for us. Sorry we won't be around to chat anymore, but you see how it is. My sister's health is a trifle fragile. Has been ever since . . . well, since the tragedy."

So he was blaming our early departure on me, was he? Well, I couldn't say as how I blamed him. One almost has to make up little white lies occasionally in order to abide by the rules of social convention.

Mr. Stackville bent over and peered at me through the window. "Where will you be going?"

And why, exactly, was our destination of interest to Mr. Stackville? I thought he was being quite pushy. As usual. Therefore, before Harold could reply with our complete itinerary, I said, "Oh, we haven't decided yet. We'll take the train to Constantinople and decide where to go from there."

Harold blinked at me but didn't contradict me.

"Are you sure you want to leave Egypt so soon? Before you've seen everything? I'm sure the weather will break before long." Stackville was beginning to sound downright worried, and I recalled the letter from Sam I'd read the night before and which had annoyed me so much.

Hmm. Perhaps Sam wasn't merely being an obnoxious butter-inner after all. Could Stackville be . . . ? But no. The notion was absurd. White slavery was utter nonsense, and to think that Mr. Stackville was an honest-to-God white slaver was merely silly.

Maybe.

Before Harold could say anything more to Stackville, I spoke rather sharply to him. "Come along, Harold. We'll miss the train. Good-bye, Mister Stackville." You may notice I refrained from saying it had been a pleasure meeting him.

"But . . ."

But nothing. Harold climbed into the automobile next to me, tapped the driver on the shoulder, and we took off, leaving a huge plume of dust to follow along behind us. I hoped Mr. Stackville and his pretty white suit got smothered in the stuff.

As soon as he was settled and the car was moving, Harold turned to me. "I know you don't like Stackville, but why were you in such an all-fired hurry to get away from the hotel? We have plenty of time to catch our train. We could at least have had a last drink with him or something so as not to appear totally rude."

I contemplated a lot of things before answering Harold's question. Should I bring up Sam's letter and his reference to slavery gangs preying on tourists? If I did, Harold might well scoff. I'd scoffed at first when I'd read the letter. But Stackville's behavior when he saw us loading our trunks into the car that would take us to the train station added a certain amount of weight to Sam's words. Still and all, just because I disliked Stackville didn't mean he was a criminal. And I didn't like to be laughed at any more than anyone else does.

Therefore, I said merely, "I just wanted to get away from him before you invited him to come with us."

"I wouldn't do that!" Harold was plainly incensed.

"Sorry, Harold, but you have to admit you've invited him to join us a whole lot since he intruded into our lives."

Harold frowned, but only said, "That's only because I want

you to meet new people and have new experiences."

"I am meeting new people and am having new experiences. I just don't happen to like that particular new person, and would just as soon end our acquaintance now rather than later."

"Well, we're on our way now, and Stackville isn't with us, so I guess there's no point in arguing about it."

"My sentiments precisely."

As Harold anticipated, we arrived at the train station early. We waited on a couple of dirty benches under a dusty awning in the relentless heat—but at least we were in the shade. It wasn't much fun, but at last the train arrived, and we boarded, Harold making sure our luggage was stored safely in the compartment designed for that purpose. Fortunately, Harold got us first-class accommodations, so we didn't have to sit with a bunch of people carrying chickens and goats and stuff like that. I'm not kidding. I'm also not a snob. However, I found a nice, clean first-class compartment ever so much more to my liking than the third-class accommodations provided for the poor folks to ride in. Mind you, we have poor folks in Pasadena, too—at least I'm pretty sure we do—but they don't take their livestock on the red cars or bus lines with them.

We had an uneventful trip to Constantinople—Istanbul—oh, bother, I'm going to call it Istanbul from now on. I again enjoyed the variety of scenery as the train chugged along. Boy, it didn't look like anything I'd seen in the USA, probably because all the people we saw were clad in their native costumes, which were nothing like ours. If we have a native costume. Hmm. Interesting thought. I'd have to chat with Harold about it one of these days.

In Istanbul we had to stay the night in a hotel, but it was another beautiful one, called the Sultanahmet, a rebuilt palace of some ancient sultan or other, and which was on a par with Shepheards. Somehow, however, between Egypt and Istanbul,

I'd managed to come down with a dreadful illness. I suspect my indisposition was the result of drinking the local water, because it took the form of . . . never mind. You don't want to know. At any rate, I was *really* sick.

"Are you sure there's nothing I can do for you, Daisy?" Harold appeared quite worried about me.

I appreciated his concern, but I wanted him to go away and leave me alone to be ill in private. "I'm sure there isn't," I told him. "If you can find some kind of bottled drink, like ginger ale or something like that, it might help settle my stomach."

"Will do. I'm sure this hotel will have what you need."

I loved Harold with all my heart—as a brother, of course—but I was so happy to see him scurrying away down the hotel hallway that I darned near cried. Then I resumed my stay in the bathroom. There's a lot to be said for first-class accommodations, and among the most wonderful of them is having a bathroom all to oneself when one was under the weather. Whatever that means. I mean, is anyone ever *over* the weather?

Oh, never mind.

Chapter Sixteen

Harold managed to get hold of a gigantic supply of ginger ale, bless his heart.

"Thank you *very* much." I was so happy to see the bottled stuff, I nearly cried, but I always get weepy when I have the stomach flu.

"You'll never guess who I saw in the bar while I was fetching your ginger ale," he said as he set the crate holding a couple of dozen ginger-ale bottles in the corner of the room.

Although I'd been flopped, aching and feverish, on my bed, wishing I could just die right then and there and join Billy in the hereafter, Harold's words made me sit up. Well, I sort of leaned on my arm, but it amounted to the same thing. "Stackville?"

He shot a glance at me and frowned slightly. "No, not Stackville. Good Lord, Daisy, you make him sound like the veriest villain."

Sinking back onto my pillows, I whispered, "That's because I think he is one."

"Tut," said Harold, opening a bottle and bringing it to the bed. Before he gave it to me, he felt my forehead. "Lord, Daisy, you're burning up. Would you like the hotel doctor to see you?"

"No. Yes. Oh, I don't know. Yes, I guess. But whom did you see in the hotel bar?"

"Mister Pierre Futrelle."

"Hmm. One of Mister Stackville's accomplices."

"Accomplices? Are you serious?" Harold set the bottle on the nightstand then thoughtfully went to the bathroom and fetched a washcloth, soaked it in cool water and placed it on my forehead.

"Thank you, Harold."

"You're welcome. Why do you call Stackville and Futrelle accomplices?"

"I don't know. But I think they're crooks and are accomplices in something shady." I thought about telling Harold about Sam's fear of white slavers, but even in my weakened condition that sounded too ludicrous, and I didn't care to be laughed at, so I didn't.

Harold didn't speak for the longest time. When he did, he merely said, "I'm going to go get the hotel doctor now."

"Thank you." I think I whimpered the two words.

Very well, maybe I was relying too much on the last of Sam Rotondo's letters to me, but the more I thought about what he'd written in it, the more Stackville's constant presence in Harold's and my vicinity every time we so much as stepped foot out of our rooms seemed suspicious. And, since I couldn't imagine any other kind of crookery (is that a word?) he might be up to, Sam's notion of white slavery, while absurd on the face of it, maybe wasn't. Absurd, I mean. Or—

Maybe they were drug smugglers! That sounded more probable to me, although I couldn't imagine what a drug smuggler would want Harold and me for. Heck, maybe they just wanted to rob us blind.

On the other hand, I was really sick, so maybe I was merely hallucinating. I must have dozed off for a moment, because I was startled by a soft knock on the door.

Every single muscle in my body ached, including the one between my ears, and I groaned before calling out in a feeble voice, "Harold?"

Someone in the corridor outside the door said, "Oh. So sorry. Wrong room." What's more, the person said those words in a heavy French accent. If I hadn't felt so puny, I'd have leapt out of bed and rushed to the door to see if the knocker was Futrelle. Unfortunately, the moment I swung my legs over the side of the bed, I knew I'd have to make another trip to the bathroom before I did anything so extravagant as check the hallway. Lordy, I felt awful.

When I emerged from the bathroom, sweaty and miserable and with a headache so ghastly I was surprised I wasn't seeing double, Harold had returned to the room with the doctor. I grunted a hello to the two men and collapsed once more on the bed.

"Daisy, this is Doctor Weatherfield. He's an American, believe it or not."

"Why shouldn't I believe it?" I asked, my eyes closed. I managed to pry them open far enough to greet the doctor. "Thank you for seeing me, Doctor Weatherfield. I don't think I've ever been this sick in my life."

A handsome specimen, the doctor was probably about fifty years old, with white hair and a white mustache. He'd been burned to a crisp by the weather, but on him a dark complexion worked very well with his white hair and azure-blue eyes. I know you can't really tell these things from looking, but he appeared competent. I prayed he was. He seemed nice enough.

"It looks to me, young lady, as if you've managed to get yourself a good case of what we sometimes call Pharaoh's Revenge here in these parts."

"I thought we were in Turkey," I muttered, unamused.

His smile showed gleaming white teeth. "We are in Turkey, but the term fits here as well. I understand that in Mexico, they refer to it as Montezuma's Revenge."

"You'd think they'd call it Atatürk's Revenge here in Turkey,"

I muttered, still feeling puny and not much like joking around.

"Better not say that to a Turk. Atatürk is a most revered figure here."

"Sorry." People were so sensitive about their heroes. I guess that's true everywhere, but I didn't feel like having a philosophical discussion at the moment, as ill as I was. "What about this stuff I have?"

"It really doesn't matter what you call it," said Dr. Weatherfield. "What it boils down to is a bad case of dysentery, but I think we can get it under control without too much trouble."

"I hope you're right," I whispered. "Because I feel like death warmed up."

Dr. Weatherfield proceeded to take my temperature—I had a fever of 102 degrees, which accounted for the warm part—asked about my symptoms, and nodded thoughtfully throughout my narrative, which was extremely short since I didn't feel like talking. "Yes, indeedy, that's it, all right. I'm afraid you're going to have remain in bed for at least a couple of days." He turned to Harold. "Is that going to play havoc with your travel plans?"

With a shrug, Harold said, "We don't really have any plans that can't be changed. We decided Egypt in August was too hot for us."

"My goodness, yes," agreed the doctor. "I'm glad you don't have to go anywhere instantly, since your sister has an acute case of the miserable stuff and truly does have to rest for a few days. But with a few doses of these powders"—he held up a bottle—"aspirin tablets and apples, we'll have her right as rain again in no time at all."

I squinted up at him. "Apples?"

"Apples." He gave me another sparkling smile. "When Eve ate that apple from the tree of life, God might have been displeased, but she did mankind a good service. Why, apples are used to cure everything from constipation to diarrhea to almost everything in between."

"Is that why they say an apple a day keeps the doctor away?"

"Probably." The doctor chuckled. "But your illness, while I expect you to recover from it shortly, can be an honest-to-goodness killer. Did you know that more soldiers during the Civil War died of dysentery than they did of gunshot or bayonet wounds?"

"Actually, yes. My husband read that to me out of an article in the *National Geographic*." And then, because I was so darned weak and feeling so darned miserable, and because, as I've already said, the intestinal flu always makes me cry, I cried. After the doctor handed me a clean handkerchief from his black bag and I'd wiped my eyes and blown my nose, I apologized. "I'm sorry. I guess I just feel so weak."

"That's perfectly all right, Missus Majesty. Your brother told me of your recent bereavement. I'm so very sorry. What with you knowing about Atatürk and the dysentery deaths of Civil War soldiers, your husband sounds as though he was a well-read young man."

Well-read? Hmm. I guess Billy had been well-read. The good Lord knows there wasn't much of anything else he could do except read. Therefore, I said, "Yes. He was. And I miss him awfully."

Dr. Weatherfield patted my hand. "I'm sure you must, my dear. But in a very few days, if you follow my instructions, at least you won't have to contend with illness as well as grief."

"Thank you." I sniffled some more, feeling stupid.

But the doc turned out to be correct. He sent up a half-dozen apples with strict instructions to wash them with soap and boiled water and to remove the peel before I ate one—not that I was in any condition to eat anything that day. I think the powders he left were nothing more than bicarbonate of soda, although I'm not sure, and as soon as I was able to keep anything down, I took three aspirin tablets with a glass of previously boiled water into which the bicarb was mixed, which eventually helped my headache. I was weak as a kitten, but at least I was no longer throwing up or—well, never mind.

Bless Harold's heart, he practically hovered over me all that day after the doctor left. "Are you sure you don't want anything besides ginger ale?" he asked more than once.

"Thank you, Harold, but no. I'll just sleep, if you don't mind. You go and do anything you want to do. I'll recuperate just fine in my bed here. Thanks for bringing the doctor."

"He told me he'll be back to check on your progress this evening."

"I appreciate being taken care of so well," I said. "Thank you, Harold." Then I had to wipe away more tears. Good heavens, I was a pathetic mess!

"God, Daisy, you're turning into a garden hose. I've never seen you cry before, and you're crying every other minute today."

"I know. It's because of the flu. I always get this way when I have the stomach flu."

"I hope you don't get it often."

"No, I don't." I managed a weak smile for his sake.

"Well, if you're sure you don't mind being left alone for a while, I think I'll go downstairs and see what's to be had for dinner."

I groaned at the mere thought of food, and my stomach gave a hard cramp in reaction. "Don't even mention food to me for a day or so, will you?"

"Sorry, sweetie."

"That's all right."

"I'm not sure when the doctor will be back, but I'll try not to take too long over my dinner."

"Don't worry, Harold. Take your time. If Doctor Weatherfield returns before you do, I'm sure I'll manage just fine."

"I don't know," said Harold doubtfully. "I've never seen you cry so much before. Not even—"

His pudgy cheeks flushed, and I knew he was thinking of the day of Billy's funeral. "That's because I wasn't sick in the body then. Only sick at heart. I'm not kidding about the stomach flu making me cry. It really does."

"Indeed. Well, I'll be off then. Do you need me to—"

"Harold!" I spoke as loudly and sternly as I could, which wasn't very. "Get out of here. I'll be fine."

He saluted, clicked his heels, bowed and left. Thank God. I sank back down into my pillows and slept, already feeling a little less feverish, although my insides hurt as though some giant hand had reached inside my body, stirred them with a spoon and every now and then gave them a quick, hard kick for good measure.

I don't know how long I'd been asleep after Harold left before another soft knock came at the door. I opened a bleary eye or two and managed to croak, "Harold? Doctor Weatherfield?"

No answer rewarded my curt questions. Rather, I heard a sharp word that I couldn't make out, and then all I heard were footsteps hurrying away down the hall.

Curious. First somebody with a French accent knocked at my door, and now somebody who didn't speak at all knocked. I recalled Sam's letter, endured a little sizzle of alarm along with another intense intestinal cramp, and slowly and painfully got out of bed. After assuring myself I wouldn't fall flat on my face, I dragged myself to the door, which I opened. Peeking at the long, empty hallway, I saw nobody. Of course, whoever the knocker was had had plenty of time to escape my prying eyes, as I was moving at a very slow snail's pace—perhaps the pace of a grandfather snail who was on his last slime. Still and all, I made sure the door was locked when I shut it, and then I pretty much crawled back to the bed and fell into it.

I have no idea when Harold and Dr. Weatherfield showed up again or how long they'd been knocking when I finally awoke. Their battering at the door had somehow become mingled with a bad dream I was having, in which I was being sold to the highest bidder at a slave auction—I didn't fetch a very high price, which was moderately discouraging. It wasn't until Harold cried, "Daisy! Answer me! Good God, Doctor, do you think she's suffered a relapse? She couldn't possibly have died, could she? Daisy! *Daisy!*"

Oh, dear. That's right. I'd locked the door. Feeling like an utter fool, as well as a sick one, I fell out of bed, threw on a robe and hurried as fast as I could to the door—my stomach still had a tendency to cramp painfully, so I was almost bent double—and opened it. "I'm so sorry. I was asleep."

"You scared me to death, Daisy Majesty," Harold said. He sounded honestly peeved, which is, I think, the usual reaction one has after having been frightened for another person's safety. He was quite gentle when he led me through the sitting room and back to the bed, so I guess he wasn't too mad at me.

"I'm sorry. Your knocks got entangled in a dream I was having."

Dr. Weatherfield smiled kindly at me. "I'm glad you were able to sleep, Missus Majesty. Sleep is probably the best medicine for you, after the powders. Pretty soon, you can start on the apples."

"Uhhh," I said.

He chuckled as he took my temperature, asked about my cramps and the general state of my insides. He seemed pleased to know I hadn't thrown up once since he'd seen me last, and that I'd . . . well, never mind what, but I'd only had to use the bathroom for the purpose two or three times. His chuckle annoyed me a bit. I mean, did it make him happy to see people suffer? But no. His chuckle was probably only part of what people call a doctor's "bedside manner." I longed for Dr. Benjamin, our kindly old physician back in Pasadena. He never chuckled when someone was in pain.

"What you need to do is drink plenty of liquids to replace the water you've lost due to your illness," he said after noting that my fever had gone down to under a hundred degrees.

God bless whoever invented aspirin.

"So she's getting better?" Harold sounded worried.

"Oh, yes. I'll know more tomorrow, after I see how she's progressed overnight. The main thing you need to do, Missus Majesty, is drink lots of liquids. We must guard against dehydration, which is the main worry in cases of dysentery."

"But you think she'll be better? I don't want a corpse on my hands, Doctor Weatherfield. If Daisy dies, I won't be able to go home again. Both my family and hers will kill me."

"Harold!" cried I, appalled both at his question and the fact that, while he posed it in a joking manner, I sensed he'd really meant it.

The doctor glanced between us curiously, and it occurred to me that he didn't understand Harold's reference to his family and mine, since we were supposed to be brother and sister. Too bad. I didn't feel like explaining something that was none of his business in the first place.

"Well, dash it, Daisy, Doctor Weatherfield said people can die of this stuff. I don't want you dying on me."

"Modern medicine is a wonderful thing, Mister Kincaid," said Dr. Weatherfield. "Missus Majesty won't die. She'll be laid up for a few days, but she definitely is on the mend."

"Thank God."

I do believe that had been an honest prayer on Harold's part. Hmph. Probably the first one he'd uttered in years. He'd told me more than once that he didn't think much of religion and that his partner in life, Del Farrington, who was quite devout, went to a church called "Our Lady of Perpetual Misery" in Pasadena. He meant that Del, a fine gentleman even if he was a Roman Catholic—a species my aunt Vi despised as much as she despised Baptists—attended Saint Andrews Catholic Church.

"I'm going to leave a bromide for you to take before you retire for the night, Missus Majesty," said Dr. Weatherfield, ignoring Harold's heartfelt prayer of thanksgiving. "The bromide will help you sleep soundly. I expect you still feel pretty wretched."

I nodded.

"When you believe you're ready to go to bed for the night, take another dose of the powders I left earlier, and stir this packet of bromide into boiled water and drink it down, too. Remember to drink lots of fluids. I see a crate of ginger ale in the corner. That's good. It's best not to drink the local water unless you boil it first, and one can never quite be sure it's been boiled unless one boils it oneself."

"And we don't have a stove handy," said Harold.

"Exactly." Dr. Weatherfield beamed at Harold, who'd sounded kind of sarcastic to me, but as a hotel doctor, perhaps Dr. Weatherfield was accustomed to treating snippy tourists. "I have given instructions to the kitchen staff regarding Missus Majesty's needs, however, so I think you'll be safe eating and drinking anything they bring up to you."

"I don't want to eat anything," I said, revolted at the notion.

"Not yet," said he, still smiling and friendly, "but eventually you'll get hungry again."

"We can always hope so, anyway," muttered Harold. "She hasn't been hungry for nearly three months now."

Although the doctor peered at him questioningly, neither of us told Dr. Weatherfield about my recent weight loss. Still and all, I guess this wasn't the absolutely best time for me to be

stricken with a case of the stomach flu. I'd probably lost even
more weight and now weighed less than I had when we'd begun
this voyage. Ma and Pa would be really upset if I returned home
to Pasadena even skinner than I'd left it. Nuts.

"I'm going to send up a chambermaid to change your sheets,
Missus Majesty," said Dr. Weatherfield. "You'll probably want
to sleep on clean sheets tonight. This illness causes people to
perspire, due to the fever attached to it. That will help you feel
better, too."

"Oh, boy, you said it! Thank you, Doctor."

He smiled at me.

After a bit more chitchat, Dr. Weatherfield left, and Harold
stared at me critically. "You look absolutely awful, Daisy. Do
you really think you're getting better? If you want me to, I'm
sure I can find another doctor somewhere. Isn't modern
medicine supposed to have had its roots in some Arabic country?"

"I have no idea. Billy never read me any articles about Arabic
medicine. But, yes. I still feel horrible, but I don't feel quite as
awful as I did before the doctor came to see me, so I think the
stuff is passing. At home, it usually doesn't last too much longer
than twenty-four hours, although this is, I think, the sickest I've
ever been with it."

"Please don't give it to me."

"I'll try not to. But why don't you go to your room. Or go
downstairs to the saloon and see if you can find someone to talk
to or play cards with or something? I'm well enough that as
soon as the chambermaid comes to change the sheets, I'm going to get out of this sweaty old nightie and take a soothing
bath. I think I'll feel better after that."

"Are you sure you should bathe? Won't the water give you a
chill or something?"

I didn't even bother answering that question. I only stared at

Harold for a minute or so.

At last he shrugged and lifted a hand in a gesture of defeat. "You're right, of course. The weather's too hot for anyone to get a chill."

"Exactly. And I know I'll feel better if I have a nice, hot soak to soothe my aching bones. I bought some lovely bath salts when we were in France. I was going to give them to Aunt Vi, but I think I'll use some of them now and replace them for her later."

"Good idea." Then Harold slapped his forehead with the palm of his hand and said, "Dammit!"

Before I could wonder if he'd managed to get himself possessed by one of his mother's pharaonic spirits and gone insane, he said, "I forgot to tell you I stopped by the front desk. There's some mail that's been forwarded to us from Egypt. Here are your letters." And darned if he didn't come to the bed where I sat and hand me three envelopes.

"How nice," I said, genuinely happy for the first time all day. Oddly enough, I was primarily hoping there would be another letter from Sam, even if he'd probably scold me about something or other. Which made me think of his last letter. "By the way, Harold, while you were out, somebody knocked on the door. When I asked who was there, whoever it was went away again. That happened twice and it made me uncomfortable, so I locked the door. That's why it was locked when you and the doctor came by."

"I wondered why the door was locked. Actually, what I wondered about was why you didn't answer our knock. I thought you'd died while I was gone."

"I'm sorry to have frightened you," I said, contrite.

"That's all right." He sat on the bed next to me. He popped up again a second later. "Do you think you're contagious?" He began brushing at his sleeves and trousers, as if by doing so he

174

could rid himself of any germs that might have attacked him.

"I don't know. I don't know how I got this stuff. If it was from the local water, I doubt I'm contagious. If it's the regular old stomach flu, it's probably already too late for you to begin worrying. That stuff spreads like wildfire."

"Wonderful. Maybe we'll just spend the rest of our time on holiday in Constantinople being sick."

"Well, I'm sorry I got sick, but I honestly didn't do it on purpose, you know."

"I'm not blaming you, sweetie. I've never seen anybody so ill." He shuddered. Harold was what one might call a sensitive plant. I was actually kind of surprised he was being such a good nurse. "Just get better, will you? I'm going to go down to the bar and see if good alcohol can kill any germs you might have given me."

"When I get better, maybe we can see more of Istanbul. It's supposed to be a really interesting city."

"That's all right by me. It's still hotter than Hades, though, so I don't expect you'll feel up to walking much any time soon."

"Probably not." I sighed dolefully. My one and only opportunity to see the world, and not only was I in no emotional state to appreciate it, but now I was sick as well. I think God likes to play with us lowly creatures here on earth sometimes just to let us know how little real control we have over anything.

A timid knock came upon the door at that point. After Harold and I exchanged a glance of curiosity, he went to the door and opened it. A swarthy chambermaid in a white uniform and with a sort of snood-like thing on her head stood there, looking nervous and holding a stack of sheets and pillowcases. I was so happy to see her, I darned near cried again.

"Come in, come in," I said from the bed, out of which I slowly crawled. Then I made my way to a chair in the sitting room and collapsed into it.

The maid glanced between Harold and me as if she thought we might be devils in disguise, but she scurried in and did her duty. As she was leaving, Harold handed her a whole bunch of coins, and she nearly dropped the dirty sheets. Her thanks were profuse and long, and I think she was still thanking Harold when he closed the door on her.

"There. At least you'll have clean sheets to sleep on."

"Yes. I'm so glad the doctor thought of the chambermaid. I never would have, you know, not being accustomed to having chambermaids at my beck and call."

"You can get used to anything," said Harold in a relatively sarcastic tone.

"I don't think I'd mind getting used to being waited on."

"It's not bad," agreed Harold. "Well, I'm off now, Daisy. I'm sure the doctor will want to see you again in the morning, but I won't bother you again tonight unless you call for me."

"Thanks, Harold. Just don't forget that I'm locking the door."

"I promise I won't forget. Have a nice bath."

"I plan to. Thanks."

As soon as the door closed behind him, I locked it. Then I glanced through the envelopes he'd given me. Ma. Flossie Buckingham. Sam Rotondo. My heart gave a little jump, which made no sense at all. I chalked it up to my being so sick.

Before I opened any of the letters, I did exactly as I'd told Harold I'd do: stripped off the nightgown in which I'd been so miserable, found a clean one in a drawer—when you're rich, you see, maids in hotels unpack your stuff for you. As I'd told Harold, it's actually kind of nice not to have to do anything for yourself, although it might get boring after a while—and set it, another robe, the letters and a hand towel on a marble stand in the bathroom near the tub. Then I found the bath salts I'd bought for Aunt Vi, turned on the tap and sprinkled some of the salts in the water. The fragrance of lavender was heavenly when I stepped into the tub and lowered my aching body into the water.

I'm pretty sure I slept again for a while, because when I next opened my eyes, the water had gone tepid, and I'd sunk so low into it, I was in danger of drowning. My aches didn't ache so much, though, so I pulled the plug to let some of the lukewarm water out, refilled the tub with more hot water, leaned back, and reached first for my hand towel and then for my mail. It pays to be organized.

Ma's letter was full of news from home. Pudge Wilson had broken his arm falling from a tree, but Dr. Benjamin fixed him up, and now he wore his cast proudly. Pudge missed me. She missed me. Pa missed me. Aunt Vi missed me. Spike missed me. I admit to shedding a few tears into my bath, since I missed all of them, too.

Setting that letter aside, I opened the one from Flossie. She was fine. Johnny was fine. Their Salvation Army flock was fine. Dr. Benjamin had given her a clean bill of health, and the baby seemed to be progressing quite well in Flossie's nice, warm womb. Lucky kid, to have two great parents like Flossie and Johnny. I admit to shedding another tear or two, mainly because—as I've mentioned probably too many times before—Billy and I had been unable to have children, thanks to the blasted Kaiser's foul bullets and mustard gas.

I set Flossie's letter aside too, and steeled myself before opening the letter from Sam. I was glad I'd done so before I'd finished reading the first paragraph.

CHAPTER SEVENTEEN

Dear Daisy,

I'm really uncomfortable about you traveling the world with Harold Kincaid. I know he's a good friend of yours, but even you have to admit he wouldn't be much good if you got into a jam, and you're always getting into jams.

"Darn you, Sam Rotondo! How dare you!" Not only had he insulted Harold, who was a wonderful friend, but he'd also insulted me. I was *not* always getting into jams! Just because he had a bee in his bonnet about criminal gangs and drug smugglers and white slavers . . .

Oh, wait. The drug smugglers were my idea. Still . . .

I remembered the two knocks on my door while Harold had been away; I frowned.

No. It was too absurd to think that the instant Sam had mentioned criminal gangs targeting tourists, a gang of criminals had miraculously appeared in my life. The world didn't work like that. Furious with Sam, I read on:

You're probably steamed at me for telling the truth, but I swear to God, Daisy, I've never met anyone else in my life who manages to get herself into trouble with the ease and frequency you do. You used to drive Billy crazy with your shenanigans

*and, damn it, he asked me to look out for you after he died, and
I'm not going to let him down now. Watch yourself. If you notice
some stranger hanging around you and Harold, call the police.
Oh, hell, I don't even know if there are police in some of the
places you're staying. Just try to be careful, will you?*

Darn it all, I was being careful! I'd locked the stupid door,
hadn't I? And Sam had no business saying I was always getting
into trouble. I wasn't, either!

True, Pierre Futrelle had just happened to appear in Istanbul
when we did, after we'd surprised Mr. Stackville by leaving
Egypt early. And a person with a French accent had knocked on
my door while Harold was away.

But that was stupid. I was sick. That's why I was connecting
Sam's insane suppositions with Stackville and Futrelle. They
were probably both nice gentlemen who were . . . merely a little
pushy. And who just happened to be traveling in the same places
we were. Hmm . . .

Someone had been in my room at Shepheards while was
away from it. I hadn't found anything missing, but had
something been added? Drugs or something? Added where?
No, it was too absurd.

"Fiddlesticks!" I read on.

*I'm worried about the gangs I told you about in my earlier
letter. According to the bulletins we keep getting at the department, tourists are their primary targets—and don't ask me for
what, because I don't know. I've heard rumors of white slavers,
antiquities thieves, drug smugglers, political spies, and even illegal liquor sources. Pick your poison. Since the two of you
decided to go to Egypt in the middle of the summer when nobody
else in his or her right mind would want to go there, you're
probably among the very few people the bad guys can choose
from. So be careful, will you? I know that's kind of like telling*

the earth to stop in its orbit, but do it for Billy, if you won't do it for your parents or me.

I've decided to take the vacation days I've earned and come after you. I know you won't want me around, but I can't stand knowing you're all alone in the world with no protection except Harold Kincaid, with gangs of vicious criminals running around everywhere. Knowing you, you'll decide to befriend an entire gang. I've got lots of vacation time accrued since I never go anywhere or do anything, so I'll see you wherever you are when I get there. If you get there. Damn it, I'm worried about you!

"Good God." The words left my lips in a whisper. Sam was coming after us? Because he was sure I was going to befriend a gang of . . . something or other? The man was out of his mind!

A knock came at the door, and I darned near dropped Sam's letter into my delightfully scented water.

"Yes?" I called from the bathroom.

No answer.

"Who is it?" I called, louder than before.

Nothing.

"Blast and heck, Sam Rotondo! Now you've got *me* worrying!"

Since he'd already spoiled my bath for me, I decided I might as well pull the plug and get out of it. If a gang of thieves was going to break in and either steal me blind, fill my luggage with drugs, kidnap me to sell to a sultan or plant coded messages in my underwear drawer, I sure didn't want to meet them naked. So I dried myself with one of the hotel's fluffy towels, put on my clean nightie and robe, and went back to bed, mentally thanking the doctor and the chambermaid for the fresh, clean sheets.

And then, so exhausted I could hardly maintain my annoyance with Sam, I crawled under the covers and went to sleep.

★ ★ ★ ★ ★

It beats me to this day what awoke me in the middle of that miserable night. Groggy and aching in every bone and muscle, and with eyelids that felt as though they'd been glued together after someone had thrown sand in my eyes, a very slight noise gradually penetrated another dream in which I'd been captured by a handsome sheik and carried to his tent on the desert. Yes, my family and I had gone to see *The Sheik,* starring Rudolf Valentino, earlier that same year.

I turned over with a soft groan, the noise stopped, and that's when I became fully conscious. Well, more or less. I still felt as though I'd been dropped onto the shimmering desert from the top of the Great Pyramid on the hottest day of the year, from which I gathered that my fever had returned. The doctor had said it might get worse at night, but that he believed the illness was running its course.

And then I recalled the forgotten bromide powders I was supposed to have stirred into some boiled water and drunk down before I went to bed. Huh. If I'd taken them, that noise probably wouldn't have awakened me.

That noise . . .

Then it dawned on me that there shouldn't have been a noise in my room in the middle of the night, and fright fought with fever. I wanted to pull the covers over my head and pretend the noise had been a figment.

But it hadn't been.

Oh, Lord. Now what? Could one of Sam's slave-stealing gangsters have invaded my room for some fell purpose? Could Sam himself have done so? How'd he get here so fast, and what was he doing in my room?

No. No. I wasn't thinking clearly.

The noise came again. It sounded as if it was over by the

closet, which was where my vision would land if I could pry my eyelids apart. Wonderful. Very carefully, I opened my gummy eyes and tried to focus them in the dark room. Couldn't do it. And the noise came again. Someone had just opened the closet door, from the sound of it.

If I rolled out of bed and ran for the sitting-room door, assuming I could stand on my rubbery legs and my head didn't fall off—which it felt as if it might do even as I lay there—I probably wouldn't get to the door before the crook did. Should I merely open my mouth and confront whoever it was or scream bloody murder?

No. Definitely not. Not only was I unsure that my voice would work the way I wanted it to but my head already hurt. Having it bashed with a big stick or the butt of a gun or whatever this particular villain carried on his person wouldn't help my condition at all.

Well . . . there was always ginger ale. Harold had set two bottles of the stuff on my bedside stand along with a bottle opener in case I got thirsty during the night. For my purpose, I didn't want to open the bottle.

As silently as possible, I tested my various muscles. They seemed to work, even if they ached. Slowly and carefully, I reached for a bottle on the bedside table. Since I couldn't see in the dark, I bungled the job, knocking one of the bottles over. I swear, that was the loudest noise I'd ever heard in my life.

Whoever was at the closet jumped back out of it—I saw that much—and made a flying run out of the bedroom and headed for the sitting-room door. I figured what the heck, did some leaping of my own, which wasn't quite as successful as the other person's, grabbed the bottle I hadn't knocked over, and gave chase, out of the bedroom and across the sitting-room floor. We were definitely not evenly matched. I managed to get one good whack at the person's head before he disappeared out through the door of my room.

Then it was that I set up a screech that would have done a Halloween witch proud. The *suffragi*—or whatever those guys are called in Turkey—who, as usual, was napping on his chair in the hallway, fell out of same, jumped to his feet, and gave chase to the retreating figure. But whoever my nighttime visitor had been, he took the stairs and was out of there lickety-split. I stood swaying in the doorway, one hand holding a broken ginger-ale bottle and the other clinging to the jamb, when other doors along the corridor began opening and people started pouring from their rooms, alarmed by my screech, I suppose.

Harold, whose room was next to mine, rushed up to me, tying the sash of his dressing robe. "Daisy! What the devil just happened?"

I dropped the broken ginger-ale bottle and flung myself at Harold, crying. Honest to goodness, I don't really cry all that much as a rule, but you have to remember that, even without my midnight visitor, I'd been through an ordeal that day, and I was still sick as a dog, not to mention grieving over the death of my husband. "Harold! Somebody broke into my room! I hit him with a ginger-ale bottle, but he got away."

"Good God." I'm sure Harold didn't mean to be less than gentlemanly when he took me by the shoulders and moved me aside so he could enter my room, where he turned on the electrical lights and glanced around.

"Be careful of the glass, Harold."

Harold checked the floor and managed to elude the fragments of ginger-ale bottle. "What was he doing in your room? Did he try to . . ." Harold's face was white as a bleached sheet when he turned to gape at me, a horrified expression on his face.

I knew what he was worried about, and I hurried to assuage his worst fears. "No. Whoever it was wasn't after me. He was after something in the closet."

"The closet? What the devil did he want in the closet?"

"I don't know. According to Sam Rotondo, there are criminal gangs all over the place in this part of the world, doing everything from smuggling drugs to kidnapping women to be slaves, and they prey on hapless tourists. I suspect I'm a hapless tourist." And then my legs gave out. Harold caught me before I could hit the floor.

Some hotel official, looking regal and with a magnificent mustache, bustled up as Harold led me into my room, and I allowed Harold to explain what had happened to him. As for me, I stumbled into the room, avoiding broken glass and spilled ginger ale, and managed to get my robe on before I flopped onto a chair, where I proceeded to ache all over. I really wanted to take some more aspirin, but couldn't quite summon up the energy to go to the bedside stand and get myself some.

Harold and the hotel official, who appeared totally shocked, entered the room, and I managed to warn them about the broken glass before either of them could step on it.

"I don't understand," said the hotel fellow. "Things like this don't happen in the Sultanahmet. We're top of the line, you know. A first-class establishment."

"I'm sure that's so, but evidently a thief managed to get in anyway."

Shaking his head, the hotel man muttered, "Impossible."

The uneven temper that had been plaguing me since Billy's death, suddenly soared as high as my fever, and I snapped, "Clearly it's *not* impossible, because it happened. Or do you think I broke that bottle for the fun of it?"

Clad in western clothes, but with a fez on his head, the man pressed his hands together and bowed at me. "I beg your pardon, madam. You're right, of course. Did you see what the man looked like?"

Had I? I pondered the question for a moment before answering. I hadn't seen his face at all, but he sure wasn't dressed like a westerner. "Actually, I think he wore a short robe, belted at the waist. I'm pretty sure he had on some kind of trousers—you know. The kind that look as though they're wrapped about someone's legs. And I think he wore a fez." Which made me wonder if maybe I'd hit his shoulder rather than his head, which might have been protected by the fez. I wanted to get Pa one of those fezzes as soon as I was up to shopping. I thought they were ever so much more attractive than turbans. Not that it matters at this point in my narrative. Sorry for the diversion. "I don't think he was a westerner, I mean. His clothing was light-colored."

"Good God, Daisy! Do you mean to tell me one of those poor fellows from the street had the effrontery to invade your room?"

The hotel guy shook his head. "Highly unlikely. Those peasants never darken these doors."

"Maybe somebody paid him to do it," I suggested, my own personal middle-class roots bristling at his referring to the populace of his own country as *peasants*. What the heck did he think he'd be if he hadn't been lucky enough to snag a job in a fancy hotel, anyway?

Harold, fists on hips, surveyed the room. "Well, will you get someone up here to clean up the glass and the ginger ale? I think Missus Majesty should be moved to another room."

"No!" I didn't mean to holler, but the notion of moving all my things and my suffering sick self to another room made me want to cry again. "Please. Just clean up the mess and . . . and . . . I don't know. Post a guard at the door or something. Heck, we're on the third floor, aren't we? Can anyone get in through the windows?"

Harold moseyed over to the window, opened it and looked

out. "There's no balcony or anything, and we're three stories up. I doubt anyone could gain access this way. Anyhow, the window was closed just now, and you said the fellow escaped via the door."

"Right," I said. It was comforting to know I didn't have to worry about thieves—or whatever the reverse of a thief is— accessing my room by way of the window.

"But why would anyone want to break in to your room, Daisy?"

"I don't *know,* Harold. Unless Sam Rotondo was right and some smugglers stashed something in my suitcase. But I searched through all my bags and didn't see anything in them that didn't belong there. And everything that was supposed to be there was. If you know what I mean."

"I understand. Hmm. Perhaps I should go through my own luggage."

"Might not be a bad idea." The hotel man—I guess he was the manager or held some other important post—still stood in the middle of my room wringing his hands, and my temper rocketed again at his uselessness. "Will you *please* get someone in here to clean up this mess? I've been very ill, I still feel horrid, and I need to get back to bed."

"Yes, yes. Of course. Right away." The poor man scurried away, and I felt guilty for having barked at him.

Slumping, muscles aching, insides churning, I pleaded with Harold, "Will you please get me three aspirin tablets and another bottle of ginger ale? I feel so awful."

"Do you think you'll be able to keep the aspirin tablets down?"

"I don't know, but I sure hope so. My head's about to fall off. I forgot to take the bromide powders the doctor left. I suppose I should take them, too, if you wouldn't mind mixing them for me."

"Happy to," said Harold.

I'd been resting rather like a limp beanbag in my chair. When I managed to lift my aching head, I saw that the hall was still full of people clustered about in a big clump and peering into my room. I glared at them all and said, "Of all the nerve! Go away, will you? The excitement's over."

Harold evidently hadn't been paying attention to the crowd at the door, because he went over and shooed them all away. "Sorry to have disturbed your sleep. Missus Majesty's room was invaded by an intruder, but he got away. I recommend everyone lock your doors."

This explanation and word of caution provoked many shocked exclamations in a variety of languages. But everyone hurried back to their own rooms, which was all I cared about. As soon as they left, a chambermaid showed up and did an excellent job getting rid of the glass from the broken ginger-ale bottle and mopping up the spilled liquid. A dark, damp blotch remained on the lovely rug—a Turkish one, I'm sure, given that we were in Istanbul—but I figured it would probably dry out and be not much the worse for wear eventually.

Bless Harold's heart, he brought me the aspirin, ginger ale, and a glass of boiled water into which he'd stirred the bromide powders. I downed the aspirin, then the powders, which tasted ghastly. Fortunately, there was more ginger ale left in the bottle, so I drank it down, too. By that time, the chambermaid had finished her work.

I said, "Thank you," because I'm polite, even though I've read that people in other countries tend to ignore their servants.

"Yes," said Harold. "Thank you very much. Here." He handed the woman a bunch of coins, which seemed to startle her a good deal. Smiling broadly, she bowed herself out of the room, shut the door behind herself, and Harold and I were alone.

"Do you want me to stay here the rest of the night, Daisy?" he asked. "I could sleep . . . um . . . somewhere." His gaze swept the room, as did mine, and I assumed neither of us could find anywhere suitable for Harold to lay his head except the bed, and that was mine.

A knock at the door startled the both of us. After we exchanged a glance of mingled suspicion and alarm, Harold walked to the door and said, "Who is it?"

"Mister Ozdemir, the manager. I've brought a guard, who will sit outside Missus Majesty's door for the remainder of the night."

Opening the door, Harold revealed the hotel fellow who'd recently left the scene of the crime and a largish fellow clad in big, puffy trousers tucked into black boots with tassels on the sides, a short jacket and a striped head scarf, which I'm sure has a name although I don't know what it is. He had what looked like a serviceable and extremely large knife or dagger thrust through the red sash at his waist. His appearance was exotic, to say the least, and he was one of the most astonishingly handsome men I'd ever seen in my life. Even in my enfeebled condition, I couldn't help but stare and wish I didn't look so terrible myself.

"Thank you very much, Mister Ozdemir. And thank you, too, Mister . . . ah . . ."

"This is Ali," said Mr. Ozdemir. "He is a hotel employee who generally serves as required when guests of particular eminence stop here."

"I see. Well, thank you for allowing us to use his services," said Harold. "I don't know what's going on that Missus Majesty's room was entered, but I appreciate the guard."

Mr. Ozdemir bowed, Ali bowed, Harold bowed, and then he shut the door.

"Good," said he. "I feel better about leaving you alone now."

"Me, too." It was kind of good to feel better about something. The rest of me didn't feel much better at all.

No. That's not true. I was no longer throwing up, and it looked as though the aspirin tablets were going to remain where they belonged, in my tummy. And since earlier in the evening, I'd only occasionally been hit by hideous stomach cramps which made me run for the bathroom. While my stomach still cramped as I sat in the chair, I felt no particular need to . . . well, never mind. Whilst sitting in that chair, watching Harold, Mr. Ozdemir, the chambermaid and Ali, I'd had time to think about things, however, and I decided upon a course of action. It wasn't one I particularly wanted to take, but having had someone invade my room in the middle of the night had scared me enough to do it anyway.

"I'm going to send Sam Rotondo a telegram in the morning, Harold."

He'd been bending over, smoothing the covers on my bed— which I considered quite kind of him—and he straightened so abruptly, I thought his spine might crack. "You're *what?*"

"He's already said he's worried about us and is going to meet us somewhere. He probably expects to find us in England, but as long as we're staying in Istanbul for a while, I'll just let him know we're here." I mulled and frowned for a second. "Although I suppose I'd better call it Constantinople, just in case he doesn't know where Istanbul is." Bother. It was hard enough when my female friends got married and changed their names. But a city? I didn't approve. Not that anyone in Turkey or anywhere else cares what I thought.

"But . . . how long did it take us to get here? Surely we'll be long gone by the time he gets here."

I shrugged. "Knowing Sam, he's probably already on his way. Knowing how he uses his police connections, I'm sure he's made arrangements for correspondence to reach him wherever he is, and to get here by a faster means of travel than the ones we used."

"Good God. But why do you want to wire him, Daisy? That doesn't sound like you at all. Are you sure you're not suffering a relapse?"

"Only maybe a relapse into common sense. I've received two letters in two days from him, warning me about gangs of various sorts who prey on tourists. Lots of people have knocked on my door and then run away when I asked who was there, and now somebody has actually invaded my room in the middle of the night. As much as I hate to admit Sam might be right about anything, I'm afraid he's right about us being targets of some kind of criminal activity." I shook my aching head. "But I can't figure out what kind. I swear, Harold, I've gone through every bag and suitcase I brought with me, and I haven't seen anything that's not supposed to be there—or anything missing, either."

Harold stared at me for what seemed like a minute or ten before muttering once more, "Good God."

I understood his astonishment. I wasn't in the habit of calling upon Sam for help. Quite the opposite, in fact. But things had changed drastically, and I wouldn't mind having a trained police detective around, even one who annoyed the heck out of me more often than not.

CHAPTER EIGHTEEN

I stayed in bed for another two days and only got up and about briefly on the third and fourth days of my ordeal. During those two days, I managed to write a couple of letters in between naps and assure Harold that I was getting better. Which was true, although I remained weaker than your average kitten.

Dr. Weatherfield visited me twice each day and reported he was satisfied with my progress. My fever still showed up in the evenings, although it had gone down to almost normal during the day, and my body still ached, although not as much as it had when I'd first got sick, so I supposed his diagnosis was correct. I was no longer nauseated and no longer had the other problem and, while I still didn't feel like eating anything, I did manage to get down a couple of the washed and sanitized apples. Along with copious amounts of liquid, which Dr. Weatherfield assured me over and over again at every visit, was essential.

"You need to replace the water your body lost while you were so sick, you see. I've spoken about the matter with Mister Kincaid, and he's agreed to keep you supplied with lemonade and ginger ale."

"Thank you." Dr. Weatherfield was a nice man, but I longed for Doc Benjamin almost as much as I longed to be home. There's nothing quite as icky as being sick when you're thousands of miles away from the comfort of home. And my dog. I needed Spike next to me in bed, offering fur and sympathy.

Harold had taken my message to the telegraph office early the morning after the break-in, and he might as well have waited there for a response, one came so quickly. It was terse to a degree:

On my way. Don't move. Sam

"Good God, does that mean we have to remain in Istanbul while your tame detective makes his way from Pasadena, California, to Turkey?" Harold asked, staring with dismay at the telegram.

I shook my only nominally aching head. "Naw. He's probably already halfway here. Anyhow, we might as well get back to London and stay there where it's cooler and everyone speaks English. As soon as Doctor Weatherfield says I can travel, and after we see some of the sights in Istanbul, let's just go. Sam can't stop us, and he might just make it to Istanbul before we leave." It occurred to me that whoever seemed to be after us possibly *could* stop us, but I didn't care a whole lot at that point. I wanted to go home.

"Do you think it's safe? I mean, we don't even know who's after you."

"Me? Do you really think it's just me? Maybe whoever it is *is* after the both of us. Has your room been ransacked or anything?"

Harold grimaced at me, which was no more than I deserved. "Do you honestly think I wouldn't have told you if my room had been ransacked, Daisy Majesty? I know you've been sick, but your brains haven't fallen out of your head, have they?"

"All right, all right," said I pettishly. "No need to get nasty."

"However, I'm not all that keen on taking off to London all by ourselves. Not only do I want to see the sights with you with some kind of protection along, I'm also not that keen on us traveling alone anywhere. Perhaps I should hire someone to act as our guard on the Orient Express to France."

"That might not be a bad idea, but where would you find someone to guard us?" Then I bethought myself of the devastatingly handsome Ali, but I didn't mention him because my appreciation of the young Turk seemed disloyal somehow to Billy. Silly, I suppose, but it was true.

The day after the break-in of my room, the Turkish police authorities were summoned to the hotel, where they questioned Harold and me, Mr. Ozdemir, Ali (whose last name I eventually learned was Bektas) and what seemed like the entire hotel staff. The main policeman, or whoever he was, told us that such an occurrence in such a high-class hotel was practically unheard of, and implied that we were somehow at fault for our own misfortunes. I set him straight in no uncertain terms, and he left quivering, probably with wrath. At any rate, I doubted we'd get much help from that quarter should we ask for it.

"Damned if I know what's going on," said Harold. "If you hadn't been so rough on that police fellow . . . but that's all water under the bridge." He added the latter part of the sentence hastily, I presume after catching a gander at my face, which was moderately wrathful itself. I was still sick, darn it, and didn't feel the least bit diplomatic.

"We still need to hire a guard when I'm well enough to visit the sights in Istanbul." I decided not to discuss my rudeness to the poor policeman.

"I wonder where one finds a guard in Istanbul."

"Maybe Mister Ozdemir could advise us," I proposed. So far, I didn't think I'd aggravated Mr. Ozdemir beyond bearing. "Perhaps he could lend us Ali."

Harold brightened. "I like that idea. A lot."

Evidently I wasn't the only one who appreciated Ali's looks. I frowned at Harold. "You're married, remember."

"Am not."

"Might as well be."

"There's no harm in looking."

Hmm. Maybe Harold was right about that. His words made me feel minimally better about my own tendency to stare at Ali whenever he was around.

"Do you think you'll be up to taking in the sights of the city any time soon? I don't want to rush you," Harold hurried to explain, probably because he didn't want me to treat him as brutally as I had the policeman, "but let me know when you're ready."

"I'm sorry, Harold. I'm not being fair to you, making you wait around at the hotel while I'm sick. Why don't you go out and about a little yourself? Aren't there any interesting people in the hotel with whom you can visit mosques and palaces and stuff like that?"

Harold huffed. "Thanks to *you*, I'm afraid even to talk to strangers. Until we discover who's harassing you, I don't dare trust anyone."

"I haven't been harassed in a couple of days," I said in a small voice.

"That's because nobody can get at you." He smiled. "But do let me know when you feel up to it, and I'll ask Mister Ozdemir if we can borrow Ali."

"Ali's last name is Bektas, by the way, if you want to be polite and call him Mister Bektas."

Harold eyed me suspiciously. "How'd you find that out?"

I shrugged. "I asked him."

"Oh? And when did you do that?"

"Yesterday, when I was feeling slightly better, I brushed my hair, washed my face, put on a long robe, opened the door and asked him. He speaks pretty good English." I laughed. "In fact all of these people speak English. We should be ashamed of ourselves for not learning other languages if we expect to travel in other people's countries."

Harold blinked at me, and I sighed.

"Never mind. I'm not propounding a revolution or anything. I know you're rich, and when you're rich, you don't need to learn other people's languages because they'll cater to you no matter what language you speak."

"Are you a Socialist, Daisy Majesty?"

"No. Just from a lower class of American society than you."

"I thought we were a classless society."

I only looked at him until he gave up.

"Oh, all right. We're no more classless than any other society, I suppose."

"I suppose. Anyway, I can appreciate the feelings of other people who aren't rich, is all."

"Hmm. Well, whatever your politics, you sound as though you're getting better."

"I am. Maybe the day after tomorrow we can take in a mosque or something. I doubt if I'll be ready by tomorrow. I still feel as though I might fall down when I walk across the floor." I thought of something. "Gee, do they allow women in mosques? I don't want to break any rules or anything."

"I'll ask Mister Ozdemir. I'm sure he has packets of information about the sights to see in Istanbul, and he can probably hire us a guide, too."

I sighed, regretting the loss of Ali Bektas already. "You're certainly right. These fancy hotels cater to tourists."

And indeed our hotel and Mr. Ozdemir did cater to our urge to see the ancient city of Constantinople/Istanbul. What's more, he offered to allow us to hire Ali Bektas for only a slightly extortionate rate. Harold, having come from money and never having been in need of anything in his life, didn't even blink when he accepted Mr. Ozdemir's offer.

"He's going to charge you *what?*" I demanded when Harold came to my room that evening and told me of our good fortune.

"It's fine, Daisy. Mister Ozdemir said that Ali is not merely an excellent tour guide, but he's strong as an ox and can protect us if anyone tries anything untoward."

"Well . . . do you want me to give you some money to help pay for him?" Lord, it felt odd to talk about a human being as though he were merchandise. Not only would I make a lousy queen, but I don't think I'd have done very well as a belle at an old southern plantation, either.

"For heaven's sake, Daisy. This trip is my treat to you. I'm practically dripping money, and you know it. So shut up about the money, will you?"

I saluted. "Yes, sir."

That day I'd actually felt well enough to get into real clothes—a plain skirt and shirtwaist—which made me feel less like a dying diva and more like a real, live human being. I'm not sure why, but being in my nightie and robe all day long is to me a sure sign I'm really, really sick. Perhaps this is only one more indication of my working-class roots.

"I didn't realize how much there was of historical interest in Turkey," said Harold, browsing a brochure.

"Sure it's of historical interest," I said. "Istanbul used to be Constantinople, for Pete's sake—well, it still is to lots of people—and it was the center of the ancient world."

"Really? I didn't know that." He'd handed me another of the same, and I opened it and began looking too. "We need to see the Blue Mosque and the Topkapi Palace, for sure."

"Yes. And I'd like to see the old city walls. I guess lots of important cities used to have walls around them to keep invaders out."

"Indeed they did."

I heaved a sigh. "Billy used to read to me about the various walls in England. I'm sure you've heard of Hadrian's Wall. Maybe we can see that when we return to England."

"Maybe. I don't know if we'll be there long enough."

"I'd rather return to Pasadena than see Hadrian's Wall, if that makes a difference in our plans."

Glancing up from his brochure, Harold said seriously, "I hope this trip wasn't an awful mistake, Daisy. I was trying to help you out, and so far, you've been harassed by persons unknown and been deathly ill."

"Pooh, Harold. Neither of those things is your fault." I recalled Sam's last letter. According to him, everything that happens to me is always my own fault. I hadn't received another letter from him. That terse telegraph was his last communication, and I didn't know where in the world, literally, he was when he sent it. Although it sounds silly, I almost hoped he'd find us in Istanbul. I'd be happy to see anyone from home at that point in time, even Sam Rotondo.

"Well, I still feel responsible for your welfare."

"Thank you, Harold." I peered down at the brochure, feeling homesick and not wanting Harold to know it. "Oh, look! There's a Grand Bazaar here, too. I'll bet they have beautiful things there. Turkish rugs and fabrics. I love the few examples of Turkish art I've seen so far. It's so . . . colorful and exotic. And I definitely want to get a fez for Pa and Pudge Wilson."

"Yes. Me, too. I think I'll get Del a rug."

I glanced at the rug decorating my room. One couldn't even see where the ginger ale of the other night had puddled anymore. "They certainly seem to be sturdy. Personally, I'd like to see if I could find a couple of those camel blankets, preferably cleaned. Do you suppose they have camel blankets in Turkey?"

"I have no idea. I'm sure you can find almost anything at the

Grand Bazaar."

"I hope so. Oh, and look at this! There's a place called the Galata Tower. It used to be called the 'Jesus Tower' by the Genoese, but the Byzantines called it the 'Great Bastion.' What an odd combination of names."

"You're right about that."

"It seems funny to me that all the Turkish folks we've met have been so nice and helpful. Didn't the Turks pretty much take over this part of the world in times past? All that pillage and plunder and death seems far removed from the country we're in now."

"From what I've read, they're ferocious fighters even to this day."

"Hmm. Well, I'm glad they're nice to tourists."

A hard knock came at the door, and Harold and I glanced at each other uneasily. As far as I knew, Ali still stood guard out there, and that didn't sound like one of his polite knocks. At all.

"I'll see who it is," said Harold, quite gallantly, I think. I mean, for all we knew, the knocker with the knuckles had murdered Ali and was now going to do us in for the purpose of getting whatever I seemed to be in possession of—and boy, I wished I knew what it was, because I'd hand it over in an instant—or kidnap me and pawn me off to a white slaver.

Picking up an unopened ginger-ale bottle, I said, "I'll be your backup."

Frowning at me, Harold said, "I don't need backup, for God's sake."

"You never know," said I, and I followed him to the door whether he wanted me to or not.

Harold, being no dummy, didn't instantly open the door. Rather, he said, "Who is it?"

"Damnation, let me in!" came a voice I'd recognize anywhere.

Bolting past Harold, I flung the door open. "Sam! How in

the world did you get here so fast?"

Glaring at me in his old Sam-like way, Sam Rotondo shot a glower at Ali, who rolled his eyes in a great imitation of Sam himself, then stomped past me into my sitting room. He stopped a couple of paces from the doorway and glowered around. "The two of you aren't taking it easy with the money, are you?"

Before tackling Sam, I smiled at Ali and said, "Thank you very much, Mister Bektas."

He bowed, but appeared doubtful about our guest. I must say I couldn't blame him.

After gently closing the door on Ali, I turned on our latest arrival. "Sam Rotondo, if you aren't the rudest, most boorish man I've ever met in my—"

"It's all right, Daisy," said Harold in a placatory voice. "We're glad to see you, Detective Rotondo. I didn't want to travel alone with Daisy because someone seems to be dogging her footsteps, and it will be good to have you with us."

I stared at Harold, open-mouthed.

Before I could argue with him or scold Sam for being impolite some more, Harold rushed on. "Daisy's been quite ill for the past few days, and—"

"You've been *sick?* What the devil's the matter with you?" Sam rounded on me and looked as though he thought my getting sick was merely one more example of my incompetence.

"Darn you, Sam Rotondo, getting sick wasn't my fault! The hotel doctor called it Pharaoh's Revenge. What it boils down to is I got a case of dysentery, but I'm feeling much better now. In fact, Harold and I were just planning a tour of the city of Istanbul for the day after tomorrow."

"Where's Istanbul?" asked Sam belligerently.

I almost rolled my own eyes. "You're in Istanbul right this minute, Sam Rotondo. If you'd bothered to do any research, you'd know that people are calling Constantinople Istanbul these days."

"Huh."

"And we're going to see the sights," I said, my voice tight with annoyance.

"In which activity, of course, you'll join us," Harold said hurriedly, as if trying to prevent a bout of fisticuffs breaking out in my hotel suite.

Sam eyed me balefully. "You've lost even more weight, haven't you? You look like a damned skeleton."

"Blast you, Sam! Of course, I've lost weight. I was *sick*. I couldn't keep anything down for days! I'm still being careful, as a matter of fact." I placed a hand on my sensitive tummy, hoping Sam's bursting into its presence wasn't going to upset it again.

"I was trying my best to feed her before she got sick," Harold said in a conciliating tone, as if trying to prevent Sam from attacking him next.

"You don't have to explain anything to *him*," I told Harold, still frowning at Sam. "Well, don't just stand there, Sam Rotondo. Sit down and tell us why you're here."

"I'm here because you wired me, for God's sake!"

"Yes, I know we wired you, but you were on your way here before you got our wire, and you know it, or you couldn't have got here so fast. Now sit down and tell us what you know about the problems we've been having. *If* you know anything at all, which I very much doubt. I'll have you know I've been through every piece of luggage I brought with me, and haven't found a single, solitary thing that doesn't belong there, and not a single thing has been taken, either." Sam looked around the room as if searching for a chair, of which there were plenty. "And take your hat and jacket off, too, for pity's sake. You're not at a crime scene in the flickers. It might not be as hot here as it was in

Egypt, but you'll be more comfortable if you stop berating us and relax."

"Huh." Sam selected a chair, but before he sat, he did as I'd suggested and removed his hat, which he dropped onto a table, and draped his jacket over the back of the chair. He wore his policeman's clothes: dark suit, white shirt, big black shoes and dark tie. Not a tourist ensemble for Sam. He was at work, whether in Pasadena or Istanbul. I swear, I despaired of the man.

"Want a drink?" asked Harold. "Daisy's been drinking ginger ale as if it's going out of style, and we have lots of bottles here. I keep having to restock, because the doctor told her she has to rehydrate."

"Ginger ale?" Sam kept his scowl going for another several seconds and then dropped it. Thank God, I might add. I was afraid he'd keep it up for the rest of the day. "Sure. Thanks. I am thirsty."

"I'm not surprised," said I with a sniff. "You really need to get some lightweight duds, Sam, if you're going to be touring Istanbul with us the day after tomorrow. You'll be terribly uncomfortable in your copper clothes."

"I brought some other clothes with me," Sam said, as if he didn't want to. "I knew it was going to be hotter than hell in these parts in August."

Harold and I exchanged a glance, but neither of us said anything. After opening a ginger-ale bottle, Harold handed it to Sam. "Would you like it in a glass?"

"Thank you, and no thank you," barked Sam.

I'd had enough of his incivility. "That's enough, Sam Rotondo. Quit sounding like a copper interrogating a couple of murder suspects and relax. This is supposed to be a holiday."

After swallowing, Sam said, "Huh. For you maybe. I just want to make sure you both get home in one piece."

"Two pieces," I grumbled. "There are two of us, after all."

It didn't surprise me a bit when Sam rolled his eyes.

"Um, Daisy said you know something that might relate to some of the incidents that have taken place since we arrived in Egypt and moved on to Istanbul—I mean Constantinople. Daisy's room was broken into once while we were at supper and once while she was asleep one night, but Daisy drove the intruder out."

Sam eyed me over his ginger-ale bottle. "How'd you do that?"

"It was the first night of my illness, and I was so sick I could scarcely move. But I heard a noise in the night and sort of woke up."

"Sort of?" Sam recommenced glowering at me. "What the devil does that mean?"

"I was sick, darn it! I rolled over and the noise stopped, and I thought maybe I'd dreamed it. Then I heard it again, opened my eyes, and saw something that looked like a person at the closet door. I tried to grab a ginger-ale bottle so I could conk the guy on the head, but another bottle fell off the bedside table and made a big noise, so he ran for the door. I ran after him, but I was sick and feeble, and only managed to hit part of him with my bottle. I don't know what part. The bottle broke," I added, although I'm not sure why.

"How'd he get in with that guy at the door?" Sam gestured at the door with his thumb, indicating Ali.

"Ali wasn't there then. He was hired to guard my door that very night."

"Ali? You're pretty chummy with him, aren't you?"

Lord, please grant me patience. I'd asked the Lord to do that before, and so far my prayers had gone unanswered. I really tried to keep my temper that day, however. "His name is Ali Bektas. Mister Ozdemir, the manager of the hotel, posted him at my door the night of the break-in. The police didn't seem interested. In fact, they said it was impossible for anyone to break into a first-class hotel like this one."

"Huh," said Sam. "I sure as hell can't afford it. I'm staying a few blocks away, at a place called the Bosphorus."

"You can stay here," Harold said in a rush. "I'll be happy to—"

Sam didn't even have to speak to Harold to make him shut up. He merely looked at him with his cop's eyes, and Harold's generous offer gurgled to a stop.

"I'll pay my own way, thank you," Sam said, sounding extremely grumpy and not at all thankful.

Harold shrugged. "Just trying to be helpful," he mumbled.

"Sam Rotondo, you're about as gracious as a hippopotamus. Did you know that?"

"Huh. What's a hippo have to do with anything?"

"Billy read that more people are killed by hippos in Africa than any other animal, including the ever-popular lion. You're about as gracious as that."

"Well, I don't like taking things from other people. I'd rather pay my own way."

"Fine," said Harold, throwing up his hands.

Silence filled the room for a moment. Then Sam said, "So, do you want to hear what I've learned about what might be going on here, or not?"

That's when I truly lost my temper.

CHAPTER NINETEEN

Sam held up a hand after listening to me rant for several minutes. "All right, all right! If you'll shut up, I'll tell you."

"I asked you to tell us what you knew the minute you entered the room, darn it!"

"So quit hollering at me, and I'll tell you now."

My gaze paid a visit to the ceiling, and I prayed once again for patience. Again, it was not granted unto me. I did, however, remain silent.

"It's like this," Sam said, once he decided I wasn't going to interrupt again. "There are gangs of antiquities thieves running riot all over the Middle East, and especially in Egypt, where new antiquities are being discovered all the time."

"New antiquities. That sounds like an oxymoron to me," I muttered.

Both Sam and Harold looked at me as if I'd just spoken to them in ancient Greek or something. I tried to explain. "New antiquities. It's funny calling something so old as to be ancient new. Kind of like calling somebody pretty ugly. Or saying something's a little big. Phrases like that are called oxymorons."

Harold said, "If you say so, sweetie."

Sam said, "Huh. May I please continue? Or do you have more vocabulary words for us to learn today?"

I huffed. "Go on. I didn't realize how scanty your vocabularies were, or I never would have used the word."

"Good," growled Sam. "There are also gangs of white slavers

who like to get their hands on unattached females. Then there are the drug smugglers. At any rate, some of these gangs are really smooth, and they like to get in good with tourists. After they pal around with a tourist for a while, they'll manage to stuff drugs or small antiquities or antique coins or whatever into the tourist's luggage or what have you. Then, when you get back home or to England, or wherever the gang is stationed, they'll get it back from you again, and nine-tenths of the time, the sucker never even knows he's been used. If the customs guys do happen to find whatever it is that's being smuggled, the tourist will be called on the carpet for it, and the gang members get away scot-free. Of course, if it's a gang of slavers, you'll be snatched, and nobody will ever find you."

"How very comforting," said I.

Sam, as I might have predicted, said, "Huh."

"Anyhow, Sam, I've been through every piece of baggage I brought with me, and there's nothing there that shouldn't be. I swear it."

"I've gone through my stuff, too," added Harold, "even though nobody's bothered me."

Sam frowned. He had formidable eyebrows, and he looked mighty fierce when he was unhappy. "I don't understand this. Clearly, something's going on."

"Clearly," I agreed a trifle snidely.

"Well, I don't know what the devil is going on, but I'm going to be with you from now on, so nobody can get at you."

"We've already hired Ali to be our escort and guard when we tour the city."

"That's fine. You'll have me, too. If we figure out what these guys who are after you want, maybe we can set up some kind of sting."

Harold and I gazed at each other blankly for a second before I asked, "What's a sting?"

"You just carry on with your business. My copper pals—"

"What copper pals?" I demanded.

Sam shrugged. "A couple of fellows from Scotland Yard came with me. Anyhow, they'll hang around out of the way, and when the thieves approach you, we'll pounce."

"You'll pounce?" I repeated, still unable to grasp what Sam and his British cohorts were up to.

"Yeah? See, you'll go on about your business as if nothing's the matter. Since I'm here and I've already made contact with you, I'll just be a friend who's joined you from the States. But the London fellows will hang out in the background and see if they can determine who's behind the odd things that have happened to you two and what the perpetrators are after."

"That sounds really lame, Sam," I told him. "But if your friends want to follow us around, I guess that's okay. I can't imagine why we've been targeted. Nothing's been stolen and nothing's been added to our stuff."

"Not that you've seen," said Sam. "These gang guys are pros, don't forget."

"Good Lord," murmured Harold.

"And they're mean as snakes, too, so don't expect to do any detecting on your own," Sam growled.

"We have no intention of doing any *detecting*, Sam Rotondo, curse you!" After a moment of silence in the room, I decided to tell Sam the names of the people I thought were behind the plot, if there was a plot, being carried on in and around my luggage and me. Well, you know what I mean. "However, I can give you three names that might comprise some of this so-called *gang* of yours."

"Oh, cripes, Daisy," said Harold, running his hands through his hair. "You can't really mean you suspect—"

"Yes, I do suspect them, although I'm not sure of what."

Sam held up a hand that was big enough for a family of four

to eat from. "Hold on a minute. Who are these people and what do you suspect them of?"

"I don't know what I suspect them of, but I suspect them of something. Harold disagrees."

Sam rolled his eyes once more and said, "Will you please just give me the names and tell me why you consider them suspicious?"

"All right. The first one is Mister Stackville." I glanced at Harold. "Do you remember his first name, Harold? It was something strange."

"Wallingford," said Harold resignedly. "Probably an old family name or something."

"Wallingford Stackville?" Sam, who'd used his big paw to withdraw a policemanly notebook and pencil from his pocket, wrote the name down, although he did so with clear distaste, as if he didn't approve of Mr. Stackville's name. Huh. Wait until he met the man himself.

"He's the leader of the gang, if you want my opinion," said I. Rather than hesitate long enough for Sam to tell me he didn't, I hurried on. "Then there's a Frenchman named Pierre Futrelle and another British guy named Gaylord Bartholomew."

"Huh," said Sam.

"Any of those names ring a bell? I mean, if your London brothers-in-uniform have any names."

"No."

"Well, there's something odd about them."

"Daisy," said Harold, in a warning sort of voice.

"There is, too, Harold. Stackville stuck to us like glue when we were in Egypt, and he was horrified to see we were leaving Egypt earlier than we'd planned."

"Yeah?" said Sam, his interest piqued.

"Yeah. And then who should show up at this very hotel but Pierre Futrelle!" I announced triumphantly. "What's more, somebody with a French accent knocked at my door when I was sick, and when I asked who it was, he went away again."

"How do you know he had a French accent if he went away again?"

I frowned at Sam. "Because he said something and had a French accent, of course."

"I haven't seen him since that one time, Daisy, and I only caught the one glimpse of him, you know. It might not have been him at all."

"You said it was he," I told Harold, feeling as though he were abandoning me on a field of battle.

"Well, I thought it was, but I didn't talk to him or anything."

"Anyhow, it wasn't the last time someone knocked on my door and then went away when I asked who it was. I think that's suspicious behavior."

"Hmmm." Sam. "Well, it sounds as if you might be right about those men being in a conspiracy of some sort. But darned if I can figure out . . ." His voice trailed off.

"You mentioned political spies, didn't you? What might they want with little old me?"

Sam frowned at me some more. Then he said, "Damned if I know."

I sighed. "I can't imagine what an antiquities thief would want with me, either. I guess I can see a political spy sneaking something into my handbag or something, but I swear to heaven, nobody's put so much as a pottery shard in my luggage. I think smuggling antiquities is really a stretch."

"I guess. Although that's what the London folks are here for. Egypt was a British protectorate for years, you know, and it's only recently that the Egyptian government has taken an interest in keeping their antiquities in their own country. Hell, Europeans have looted the place—with the complicity of the natives, mind you—since before Napoleon's time."

I blinked. "That is a very long time, isn't it?"

"Very," said Sam dryly. "But now everyone's up in arms about the problem, so folks are trying to stop it. I don't know about drugs or spies, though. That's . . ." Again his voice sort of sagged to a stop.

"You'd think Turkey would be the place for drugs," Harold said, rather unexpectedly in my estimation. "Isn't Turkey where the opium poppies grow?"

"Oh, my," said I, not having thought about opium poppies in connection with Turkey, even though the notion of smuggling opium sounded a bit more possible than smuggling antiquities.

Sam threw up his hands. Fortunately for all of us, he kept a hold on his notebook and pencil. "Hell, who knows what's going on? You'd better let me go through your bags, though, since I'm trained to search, and you're not."

"Darn you, Sam Rotondo. I searched everything there was to search." Besides, I didn't want him going through my more delicate, private belongings.

"Better me than a customs agent," he snapped.

"All right. All right. But does it have to be now?" With some astonishment, I placed a hand on my stomach and announced, "I'm hungry!"

This time it was Harold who threw his hands up in the air. "Hallelujah! It's about time! Let's go down to the dining room and have dinner. My treat. Please join us, Detective Rotondo."

Sam looked for a moment as if he were indignantly going to refuse Harold's offer, but he glanced at me, I made a face at him, and he finally said, "Thank you. Don't mind if I do."

I glanced down at my plain skirt and shirtwaist. "I suppose I'd better change into something more presentable for a first-class hotel restaurant."

"Hell, does that mean I have to change, too?" asked Sam, sounding aggrieved.

"You look fine, Detective Rotondo," said Harold hurriedly. "Daisy, why don't you put on that blue dress you wore before? That's not formal, but it's a bit nicer for dinnertime than what you're wearing now. I'll go to my room and change, too."

"What will I do while you guys are changing?" asked Sam, looking for the first time since I'd met him as if he felt a little left out of the party.

"Just hang out in the hall with Ali, why don't you? He speaks very good English, and maybe you can detectivate some information out of him about your gang of villains and thugs." I smiled at Sam when he shot me a thunderous scowl. "You just don't want to talk to him because he's so good-looking and exotic."

"Don't be silly," snarled Sam, grabbing his coat and hat and heading for the door.

"You're a little hard on the man, Daisy. He's only trying to help us," Harold said after Sam left my room.

"He's always been a thorn in my side." I sighed heavily. "But you're right. He's trying to help us. I shouldn't rag him."

"See that you don't in the future." And Harold wagged a playful finger at me before he, too, left my room.

It didn't take me long to change. I'd bathed earlier in the day and washed my hair for good measure so as to cleanse away the lingering remains of my recent ordeal. Then I hesitated, wondering if I should wait for Harold or Sam to come and fetch me. After all, if Sam was right, and I was some kind of target for a person or persons unknown—although I was pretty sure they were known to me even if I didn't know why they wanted me—I didn't want to be snatched away by a criminal from the hallway of my hotel. Then I recalled Ali, relaxed, and opened my door.

To my utter astonishment, I discovered Ali and Sam yukking it up as if they were long lost friends reunited after an absence of decades. I must have stared at them, because Ali shut up and straightened into his official posture. Sam turned his head and frowned at me. How typical.

"Ready at last, are you?" said he.

I decided to ignore his sarcasm. It hadn't taken me more than ten minutes to dress for dinner, after all. "I see you two managed to get to know each other. Mister Bektas, this is Mister Rotondo, from my hometown of Pasadena, California, in the United States."

"Yes. He told me. He say your—what do you say?—your . . ."

"Husband," Sam supplied helpfully.

"Ah. Yes. Your husband recently went to God, and your brother takes you on a big trip."

"Yes, that's true," I told Ali, trying to remember if we'd told Sam that Harold and I were masquerading as brother and sister. "And then I got sick and somebody tried to rob me." I shook my head. "Some trip so far."

"Most unusual," said Ali, his demeanor formal. "Not the sick, but the rob. Most unusual. This the Sultanahmet, and the Sultanahmet is the best hotel in Istanbul."

"I understand that such a thing is very unusual. But I don't want to think about that now. I'm really glad you'll be our guide when we visit the beautiful spots in Istanbul, Ali. I'm looking forward to it."

His teeth gleamed in a smile so magnificent, I darned near got weak in the knees. "Yes. I take you to beautiful places we have."

I thought of a question I'd had before, so I asked Ali, "Will I be allowed into the Blue Mosque. I mean, I'm a woman and all." I felt my cheeks heat as both Ali and Sam grinned at me. Curse all men.

"You cover your head and remove your shoes and dress respectable, and you be allowed to see the great room."

Dress respectable? I wondered if Ali considered my usual

mode of dress to be disrespectful. Boy, I never realized how complicated travel to foreign parts could be for us blasé Americans who never thought about cultures other than our own. In fact, I'd bet anything, if I did anything so foolish as to gamble, that if you asked your average American (whatever that is) if we even had a culture, and you'd get blank stares back.

My musing upon this interesting subject was interrupted by Harold, who joined us at that point. "Ah, good," said he, rubbing his hands. "Let's go to the hotel dining room and take some nourishment." Before he took his nourishment, he took my arm. "I'm so very glad you're at last feeling hungry again, Daisy." He nodded politely at Ali, who bowed politely back, and Harold, Sam and I headed for the lift, which took us to the lobby, from whence we went to the hotel restaurant, a five-star affair if ever there was one.

The waiter, who was infinitely more dignified than I and reminded me of Mrs. Pinkerton's butler Featherstone, led us to a table beside a window where we could have a view of the outdoors. Of course, by that time night had fallen, so we couldn't see much. I have to admit I was looking forward to our trip to see the sights the day after tomorrow.

"Your hotel is called the Bosphorus, Sam. Is it on the banks of the Bosphorus or something?"

He shrugged as he reared back to allow the waiter to put his napkin in his lap. Sam was no more accustomed to being waited on than was I. "I don't know. Didn't look. First thing I did after I checked in was come here to find you two."

"Oh. That was nice."

"Yes. Thank you," said Harold.

Then Harold and I glanced at each other. I do believe neither of us could figure out exactly why Sam was so dedicated to my welfare when we didn't even know why I was being pursued. If I was being pursued—although it did appear as if someone wanted something I had. But he'd been worried about me even before he knew about the room searches and break-in and so forth. Very strange. Unless he was carrying his loyalty to Billy's last request to an extreme degree.

"Don't look at each other like that," Sam growled. Trust him to notice anything a body didn't want him to notice. "We've been getting reports of strange goings-on in these parts, and it looks like you've managed to get yourself mixed up in some of them. I'm here to fix that."

"Right," I said, and I regret to say my voice was quite sardonic. "Too bad we don't know what exactly the strange thing is that we're mixed up in."

"Not we," said Harold, the rat. "You. You're the only one who's been bothered."

I heaved a sigh. "Thanks for reminding me. I just wish I knew what it was the crooks wanted of me. I'd hand it over in a minute."

"Maybe it's you they want," grumbled Sam. "Want to hand yourself over to a gang of white slavers?"

I frowned at him. "Oh, come on, Sam. Those tales of white slavery are nonsense. The stuff of fiction and the flickers. Aren't they?"

"No," he said emphatically. "They are not."

His answer sent a jolt of panic through me, but before I could ask any questions, a waiter appeared. He was another dignified bloke wearing a grand Turkish costume rather like Ali's only without the dagger thrust through his sash. I liked the way Turks dressed a lot better than the way Egyptians dressed, and I began to get ideas for spiritualist costumes. Perhaps this trip wasn't going to be a total waste after all. I forgot the white slavery question as I considered what to sew for myself when I got home. It only occurred to me later that this moment in time might have been the turning point in my recovery, both physical and emotional.

"Want a drink, Detective Rotondo? You can drink booze here, you know. Not like at home."

"I thought Moslems didn't drink alcohol," said Sam, something I'd been curious about, too.

"Perhaps they don't, but tourists do," said Harold pragmatically. "And the natives want our money, so they serve the forbidden stuff. So do you want a drink?"

"No, thanks," said Sam, who appeared uncomfortable with the very idea of consuming something that was blatantly illegal in his own country. "I'll just have coffee."

"Turkish coffee?" asked Harold, a glint in his eye—and I knew why. Turkish coffee is nothing at all like its pale and pallid cousin we Americans drink. I smiled, hoping Sam might choke on his choice of drink, or at least gasp once or twice.

"Sure. Sounds okay to me."

"I'll have a dry martini," Harold told the waiter. "Daisy, you want tea, don't you?"

He knew me so well. "Yes, please."

"Tea for the lady, and Turkish coffee for the other gentleman."

The waiter bowed and went away to fetch our drinks. Harold and I exchanged another speaking look.

Sam said, "What?" in a most suspicious voice.

"Nothing," Harold and I chorused.

"Huh," said Sam, as ever.

When the waiter returned with our beverages, Sam stared at the teeny cup of coffee the man set before him. "What's that?" he asked. I was glad he'd been polite enough to save his question until the waiter had left.

"That's your Turkish coffee, Sam," I said sweetly. "Take a big gulp."

"A gulp is all there is of it," he muttered.

"Daisy's teasing you, Detective. Take a small sip. That stuff is potent."

"Potent?" Sam stared at Harold. "Do you mean to tell me Moslems put booze in their coffee? I thought only the Irish did that."

"Do the Irish put alcohol in their coffee?" I asked, genuinely curious.

"There's no booze in the coffee," Harold assured Sam. "Trust me."

Sam didn't appear to trust Harold any more than he trusted me. Nevertheless, he spooned a lump of sugar into his coffee cup and lifted it to his lips. His huge paw dwarfed the itty-bitty cup. Then he took a sip of the coffee. And then his eyes opened wider than I'd ever seen them, he carefully replaced the cup on its little saucer before him, and he seemed to struggle for breath. After a second or two of silence, during which I prayed Sam wouldn't blow up and explode all over the restaurant, he turned to me.

"Take a big gulp, eh?"

I shrugged. "Just a suggestion." I tried to appear impish but probably didn't, given that according to all reports, I looked more like the wraith of a human being than the genuine article at the time.

"Don't mind Daisy, Detective Rotondo. She's been sick."

"Doesn't matter," Said Sam grumpily. "She hates me. And call me Sam, will you? Can the 'Detective Rotondo' thing. We don't want anyone who might be watching to know I'm with the cops."

"Thanks," said Harold. "And please call me Harold."

Stung and feeling oddly ashamed of myself, I said, "I don't either hate you, Sam Rotondo."

Sam looked hard at me. "You could have fooled me."

And, darn it all to heck and back, I felt like crying *again*. Lord, I was a mess!

CHAPTER TWENTY

In spite of the coffee incident, I managed to eat a fairly substantial meal, considering I hadn't consumed anything but pared apples, soda crackers and ginger ale for days and days. I put away a whole bowl of chicken soup with some big beans in it—the Turks favor lentils as do the Egyptians, but since I don't, I'd passed on that choice—and some delicious flat bread that we dipped in some kind of yogurt sauce. I'd never heard of yogurt before, but I guess it's quite common in those parts and is used in all sorts of different dishes, from breakfast to supper. This particular yogurt dish was kind of like thick sour milk, but it was seasoned with garlic and tiny cucumber bits and I don't know what else. It was good. That's all I knew, and I hoped I'd be able to discover a Turkish cookbook, only in English, to take home to Vi when we went on our tour of the city.

Sam, whose culinary experiences were greater than mine, as he'd grown up in New York City where, he claimed, you could get just about any kind of food you could imagine, enjoyed his meal of lamb skewered on spikes and grilled over an open flame. He called them shish kebabs and, because his knowledge of the world's foods was wider than mine, I saw no reason to doubt him. Harold had the same, and made me eat a bite of lamb from one of his skewers. I had to admit it was delicious, but my stomach was so full by that time, I couldn't eat another bite.

Gazing at me critically—the only way he ever gazed at me— Sam said, "Well, I'm glad you managed to eat something, but you still look like hell. Harold and I have to put some meat on your bones before we take you home to your family, or you'll give 'em all spasms."

"Surely I don't look that bad!" cried I—softly, in deference to our being in a classy restaurant.

"You want to risk your father's heart on it?" Sam asked.

My mouth fell open. Fortunately, it was empty at the time. "That's plain cruel, Sam Rotondo! You know I love my father with all my heart, and I'd never do anything to hurt him. Besides, it's not my fault I got sick just when I was already so . . . vulnerable." I refused to use words like *skinny* or *gaunt* or any of the others that had been flung at me recently, including *skeletal*, which had been contributed by Sam himself.

Sam said, "Huh." I glowered at him.

"We'll get her to eating again, Sam," Harold said in a bolstering sort of voice. "It's encouraging that she was hungry tonight."

"I guess," Sam grumbled.

The waiter brought us some kind of dessert, which he called *boreck* and which was flaky and fabulous, according to Sam and Harold, although I had to take their word for it, since my abused stomach couldn't hold a single other thing, not even a flake of the pastry that looked so good and which the men gobbled up like candy.

After everything had been taken away, Sam pushed his chair back a bit, looked from Harold to me, and said, "That's about the best meal I've ever eaten, except at your house, Daisy."

"I'm going to see if I can find a Turkish cookbook for Aunt Vi," said I. "Only it'll have to be in English or she won't be able to use it."

"And when did you say you're going to take this sightseeing trip of yours?" he asked.

"Day after tomorrow," said Harold. "Ali is going with us to guide and guard us. Along with you, of course." He added the last sentence hastily as if he worried Sam might berate him if he didn't. Which he probably would have, given that Sam was Sam.

"Good. We'll plan our strategy tomorrow, then."

Harold and I exchanged one last glance for the evening.

Yet the following day wasn't so bad. Sam wasn't as grumpy as he'd been the day he arrived, and he was polite as the three of us went down to breakfast, which he took with us at Harold's invitation of the previous evening. Harold and I both brought the travel brochures and maps Mr. Ozdemir had given us, and it was fun going over them together in the hotel lounge after breakfast—which, by the way, I ate. It perhaps sounds rather odd to other Americans—it sure sounded odd to me—but I had a warm yogurt soup flavored with mint.

According to Dr. Weatherfield, who had paid me a last visit the night before and who'd recommended it to me, the soup was called *yayla corbasi* and, also according to him, "It'll fix you right up. It's the perfect food for people who've been sick with dysentery." He then went on to give me something of a lecture about the joys and benefits of yogurt, but I won't go into the matter here, since you probably aren't interested in fermented milk products and so forth.

Anyhow, the soup was good, and it settled into my formerly disturbed tummy as lightly as a butterfly landing on a leaf.

"Are you sure that's all you want?" Harold asked, frowning at my empty yogurt bowl.

"Positive. I'm stuffed. Don't forget that last night and this morning, I've taken the only solid food, except apples, for almost a week."

"That stuff didn't look very solid to me," he grumbled.

"It was, though. And it was delicious, too," I assured him.

"Well . . ."

"It's all right," said Sam, eyeing me severely. "We'll make her eat more for lunch."

My gaze paid a visit to the ceiling, but I didn't scold or object, because I figured there would be no point in doing so. As for Sam and Harold, they both ate man-sized breakfasts that included some kind of spinach pie and another form of *boreck,* only this time made with vegetables (Harold said eggplant; Sam said zucchini squash; take your pick). I guess you can do a whole lot with pastry dough besides make desserts out of it.

At any rate, we had a good time planning for the morrow's visits to various sites, including the Blue Mosque, the Topkapi Palace and—at my insistence—the Grand Bazaar. "I'm still pretty weak, you know. I don't want to do too much in one day. We can see the city gates and some of the other sights the next day."

"Very well," said Harold meekly.

Sam, who was never meek, grunted and said, "I'm going to hire a car to take us around. I don't want Daisy walking on the crowded streets. Not only might she get sick again, but I don't want her getting snatched."

"I don't think anyone's interested in snatching me, Sam," I said, and quite calmly, too. "Whatever these people are after, it seems to be something I have, not me."

"You never know," he said darkly, and I decided we'd both said enough on the subject.

After breakfast, Harold and Sam went out for a while. Sam wanted to introduce Harold to his police cronies from London, and Harold wanted to see some of the city. Poor fellow, he'd been trapped in the hotel caring for me ever since we'd arrived in Istanbul.

As for me, I was directed in no uncertain terms to "Go to your room, lock the door and rest. You have to be feeling well enough to do some sightseeing tomorrow."

I saluted Sam, said, "Yes, your majesty," and watched Sam

roll his eyes. Then we all trooped back up to my room, where Sam and Ali greeted each other in Turkish—I swear, the man was totally unsociable to the rest of the universe, but he'd already made a friend of Ali—and I entered my room.

"Lock your door," Sam commanded for about the ninetieth time.

"Yes, sir. Will do."

After giving me a good hot scowl for form's sake, he, Harold and Ali waited for me to turn the key in the lock, and then I heard two sets of footsteps taking off down the hallway and Sam and Harold talking to each other as if they, too, were fast friends. Would wonders never cease?

I spent the rest of that day sleeping and catching up on correspondence. Although I wanted to, I didn't brave Sam's temper by toddling downstairs and looking for postcards, but wrote my letters on the stationery provided by the hotel. I apologized to everyone for not having written for a few days, explained that I'd been sick but that I was better now, and told my family in their letter that Sam had joined us.

I don't know why the man thinks I need a bodyguard, but he's here, and he's determined to make sure nothing bad happens to me while I'm traveling. I hate to admit it, but it was nice to see him. He, Harold and I are going to see some of Constantinople's many treasures tomorrow, and I hope I can write a more interesting letter tomorrow night.

Which just goes to show, I suppose, that one should be careful when putting what one thinks are newsy little quips down on paper.

Sam arrived the next day at nine o'clock. Harold and I had taken our breakfast in the hotel's dining room—more yogurt soup for me, and I sampled some of Harold's spinach pie, which was quite tasty.

Ali joined us in the lobby, and we traipsed out of the hotel and to the machine Sam had hired to take us around the city. A huge old Hudson Phaeton met our eyes as we walked down to the street. The machine looked like it had once maybe belonged to a sultan or something but had hit hard times since then. However, it was large enough to hold us all, and Sam had hired a Turkish driver to go along with the motor, so we seemed to be set for the day. Ali and the driver, a fellow named Ahmet Bayar, sat in front and Sam, Harold and I took the backseat. The two men sat on either side of me.

"Because I don't want anyone to be able to get at you without going over us," said Sam in his usual gruff manner.

I merely shrugged. "Whatever you say, Sam. I think they're after my luggage, though, not me."

"Huh."

Typical.

The Blue Mosque was absolutely . . . well, I don't have words to describe it. Fabulous, maybe? I made sure I was covered from tip to toe and wore a hat, and we all removed our shoes before Ahmet and Ali preceded us into the place. We didn't linger, since it was a site holy to Moslems and except for the two Turks, we weren't Moslems. I certainly didn't want to offend anyone, but I was awfully glad that we'd visited the place.

Harold politely asked if it was all right to take pictures with his Kodak and was told to go ahead, but he didn't take many on the inside of the mosque. The outside was another matter. That place is *huge,* and we spent a good deal of time walking its perimeter and stopping every second or three for Harold to take more pictures. He made Sam and me get into a couple of them, which made neither one of us awfully happy.

"Oh, for God's sake," Harold snarled at one point. "It's to

give perspective. I want people to know how big this place is, and the best way to do that is to show the two of you standing in front of it. You don't have to look as if you're being sacrificed, you know."

So, I smiled. When Harold showed me the photos later, I learned that Sam didn't. He looked, in fact, as if he were sorely aggrieved to have to stand next to me. By the way, Sam had shed his copper duds for the day and wore a typical white linen tourist's suit. It actually looked good on him, although, of course, I didn't tell him that.

We must have spent an hour or more at the Blue Mosque, and then Ahmet drove us to the Topkapi Palace. Boy. It was definitely a palace. And talk about your more-than-Oriental-splendor, as Rudyard Kipling might have phrased it. I could have spent the entire day studying the tiles alone. In fact, I became so fascinated by the tiled pool in the area that used to be set apart for the harem that I didn't notice my companions had moved along. When I glanced up from staring at the amazing tile work and discovered myself alone, a spasm of alarm struck me.

An instant later something else struck me.

After that I didn't know anything at all until I awoke on my bed in the Sultanahmet Hotel and saw Dr. Weatherfield peering down upon me with a worried frown on his face. My head ached something awful. Then I noticed Harold, who was drying his hair with a towel. That seemed extremely odd to me. And where was Sam?

"What happened?" croaked I, once more wishing I were dead.

"You were attacked," said Harold. "By three men. You were right. Stackville was one of them, and I'm pretty sure his French pal and that other fellow were with him."

"Why did they hit me?" I squinted at Harold. "And why are you all wet?"

"We realized you weren't with us after we left the harem rooms. Sam and Ali and I rushed back to see what had become of you." He gave me a fierce scowl. "For God's sake, Daisy, after everything that's gone on, didn't you think it would be wise of you to stay with the group?"

"I didn't realize you were going when you went. Where's Sam?"

That's when two other men approached my bed. I saw Mr. Ozdemir standing in the back of the room, wringing his hands. Shoot, the only people missing were Ali and Ahmet. And Sam.

"Missus Majesty?" a crisp English accent asked.

"Yes?"

"I am DI Albert Foxcroft, with the London CID. Detective Rotondo, I fear, has been captured by the men who were trying to kidnap you."

My eyes practically bugged out of my head. "Sam? *Sam* has been kidnapped?" Then, even though it made my aching head hurt worse, I cried out, "Will somebody please tell me what's going *on?*"

"Let me try to explain," Harold said, jostling his way past the London policeman. "Sam and Ali had just gone back to the harem to see where you were when they saw Stackville and his two pals carrying you off. Sam let out a roar that echoed through the whole palace, I'm sure, and that's when I ran into the room. Then he, Ali and I ran toward you and Stackville's crew. There was a huge scuffle, and I think Ali managed to slice one of the bad guys with his dagger. I ended up in the pool, and the villains somehow managed to carry Sam off while Ali picked you up after they dropped you. I don't know if that's when you cracked your head or if they conked you before they tried to carry you off."

I pressed a hand to my head. "Good Lord," I whispered. "We have to get Sam back. Great heaven, where could he be?"

"Before you go haring off anywhere, young lady, I need to make sure you didn't suffer a concussion," said Dr. Weatherfield, sounding as though he were trying to hold his emotions in check. Whatever those emotions were, they seemed to be strong. "How many fingers am I holding up?"

"Fingers? *Fingers?*" I hate to admit it, but I slapped his hand away. "I don't care about your cursed fingers! We need to get Sam back! Oh, my God, didn't anybody see where they took him?" I sat up, my head swam, and Dr. Weatherfield caught me before I could clunk back down onto the bed. "Oh," I whimpered, sounding pathetic to my own ears.

"Lie still, Missus Majesty. People are working on getting your friend back. We have to make sure you haven't permanently damaged yourself."

I resented that. "I didn't damage myself at all, darn it! Those horrid men damaged me."

"Yes, well, please lie quietly."

"I can still talk while you look at my head, can't I?" I swear, my heart, which had been behaving like a deflated balloon ever since Billy died, was now flinging itself around my chest cavity like a crazy thing. First it pounded like mad, then it sank to my toes, then it raced, then it thudded out a funereal cadence.

"No, you may not talk. At least wait until I finish examining you."

"*Harold!*" I wailed, reminding myself of his mother. "We need to get *Sam* back!"

Dr. Weatherfield turned abruptly to Harold. "Can you calm her down? I have to make sure she didn't suffer a concussion, and she's having hysterics."

"I'm not having hysterics!" I screamed.

"Can you give her a sedative or something?" asked Harold doubtfully.

"I don't *want* a sedative! I want *Sam* back!"

Those words, which I screeched for all the world to hear, finally shut me up. Astonished at myself, I closed my mouth and looked bleakly up at the doctor.

"Are you through?" he asked politely. I don't think he felt polite.

"Yes." My voice was tiny.

"Thank God," muttered Harold.

"Indeed," said Dr. Weatherfield. "Now, Missus Majesty, can you tell me how many fingers I'm holding up?"

After shooting a pleading glance at Harold and watching him mouth *Just do it* back at me, I submitted. "Two."

"Fine. And can you tell me the date?"

"August twenty-ninth, nineteen twenty-two."

"Very good. And where did you go on your jaunt this morning?"

My nerves were ganging up on me once more, but I strove to keep them at bay. Hollering at the world that I wanted Sam back had shaken me to my very soul. Therefore, I said meekly, "First we went to the Blue Mosque, and then we went to the Topkapi Palace. That's where . . . it happened."

"Yes. Mister Kincaid told me all about it. Now, can you tell me your birth date?"

Wanting to bellow at him for asking inane questions, I answered him anyway. "November thirtieth, nineteen hundred."

"Very good."

Then, instead of explaining my condition to me, he turned to Harold. Men. I swear.

"Missus Majesty has a nasty lump on her head, and I fear her head will ache for some time. Perhaps a few days. I'm leaving some chloral hydrate for her to take when the pain is particularly intense, but make sure she uses it sparingly, because it's a powerful medication."

Oh, Lord. Just what I needed. I, whose beloved husband had

become addicted to morphine after he was shot and gassed during the war and had ultimately killed himself with the stuff, had just been handed a prescription for my own death should I care to use it for that purpose. The way my heart had taken to aching in time with my head, death sounded pretty good to me just then.

But not until we got Sam back. After I knew Sam was safe, I might just decide to heck with this stupid world and go join Billy in his.

Sam came first, though. He, who'd rushed across an ocean to save me from then-unknown foes, was now in peril himself. If he'd worried about how my family would react if I came home thin, I didn't even want to think about going home and telling them we'd managed to lose Sam in Istanbul.

I absolutely hated life in that moment.

CHAPTER TWENTY-ONE

I behaved myself for the rest of that day and didn't cause another single stir. The doctor ultimately relaxed and smiled at me. Harold finally got his hair dry and put on another white linen suit, and the London coppers finally told me what they'd hoped to discover by traveling with Sam all the way to Constantinople.

Only it soon became apparent to me that they still didn't know what it was. DI (which stands for detective inspector) Albert Foxcroft and DCI (which stands for detective chief inspector) Lawrence Miller had been lured to Turkey by Sam himself, who'd told them of the perils I'd faced both in Egypt and Istanbul—only they called it Constantinople—and they'd come along with some vague notion of discovering a gang of antiquities thieves.

So, whatever it was the bad guys suspected I had, it was probably something old. Big help. And nobody would allow me to get out of bed and search for Sam as I wanted to do.

"Where would you look?" asked Harold. And reasonably, too, curse him.

"I don't know. Please tell me that Ali or Ahmet saw which way Stackville and his cronies carried him."

Harold heaved a large sigh. "I wish I could, Daisy, but I haven't seen Ali or Ahmet, either one, since the dustup at the Topkapi Palace."

I gazed at my friend in dismay. "You mean they deserted us

in our time of need?"

"I don't know. All I know is that I haven't seen either of them since then."

"Oh, Lord, Harold." Tears threatened, and I blinked them back. I'd cried too blasted much in the past two and a half months. Darned if I'd cry over Sam Rotondo, of all people.

But, oh, did I miss him! And, oh, was I worried about him! I couldn't believe that Sam had allowed himself to get captured by the bad guys.

"The London police are working with the Turkish police," Harold said, probably in an attempt to make me feel better, although his ploy didn't work.

"Yeah?" I didn't tell Harold so, but I didn't have a whole lot of faith in either set of police officials. For one thing, the coppers from London didn't know their way around Istanbul, and for another thing, the Turkish police had proved singularly uninterested in my problem when my room had been broken into. "I wish Ali and Ahmet would come back. I'd trust them over the cops any day."

"You would?" Harold seemed astonished.

"Darned right, I would. They know Istanbul better than the London police, and I don't trust the Turkish coppers to give a rap that Sam's disappeared."

"You'd be wrong there," said Harold in a decisive voice. "The authorities always become extremely interested when anything bad happens to a tourist."

That was vaguely comforting.

"How's your head?"

Dr. Weatherfield had left cold compresses—which had lost their cold long since—along with the chloral hydrate, which I wasn't aiming to touch with a ten-foot pole until after we found Sam. Good old aspirin was my remedy of choice, thank you. I removed the current compress and tenderly felt the back of my head. Ow. "It hurts. But my headache is better since I took some aspirin."

"You don't want any chloral?"

"Not on your life."

"He didn't leave you enough for you to become addicted to it," said Harold, who had an unnerving ability to read my mind at times.

"I still don't want any of the stuff. The aspirin is working pretty well." My neck ached, too, but I figured that's because when the villains smashed me on the head, my neck got twisted. From the moment I'd met him, I'd figured Stackville for an evil person, but it was proving mighty uncomfortable to discover I'd been right about him. "I'm hungry, though," I said. Then I marveled that the words were true. How very odd.

"You are?" Harold brightened as if he were a lamp someone had suddenly turned on.

"Yes. By gum, I am hungry. I want some of that yogurt soup."

"Doctor Weatherfield said it might not be wise for you to eat anything for a while. He doesn't want you to get sick."

"To heck with Doctor Weatherfield. He kept talking about fingers when I wanted to hear about what happened to me." And to Sam. I didn't mention that part.

"Right. Well, Mister Ozdemir gave us another guard until Ali shows up again, so I'll go downstairs and see about getting you some yogurt soup. Anything else?"

I thought about it for a second or two. "Yes. Some of that flat bread and some of that stuff to dip it in."

"Very good. Be right back."

And Harold left me to fret alone on my bed.

Where was Sam? What would Stackville and his villainous cohorts do to him? Would they come after me again? If they'd lead me to Sam, that would be all right with me.

Then I decided I'd gone 'round the bend and was stark, staring crazy. Sam Rotondo? My mortal enemy? Did I actually care about the man? After a while I determined I was merely worried about him because he'd been Billy's best friend and, after all, had come to Istanbul to protect me—to his own peril. Guilt. That's what it was. I felt guilty because Sam had been 'napped in my stead.

Fortunately for the state of my mental health, Harold showed up about then along with a waiter carrying a tray laden with yogurt soup, flat bread, and some kind of stuff to dip it in that didn't look the same as the kind of stuff I'd dipped flat bread in before. I lifted an eyebrow at Harold.

"Mister Ozdemir, who is very concerned about your health and welfare, said you'd be happier with this stuff, which is made with eggplant, or *aubergine*, as Mister Ozdemir calls them. He also sent you an order of what he called *dolmas*. I think they're stuffed grape leaves."

My nose wrinkled of its own accord. Aunt Vi occasionally fixed eggplant, but it was the one vegetable I didn't care much for. And stuffed *grape* leaves? Good heavens, these people would eat anything. But what the heck. I'd liked almost everything else I'd eaten in Turkey, so I decided to give this meal a go. Couldn't hurt; might help, and I had to keep up my strength if I aimed to get Sam back.

There I went again.

Carefully, I sat up. My head didn't fall off. In fact, it didn't even hurt too much. I considered that a good sign. As I arranged the pillows behind myself so that I'd have a comfy place to sit whilst eating, the waiter lowered a couple of legs on the back of the tray—I hadn't noticed them before—and gently set the tray across my lap.

"Thank you very much," I said, genuinely grateful. I thought the leggy tray was a keen invention.

The waiter, clad in one of what I'd come to recognize as the livery exclusive to the Sultanahmet Hotel—the same as Ali's, which I really liked—bowed, smiled, and backed away as if he were leaving a royal chamber or something.

"Dig in," said Harold, looking as if he wished he'd brought a tray for himself.

"Thanks. Don't mind if I do."

I started with the soup, because I already knew I liked it. It was as yummy as ever. Then, bravely daring, I dipped a ripped-off piece of flat bread into the eggplant mush and stuck it in my mouth. I felt my eyes widen. That stuff was delicious!

"Oh, my, Harold, you have to try some of this."

So he did. Then, because the flat bread and eggplant had worked out so well, I decided to try a grape leaf. Why not? I'd probably never see another one ever again after we left Istanbul. I didn't care for it as much as the eggplant stuff, but it was tasty. I offered one to Harold, who was happy to oblige.

Tilting his head to one side, he said, "Perhaps it's an acquired taste. But that bread and dip are great." He snatched another piece of bread and took a giant scoop of eggplant.

"Hey!" I said. "Go get your own meal."

"Actually, that sounds like a good idea. You'll be safe here, because there's a guard at the door."

"What's his name? Do you know?"

"Gaffar something or other."

"Gaffar. Hmm. I wish Ali would come back."

"So do I. Well, I'll see you later, Daisy. I'm going to get some chow."

"Enjoy. I think I've liked the food in Turkey best of all the places we've been so far."

Harold gave me a cynical lift of his eyebrow. "That's because you refused to eat anything at all until we got here."

I stuck my tongue out at him. Not very dignified behavior on my part, but I was tired of being ragged about my lack of appetite. Anyhow, it seemed to have come back with a vengeance, so Harold had no business teasing me about it anymore.

Just as I swallowed the last bite of the last *dolma,* a quiet knock came at my door, and I froze in my bed. Was the guard still outside? Surely, he must be. Had Harold locked the door when he left? Was Stackville out there ready to pounce on me? How had he got past Gaffar? Oh, I just *knew* Ali was the person meant to guard me! Not that he'd prevented Sam's capture, but still . . .

I lifted my tray and set it on the bedside table. Then I crept out of bed—slowly, in order to make sure pain wouldn't leap back into my head and send me reeling—tucked my feet into my slippers, and tiptoed across the sitting room to the door. I was still in the clothes I'd worn that morning, so I was decently clad. When I got to the door, I whispered, "Who is it?"

"Missus Majesty?" a voice whispered back.

"Who are you?" I demanded, refusing to give my name until I knew who was asking for it.

"Ali. Ali Bektas."

"Where's Gaffar?" I asked, although the voice calling itself that of Ali had indeed sounded as though it belonged to Ali.

"He's here. I need to speak to you."

"It is truly Ali, Missus Majesty."

I recognized Gaffar's voice, my heart leapt into my throat—it had been doing some exceptionally odd things recently—and I flung the door open. Sure enough, there he was: Ali! My Ali!

"Oh, Ali, I'm so happy to see you! Do you know where Sam is?" Now where in the world had that question come from? I hadn't even asked poor Ali if he was well or if he'd suffered any damage during the melee in the palace; I'd just popped out and asked about Sam. "I mean—"

He held up a hand as if to tell me I needn't explain. "Missus Majesty. I know where your friend is. Ahmet and me, we follow the white men. They take him to a house in Beşiktaş."

"Where?"

Ali glanced surreptitiously around him. Gaffar nodded, and Ali said, "Can come in? Need to talk. About getting friend back. Sam. Sam good man. He speak my language." Then he tilted his hand back and forth in what I guess is the universal form of "more or less."

"Oh, yes. Please, come in. Let's do talk."

Ali nodded and entered my suite, closing the door firmly behind him.

"Please," said I, "take a seat."

He sat in one of the abundant chairs in the sitting room, and I sat in a chair facing his. He sat very stiff and straight, and I got the feeling he'd rather be sitting on the rug with his legs crossed, in the posture I'd seen so many Turks and Egyptians assume. I doubted I could even take the position, much less remain in it and then get to my feet again. It's got to be some kind of learned behavior. But that wasn't the point.

"So you know where Sam is? With that information, maybe we can get the police—"

"No police," Ali said firmly.

"No police? But why not? For a long time, the police from London have been after these men who took Sam. At least, that's the impression I got from them and from Sam."

"Police too much noise. We creep up. Must creep. Be silent. Ahmet, Mister Harold and me."

"And me," I said, every bit as firmly as Ali had just spoken.

"You woman," he said.

"Yeah? So what? I'm as capable as any man!"

Ali rolled his eyes, thereby marking him a man of Sam's stamp.

"Listen to me, Ali. You Turks gave women the vote two years

before we women in America got it. You must think women are capable!"

"But not in a fight."

A fight? Hmm. I hadn't thought about a fight. Maybe Ali was right.

But, no. If there was any saving of Sam to be done, darn it, I aimed to be part of it.

"Nevertheless, I'm going with you to . . . wherever you said."

"Beşiktaş."

"Right. What's Bes . . . that place, anyway?"

"It district by water. House there with Mister Sam. Men tie him up and hit him. Ask him questions."

My hand flew to my mouth. "They hit him?"

Ali nodded. "They hitting him. Say, 'Where is it?' He tie to chair."

My brow crinkled, reminding me of my recent injury, so I uncrinkled it. "Where is what?"

With a shrug typical of those parts, Ali shook his head. "I not know. They think Mister Sam know."

"Shoot. I wish *I* knew. They've been plaguing me for what seems like forever, and I don't even know what they think I have. Maybe I do have it. I don't know if I do or not, because I don't know what it is."

Ali merely stared at me as if I were babbling, and I guessed he was right. I got up from my own chair cautiously, out of respect to my head. Then I began pacing, my nerves jumping, wanting to set out that very minute to get Sam back. "You see, these men have been after me since we were in Egypt, and we don't know why. But from what you just told me, they think I have something they want."

"Yes. You say so before."

"I did? Yes, I guess I did. Oh, dear, Ali, what will we do?"

He gave another shrug. On him those shrugs looked good.

Well, heck, everything looked good on Ali. "Go to Beşiktaş, fight men, rescue Mister Sam. Bring him back here."

I blinked at him. "You make it sound easy."

"It be easy. I get my brothers. They help."

"Oh, that's wonderful!" I clasped my hands to my bosom—what there was left of it after too many weeks of unwitting dieting.

"So you get Mister Harold, and we go?"

"Yes. I think he's eating right now."

"Mister Harold always eating."

I couldn't very well argue with that since it was true. I said, "I'll go down to the restaurant and fetch him. You wait here."

Ali rolled his eyes. "You stay here. I get Mister Harold. You don't go nowhere alone."

"Oh. Right. I forgot."

Which pretty much tells you the state I was in. "While you get Harold, I'll change into comfortable clothes so I won't get in the way, and I'll be able to help."

"How you help?"

"I . . . I don't know. I'll think of something." Boy, it galled me that Ali considered me so utterly worthless. I noticed the dagger thrust through Ali's belt. "Do you have another one of those? Maybe I can use a dagger."

He paused long enough for me to understand what he thought of that idea: not much.

"Well, then, maybe I can find a cudgel or something," I said, feeling desperate. "I want to help, darn it!"

"Yes, yes. I know." Ali sounded resigned.

Something then occurred to me that had me saying sharply, "And don't you dare drag Harold out of the restaurant and then set out without coming back to get me! I need to be there to help get Sam back."

From the way Ali looked at me then, I knew that the only

reason he aimed to return to my suite and do my bidding was that he didn't want to get into trouble with the hotel management if he didn't—or maybe he was afraid I wouldn't tip him if he refused to do what I asked of him. At that point, I didn't care.

After Ali left, I hurried to my closet and took out a white shirtwaist and my jodhpurs. I slipped on some stockings and the boots I'd worn to climb the Great Pyramid, and grabbed a jacket and a serviceable hat that looked more like a man's headwear than a woman's. But that was a good thing. I didn't want to attract attention, and I figured those clothes were about as anonymous as I could get.

Then I paced.

And paced.

And paced.

Just when I was about to bolt out the door and run to the dining room, and to heck with lurking kidnappers and/or assassins, another knock came at my door. I was rushing over to open it when Harold said, "Daisy Gumm Majesty, what's this nonsense about foregoing the police and going to rescue Sam ourselves? If that's not the most harebrained, idiotic—"

I flung the door opened, grabbed Harold's arm and yanked him into the room, Ali following hard on his heels.

"Shut up, Harold. We can't get the police involved, because they'll make a huge official fuss. By the time they get organized, those men will have killed Sam. Even if they don't kill him, they'll certainly hear the noise made by the Turkish police and those London coppers coming from a mile away. What we're going to do is sneak up on them and rescue Sam ourselves. Then we'll tell the police."

"We? Who's this we of whom you speak so glibly?"

I don't think I'd ever seen Harold so angry. And it's not that I think he was essentially a cowardly sort of person. But he wasn't your basic man of action, if you know what I mean. Harold was accustomed to running in his regular little ruts, and when he left them for any reason—like this trip, for instance—he made sure his road was smooth and his accommodations first class. He wasn't the type of person who necessarily rescued other people on a daily basis unless he had a really good reason, and even then he might hire someone to do it for him. For which he had plenty of money, of course, but in this case, money wouldn't help. What we needed was action, and Harold was going to act whether he wanted to or not.

"We can do it, Harold. Ali's bringing Ahmet and his brothers. Ali's brothers, I mean. They'll be armed." Actually, I wasn't sure about that part. I turned to give Ali a questioning glance, and he nodded. I felt better knowing we'd be accompanied by armed men who knew where we were going and, with luck, what to do after we got there.

"For God's sake, Daisy, do I look like the hero type?"

"No, actually, you don't. But you can do it, Harold. I know you can. You're my best friend, and my best friend can do anything. Heck, you helped me save a fair maiden once before. You can help me save Sam this time. And you'll have lots of backup, what with Ali and Ahmet and Ali's brothers."

"Good God." Harold hung his head for only a moment. But he knew his was a lost cause. "If I survive this day's work, Daisy Majesty, Del and I are going to be able to dine out on this story for months. Maybe years."

I grinned at him and patted his back. "That's the ticket."

"Let me change my clothes," Harold said grumpily. "I don't want to ruin a good suit."

So Ali accompanied Harold to his room so Harold could change his clothes, and I resumed pacing.

CHAPTER TWENTY-TWO

It wasn't more than twenty minutes later that we set out for Beşiktaş. My sense of geography is iffy at best, but from what Ali told us, Beşiktaş was merely one of Istanbul's various districts, in the western part of the city, and was mainly populated by fishermen because it was on the river. Which river, I couldn't tell you, being geographically challenged, as I mentioned before. The house in which Sam was being held faced the river, whatever one it was.

We grabbed a donkey-drawn cab outside the Sultanahmet Hotel, and when we told the driver where we wanted to go, he looked at us in a manner that told me people didn't often ask to be driven to Beşiktaş. Oh, well. There was a first time for everything. For instance, this would be my first time rescuing a man. As referred to briefly above, I'd helped rescue a damsel in distress once, but that was in Pasadena and not nearly so frightening a prospect. Actually, come to think of it, I was plenty scared at the time, but that was because I was trying to hide the maiden from Sam Rotondo, the very man toward whom I was headed at that very moment, and whom I intended to rescue come hell or high water this very day.

Which just goes to show you how times—and attitudes—change. There had been many times during my acquaintance with Sam when I'd have gladly seen him captured by bad guys and removed from my life. Now I was scared to death for him and wanted him back in my life.

As I watched out the window of the cab, it seemed to me that the parts of the city we were driving through were becoming less and less prosperous looking. Well, I supposed a fishing settlement wouldn't necessarily be a big tourist draw. The looks of the place didn't do my state of anxiety any good, however, and I was glad I'd downed a couple more aspirin before we set out.

"I don't like this," muttered Harold, who'd changed into something khaki, I suppose thinking he'd be less conspicuous that way than in one of his white linen suits. I agreed with him. "And where are these famous brothers of whom you spoke?"

Ali answered the latter part. "They meet us there. They with Ahmet at house."

"Ah. Wonderful." Harold turned to me. "Do you have any kind of weapon, Daisy?"

"Um . . . no."

"Well, I brought my revolver, but—"

"You brought a *gun?*" I was shocked. Perhaps I was even horrified. I couldn't imagine Harold Kincaid with a gun. The mere thought was . . . I don't know. Incongruous, I guess.

"No need gun," said Ali, sounding sure of himself. "My brothers be armed, and also Ahmet."

"With what?" asked Harold.

Ali squinted at him. "With enough weapons to get Mister Sam back."

It occurred to me that he was probably talking about daggers and swords and stuff like that. Mind you, daggers and swords are all very well in their place, but I had a strong feeling that Mr. Stackville and his accomplices were armed with guns. My heart decided to do another hectic maneuver in my chest, and my head throbbed in rhythm. Blasted head. I wished I were in better shape for this mission. But we would prevail. Darned if I'd let those blasted Englishmen—well, and that Frenchman—

get away with their hateful shenanigans.

As we traveled, the houses became taller and more exotic-looking. Made of some kind of stone or brick, they exuded an aura of the mystical Orient. Unless that was my imagination. I'd probably been reading too many Fu Manchu books; not that we were in China or anything, but boy, Istanbul sure didn't look like Pasadena. Here were the shrouded women I hadn't seen in the heart of the tourist part of the city, and the men in loose trousers and shirts belted any old how with bits of cloth. These folks didn't wear the same kinds of robes as we'd seen in Egypt. For one thing, they were slightly more colorful, but they weren't the nifty types of costumes Ali and his Sultanahmet coworkers wore, either. No glitter here. Only serviceable woolen garments—the wool was a guess on my part, Turkey, like Egypt, having lots of goats and sheep available.

The driver said something in Turkish, and Ali turned to Harold. "He can go no farther. Streets too narrow."

"Oh, wonderful," muttered Harold. Then he said, "So what do we do now?"

"We walk," said Ali.

Harold said, "If we rescue Detective Rotondo and he's injured"—my heart did another of those flippity-flop things it had taken to doing of late—"how will we get him back to the hotel?"

It was a reasonable question, although I wished Harold hadn't asked it. I gazed hopefully upon Ali, who didn't disappoint.

"We hire donkey cart," Ali said. "And I tell cab driver to wait for us here."

"Thank God," I whispered. Very well, I suppose a donkey cart might be bumpy if Sam were grievously injured, but at least I knew we'd be able to find some sort of conveyance. We'd also have the cab. I guess a donkey cart and cab would be able to carry us all, including the prisoners we aimed to take to the police station with us.

Harold shot a nasty glance at me before he said, "All right. I suppose I'm the one who'll pay the drivers?"

Ali shrugged.

I said, "Oh, for God's sake, I'll pay him!" Harold's lousy attitude was beginning to annoy me.

"Don't be silly," barked Harold. He handed the driver a bunch of coins, the driver's eyes bugged slightly, as did Ali's, and we got out of the cab.

"I wish you'd ask how much things cost and not just toss money at people," I said softly to Harold. "You're paying way too much, and you're demeaning these good people."

"Demeaning them?" Harold looked at me as if I were insane. "Does he seem to feel demeaned?"

I took a peek at the driver, who was smiling and bowing at Harold. "Well, I still think you should ask. No wonder people don't like Americans. We just toddle into their countries and throw our money around."

Another grouchy look from Harold. "Whoever said people we overpay don't like us? Did Billy read you that from an article in *National Geographic*?"

"Well, no, but it smacks of imperialism to me. We don't take time to get to know other people's cultures."

"Damn it, Daisy, we don't have time to study Turkish culture! You're the one who made me come on this idiotic rescue mission."

"You're right. I'm sorry."

As we'd talked, Ali had started shoving ahead of us through the throngs of people and donkeys and chickens and goats. At least there weren't any camels here as there had been in Egypt. Although I loved their blankets, of which I'd purchased a couple, I wasn't fond of camels. We had to hustle to keep up with Ali. Harold kept looking around nervously as if he didn't approve of the crowds. I figured they were Turkish crowds in a Turkish town, and they belonged there. We didn't. So I just tried to keep close to Ali.

I darned near bumped into him when he came to a sudden halt and held out his hand in a gesture that meant for us to stop. Three men, two of whom were as tall as Ali, and all of whom were almost as good-looking as he, surged out of the crowd and met Ali with smiles and warm embraces. His brothers, I deduced. Boy, at least in the looks department, these Turkish gents had it all over people from the other countries I'd visited. Not that I should have been noticing such things at a time like this.

Turning to us, Ali said, "My brothers. Mehmet, Demet and Barbaros."

The men bowed in turn, and I knew I'd never keep their names straight, and that didn't have anything to do with the fact that my mind kind of snagged on the last name. But . . . Barbaros? What a great name! Well, never mind that.

"Pleased to meet you," I said, and bowed in my turn. Then I felt stupid. But what's a girl to do? This was the most unusual situation in which I'd ever found myself. I turned to Harold and saw him bow, too, so I didn't feel so bad.

"Follow us," said one of Ali's brothers. I don't know which one it was, except that I knew it wasn't Barbaros, because I'd paid attention to him especially because of his name.

"You follow, Demet. Be sure nobody follow Missus Majesty and Mister Harold."

"You in trouble?" Demet asked us. I knew it was he, because he's the one who let us pass, and then he followed us.

"A friend of ours is," I said. "And thank you very much for helping us get him back."

"*Insh'Allah*," said Demet. Whatever that meant.

But I didn't have time to ruminate on the linguistic intricacies I was hearing all around me—although I did notice that I heard not a single English word spoken in this part of the city of Istanbul, which was a odd sensation. Talk about being your basic stranger in a strange land.

Ali and his other brothers kept up a stream of low chatter as we followed them through the crowds. The crowds, by the way, didn't smell awfully good, although that could probably be chalked up to a lack of running water, no proper sanitation and stuff like that. Most of us Americans don't know how lucky we are. The closer we got to our destination, the odors also became more fishy. Ah. Good. I wasn't partial to the small of old fish, but I figured the aroma meant we were nearing the place where Sam was being held captive.

Ali and his brothers turned down what appeared to be a narrow alleyway, although it happened to be merely another street, only less populated than the one we'd just left. Most of the people we saw here were barefoot and had shorter wide trousers than the rest of the populace. Then I noticed that the trousers weren't necessarily shorter, but their wide bottoms were kilted up underneath their wearers' sashes, and I figured we were amongst fishermen. Better and better, if slightly smellier.

And then I saw Ahmet! Crouching in that characteristic Middle Eastern way beside a ratty building right, smack next to the water, he was. Sam's lair! Surrounded by fishy things—nets, ropes, barrels, stray pieces of lumber and wood, and all sorts of other stuff I didn't recognize—he spotted Ali and nodded.

"Mister Sam, he still there," said Ali. Then he said, "Wait here," and we did, Harold, Ali's three brothers, and I while Ali padded softly up to Ahmet, avoiding walking in front of any windows. Mind you, all the windows I saw in that long, low building were so filthy, I doubted anyone could see out through them, but still, it was wise to take precautions.

I'm not good at waiting. I get really impatient. At that moment, my nerves were stretched so taut, I'm surprised one or two of them didn't snap right in half. I was so worried about Sam and so wanted to get him back in one piece!

And speaking of pieces . . . I picked up a bit of lumber lying on the ground, figuring it might be strong enough to smack a person with, should the need arise. I wished Ali had given me a dagger, although I suppose he was right not to do so. You probably have to take lessons to learn how to use a dagger properly. Anybody, even a phony spiritualist, can whack someone across the shins with a piece of wood.

After approximately six and a half hours—I'm exaggerating, of course—Ali crept back to where we stood, everyone waiting patiently except yours truly.

"Demet, go to the south end of the building. Barbaros, go to the water side of the building. Mehmet, you take east side. Ahmet and me, we take north end. We break down door and rush in. The three men still there, along with Mister Sam."

"What about us?" I demanded. "We want to rescue Sam, too."

"I don't," said Harold. "I'd just as soon watch."

"Don't be ridiculous! I need to see if he's all right."

"He all right," said Ali. Then he sighed, must have realized I wasn't going to hang back while everyone else did the dirty work, and said, "You follow me. But stay back. No get hurt."

"Um, do you think they have any weapons?" I asked, feeling the least little bit squeamish. A fine time for that to happen, but there you go.

Nodding, Ali said, "They have guns."

Oh, good God.

"Daisy, you'd better stay with me," said Harold.

"Nuts. Come with us and bring your gun if you want to be useful."

Ali rolled his eyes. I was getting quite tired of men rolling their eyes at me, but I'd wait until later to scold him for it. "Mister Harold, he stay here. You follow me." His voice was quite authoritative, so we did as he demanded.

My heart hammered like a kettle drum as I tiptoed after Ali, being as silent as I possibly could be, my piece of lumber held in both hands and in striking position, just in case. Ali gestured to me to crouch as we neared Ahmet, who still stood watch. Well, he crouched, too, but you know what I mean.

Putting his finger to his lips, Ali joined Ahmet. Then Ali produced a piercing whistle, clearly a prearranged signal I didn't know about beforehand, the two men smashed down the door with their shoulders and rushed into the building. Ali's brothers had also heard the signal, and they charged into the building, too, a couple through another door, and one through a window he broke out.

And then all hell broke loose, as the saying goes. Everything was so confusing there for a few minutes, I wasn't sure who was who and what was happening, but I struck out at anyone who came near me wearing a European suit, managing to get one of the villains a good one on the shins. I think it was Futrelle, because he said something in French that I was pretty sure was a swearword, although I don't speak French. I think it was Stackville who pulled the trigger on his gun, but he didn't hit anyone because Ali or one of this brothers—or maybe it was Ahmet—whacked him with the backside of his dagger and the gun went flying. I didn't see where it landed because at that moment, Mr. Gaylord Bartholomew, the third villain, shoved me aside and ran for the door.

I gave chase and managed to give him a good wallop on the back of his head with my board, but he only swore, staggered a little bit, and kept running. By that time I was out of breath— I'd been through a good deal that day already, and I had to stop and catch my breath. But I saw that Mr. Bartholomew was headed straight in Harold's direction, so I shrieked, "Harold! Stop that man!"

And, by gum, Harold pulled out his gun and fired. Mr. Bartholomew screamed, clutched at his leg, and fell down.

Then Harold fainted.

It turned out that Harold had shot Mr. Bartholomew in the thigh, and that his injury wasn't life-threatening. I, feeling pretty darned bloodthirsty by that time, said I was disappointed to hear it.

Sam, looking much the worse for wear in a filthy white suit and with bumps and bruises all over him, scowled at me. "What the devil did you come with the men for? Don't you have any sense at all?"

By this time we were all piled into the Turkish police headquarters, and the two London policemen had joined us. There were other Turkish officials there, too, although I don't know who they were. Harold was having palpitations, but Dr. Weatherfield, who'd been sent for to attend to Sam and Mr. Bartholomew, gave him a powder and he eventually calmed down.

"Darn you, Sam Rotondo! I helped in your rescue. The least you could do is be grateful we got you out of there."

"I'm glad to be out of there. I'm *not* glad you were involved. For God's sake, Daisy, don't you have the brains God gave a goose?"

I was so mad at Sam, I couldn't speak to him without hollering, so I turned my attention to Harold. "You turned out to be a genuine hero, Harold. If you hadn't shot Mister Bartholomew, he might have escaped."

"Please don't remind me." Harold's eyes rolled back in their sockets and he keeled over sideways. I caught him before he could fall out of his chair.

"Let's have some order and discipline here," said DCI Miller. "I don't like it that you civilians carried out this so-called rescue by yourselves. Why didn't you come to us? We have the firepower and the men to do the job, and you also bypassed the Turkish officials, who aren't any more happy about your shenanigans than we are."

Ah. A target for my anger. "A lot you know about it!" I cried. "You'd have taken forever and ever to get organized. Ali and Ahmet and Ali's brothers knew exactly where Sam was and how to get him back again, and they did. *And* they rounded up the crooks, too. You should be thanking them instead of moaning about how you were left out of the party!"

"My dear Missus Majesty—"

"Don't you 'dear Missus Majesty' me, DCI Miller! We rescued Sam and you didn't, and we caught the crooks, and that's that. What *I* want to know now is why they've been plaguing us ever since Egypt!"

I glared at Mr. Stackville, who appeared much less suave than usual, thanks to having been knocked about a bit by Ali and his brothers. Futrelle, also most untidy, was grumpy and kept rubbing his shin where I'd smacked him with my board. Good for me. Except for Mr. Bartholomew, who moaned a bit, none of the criminals said a word.

It was Sam who finally told us what the three villains had been after all this time.

"They tell me you bought a golden canopic jar in Cairo. The shopkeeper wasn't supposed to sell it, because it was stolen from a royal tomb, although nobody's supposed to know about the tomb yet, especially the authorities and the antiquities department or whoever keeps track of these things. Evidently the shopkeeper's nephew or brother or some other relation was running the shop for him that day, and he sold it to you."

"A golden canopic jar?" I stared blankly at Sam, who,

naturally, frowned back at me. "I don't have a golden canopic jar. I don't even know what a canopic jar is."

"I don't know what one is, either, but they think you do and, what's more, they think you have the one they want," he growled. "And they kept hitting me to get me to tell them where it was. Is."

I glared at Stackville. "I don't know what in the world you're talking about. What golden canopic jar? Which golden canopic jar? What in the world *is* a canopic jar? Whatever it is, I don't have it, and if you'd asked me instead of burgling my rooms, I'd have told you so."

Stackville only glared back at me.

Bartholomew groaned some more, probably because Dr. Weatherfield was working on his leg. I glanced at him for a mere second, discovered the doctor had scissored his pants leg off at the thigh so he could get at the wound, and quickly glanced away again. I didn't care to see any more of Mr. Bartholomew than I had to.

A shaky voice said, "I think I know what they're talking about."

We all turned to stare in amazement at Harold, who was white as table salt and looking shaky. "Do you remember that golden urn I bought at the *souk* when we were shopping in Cairo?"

"Um . . . oh, yes! I remember now. But you called it an urn."

"Evidently, the correct term for such a thing is a canopic jar," whispered Harold, who clearly didn't take the notion of shooting people, even if only in the leg, lightly.

"Well, for heaven's sake. Why didn't anyone tell us that?" I turned on Stackville once more. "You idiots! Even if I'd known what you were after, I wasn't the one who had the thing. It was Harold who had it!"

"They thought he bought it for you," said Sam. I was sorry

the doctor hadn't seen to his cuts and bruises first and left Bartholomew to fester, but I guess doctors have to abide by some kind of code, so he tended to the more grievously wounded party first.

"But they searched my room before he even bought the thing!"

"They were looking for a place to hide it once they got it. That's what these fellows do, you know. They have innocent tourists smuggle things back to England in their luggage."

"Good grief. You're truly a villainous trio, aren't you?" I glared at Stackville, Bartholomew and Futrelle. Neither Stackville nor Futrelle seemed the least little bit ashamed of himself. Bartholomew was too busy being in pain to glance at me. I heaved an exasperated sigh.

"Harold bought that thing for Del, not for me," I said, disgusted with pretty much all men at that moment. "For heaven's sake, what would I do with a golden canopic jar? Put it in the china cabinet? Maybe Aunt Vi could use it as a gravy boat. Besides that, if they were going to hide it in my luggage, why didn't they just leave us alone after Harold bought it?"

Sam shrugged. "I guess their plans changed. You two didn't stay in Egypt long enough to suit their purposes. They'd have had stashed a lot of other stolen artifacts with you if you'd done what you'd said you were going to do and taken the Nile cruise. Then, when you scooted out of Egypt before they were prepared for your departure, they wanted to get the canopic jar back."

"Why didn't they search Harold's room, then? He was the one who bought the stupid thing."

"They thought you were brother and sister, and that you were both rich and that Harold had bought it for you because you were grieving."

"I am grieving. And Harold's no more my brother than you are. And why didn't they search Harold's room after they didn't find the stupid thing in mine?"

"They didn't have time because you two left Egypt too soon."

Then I noticed that things had come to a standstill in the Turkish police office and that everyone was staring at me. Oops. Guess I'd said too much. How typical of me.

"You aren't brother and sister?" DCI Miller asked.

"We thought it would be better to pretend we were brother and sister so people wouldn't get the wrong idea," I said, feeling stupid.

"Let me see if I have this right," said DCI Miller in an icy voice. "You recently lost your husband, and now you're traveling to foreign parts with a man unrelated to you?"

"They're just friends," Sam said grouchily. "Have been for years. Nothing's going on between them."

"I have never heard of such a thing in my life," DCI Miller said. I could tell he was dreadfully offended by our breach of what he considered etiquette.

As for me, I'd taken about all I aimed to take from the snippy copper. For the second time that day, I let rip at DCI Miller. "You have absolutely nothing to say about anything Harold or I do, and you can keep your antiquated opinions to yourself! We saved the day, let me remind you, and you have your cursed gang of cursed antiquities thieves. So just stuff *that* in your pipe and smoke it!"

DCI Miller, who looked as if he'd like to use a riding crop on me, turned to Sam. "We need to get that canopic jar back."

Sam, who appeared rather grumpy with the London copper himself, said, "Well, don't tell me about it. Ask Harold. He's the one who has the damned thing."

Harold said, "I have it in my room. Come by this evening and you can take it with my blessings. But don't come before nine. I need to recover from this day's work first."

We left shortly after that, Sam eschewing the doctor's offer to see to his bumps and bruises. DCI Miller didn't speak to me again, which was probably wise of him. None of the Turkish police officials spoke to us once, which was probably wise of *them*. Ali accompanied Sam, Harold and me back to the Sultanahmet Hotel, where Mr. Ozdemir met us with much hand-wringing and congratulations. I guess word had already got around that we'd perpetrated a daring rescue and captured a gang of sinister European antiquities smugglers.

At the door to my room, Harold gave Ali about a ton and a half of Turkish coins. "For you and your brothers and Ahmet, Ali. We truly appreciate your help."

If Ali had bowed any lower, his head would have bumped the carpet.

CHAPTER TWENTY-THREE

Sam was looking pretty dilapidated when we all entered my sitting room. I told him so.

"You look like hell, Sam. You need to have your wounds taken care of before another minute passes." I turned to Harold. "Do you suppose Doctor Weatherfield has returned to the hotel yet?"

Harold, still ashen and shaky, said, "I don't know. All I know is that I'm going to my room, and I'm going to lie down. And if you still have that chloral hydrate, you might consider giving it to me as a gift."

I waved a hand. "It's all yours."

"Watch out for that stuff," said Sam gruffly. "Only take a little bit."

"Don't worry. I'm going to bathe, take a sip of chloral and lie down. Perhaps later on we can take dinner in the hotel." Before Sam could object, Harold held up a hand and said, "My treat. We all deserve it, and I won't allow you to refuse."

"What's going to happen to the jar?" I asked, truly interested.

"They can have the cursed thing. I don't care any longer."

"Do you suppose they'll reimburse you for it? You spent a lot of money on that thing."

"I don't care. It's my gift to Egypt, if that's the way they want to look at it. I've lost my taste for Egypt anyhow. I think I'll get Del a gift from Turkey. They must have lovely treasures in the Grand Bazaar."

"Oh, good. We didn't get the opportunity to see the Grand

Bazaar yet. Other . . . things intervened."

"Other things," Sam muttered under his breath.

"Farewell, all. I'll come to pick you up at seven-thirty, Daisy, and you can either meet us in Daisy's room or in the dining room, Detective Rotondo. I suppose we'll have to dine early if we're to be here at nine when the authorities come to fetch the jar."

I gave Harold the bottle containing the chloral hydrate and saw him to the door. The poor fellow was clearly suffering from the day's events. While I was there, I asked Gaffar, who still stood guard outside my door, if he'd see if Dr. Weatherfield had come back and, if so, if he'd be kind enough to come to my room and fix Sam.

Gaffar toddled off, like the good fellow he was, to fetch the doctor, and I closed the door and turned to run my gaze over Sam. "I'm so sorry about all of this, Sam. If we'd only known what those villains were after, we could have given them that wretched jar and it would have been over with."

"Except the bad guys would have escaped with a rare Egyptian artifact, and that wouldn't have been good for anybody. Besides, they'd planned to plant more stuff on you. And they might have killed you before the whole thing was over."

"Good Lord, do you really think so?"

I really didn't deserve the sour look Sam gave me. "For God's sake, Daisy, I'm not kidding about those guys being cold-blooded villains."

"But . . ."

"Yes! They've killed people before. They were going to kill me, for God's sake."

With a heavy sigh, I said, "I guess you're right. But I'm really sorry they treated you so badly. I sent Gaffar for the doctor, and he'll get you all fixed up. Then you can go back to your hotel and clean up and come back here for dinner."

"I don't need a damned doctor," Sam snarled. "What I want to know is why you put yourself in danger by coming with the search party today." He stood and glowered down at me.

"Well, I like that! We save your sorry hide and capture the crooks, and all you can do is scold me for being a party to the action. For your information, Sam Rotondo, I *forced* Ali to take me. He didn't want me to come. I made him take me! I wasn't going to trust the life and health of Billy's best friend to the hands of strangers."

Sam ran both hands through his hair, which, I noticed, was splotched with blood in spots. I grimaced. "Did they hit you in the head?"

"For the love of God, Daisy, it doesn't matter what they did to me. Do you realize you could have been hurt in that melee today? Dammit, you could have been *killed!*"

"Well, I wasn't." I was getting mighty tired of Sam ragging on me about helping to save his life.

"Listen, before he died, Billy asked me to take care of you. Why do you think I came out to this heathen place, anyway? I was trying to take care of you! Even though you seem to do everything in your power to prevent anyone on earth from taking care of you!"

"Darn you, Sam Rotondo, if you aren't the most aggravating man in the universe, I don't know who is! Billy would have been proud of me for saving your worthless life, curse it! You were his best friend. He'd have done anything in his power to rescue you, and I was only doing what he'd have done if he'd been here."

"Damn it, putting yourself in danger isn't what Billy would have wanted you to do!"

"I wasn't in danger, curse it! *You* were the one in danger! Why are you harassing me? For Pete's sake, everything turned

255

out all right. You don't have to keep carping at me!"

"Damn it all to hell and back again, you were, too, in danger!"

"I was not! Anyway, why do you care?"

"Why do I *care?*" Sam roared. "Damn it all, Daisy Majesty, I *love* you! That's why I care!"

And we both stood there in the silence that descended upon us like a cloud, staring at each other in utter astonishment.

Fortunately for both of us, a knock came at the door just then. Otherwise, I don't know what would have happened or how long Sam and I would have gaped at each other, neither of us knowing what to say next.

But . . . Sam loved me? Sam Rotondo, the bane of my existence? Loved me? The bane of his? Good Lord.

I walked to the door rather like an automaton and opened it to find Dr. Weatherfield holding his little black bag and smiling at me. "I understand Detective Rotondo is in your room, Missus Majesty."

"Yes," I said, my voice a trifle hoarse. "He is. Thank you for coming, Doctor."

"My pleasure. It's always more satisfying to help a hero than a villain."

"I'm no hero," growled Sam.

"Nonsense." Dr. Weatherfield turned to me. "Missus Majesty, I do believe it's safe for you to walk about in the hotel unguarded now, so if you wouldn't mind stepping out for about a half hour, that would give me time to see to Detective Rotondo's injuries."

"Fine. I'll go look for some postcards at the front desk." I didn't glance back as I closed the door, smiled my thanks at Gaffar, and took off down the hall, my mind in a whirl.

Could it have been love that had propelled me to save Sam and driven me nearly mad when I believed he might be in serious trouble? Could there actually be a smidgen of love for the big galoot in my own now-shrunken bosom? I'd always tried to avoid Sam, mainly because he was forever trying to thwart me in my various errands of mercy and so forth. Yet he'd been a true friend to my Billy and, I guess, through Billy, to me. He'd even come to a couple of dog obedience training lessons with Billy and Spike and me.

It had never once, in our entire association, occurred to me that Sam might have a soft spot in his heart for me. Heck, I'd always thought until recently that he didn't even have a heart, but merely a scab over his liver, as my father used to say of one of his uncles.

As I wandered around the hotel, searching for postcards and not finding any—it was thus I learned that not all hotels are set up in the same way—questions about Sam and me nagged at my brain. In fact the two words together, "Sam and me," were so incongruous that I had to stop and shake my head every now and then to get them to stay still in there. Anyone watching probably thought I was crazy as a June bug. If they have June bugs in Turkey.

Ultimately, I fetched a pretty brochure from the front desk and sat on a sofa in the lobby with it on my lap, watching the clock and mulling things over. I don't think I even opened the brochure.

Sam and me. Good Lord. I knew my family liked Sam. Heck, everyone had liked Sam from the moment he thrust himself into our lives. Except me. I hadn't liked him. He'd scared me. He was so big and so gruff and so policemanly. And, as previously mentioned, always seemed to be getting in my way. Besides that, he'd called me a *fortune-teller*. Me. Daisy Gumm Majesty, spiritualist-medium to all the best families in Pasadena, California. The person everyone with money turned to if they needed a dead relative retrieved for a chat or to read the tarot cards, a crystal ball or the Ouija board for them. Never, not once, had either Sam or Billy admitted that my job helped people. But it did, curse them both.

I didn't mean that. At least not about Billy. I wanted Billy to be at peace and without pain, finally, in our beautiful Methodist version of heaven.

Bother. I wish I could call Billy back from the dead and ask him what he thought of the Sam-loving-me issue. But I'm a fake spiritualist and can't really do the things people pay me for. I felt like burying my head in my hands, but restrained myself as this was a public lobby and I didn't want to make any more of a spectacle of myself than I already had. If I had.

I don't know how long I sat there, my hands folded in my lap, staring off into space and becoming more and more confused about life and Sam and everything, when Sam himself stepped out of the elevator. He still looked awful, but I could see the doctor had been at him because he had sticking plasters on his face, and his head sported a big bandage around it that would probably be covered by a hat, except that I guess we'd all left his hat behind at the house where he'd been held hostage. He saw me and stopped in his tracks.

Slowly I rose from the couch. "What did Doctor Weatherfield say, Sam? Do you have any serious injuries?"

"No. He said I'll be feeling better in a day or two." He fingered the bandage on his head and frowned. "Damned bandage. I look like an idiot."

"No, you don't. You look like a man who's been through a bad time. When you get back to your hotel, you can clean up, and I'm pretty sure your hat will cover that bandage."

"Hell of a lot of good that'll do at dinner," he grumbled.

"Oh, for heaven's sake, quit whining. Everyone has accidents every now and then."

"Accidents? This was no accident," he told me as if he were grievously offended at my choice of words.

Taking a page from his book, I rolled my eyes at him. "I know that, but nobody else who looks at you will. For the love of Mike, will you just go to your hotel, clean yourself up, and get back here in time for dinner?" I didn't want to talk about those few words he'd let slip when we'd been yelling at each other in my room.

Apparently he didn't, either, because he said "Yeah, yeah. I'll go to the hotel, and I'll come back here. But then I'm leaving. I'm not staying another second longer than I have to in Turkey."

I felt my eyes widen. "You're not? But . . . but I thought maybe you'd be able to do some more sightseeing with Harold and me. You haven't seen the Grand Bazaar yet, either."

"And I don't want to see it. I want to get back home and go to my job, where things make sense. This"—he waved a hand in an all-encompassing gesture—"is all too foreign to me."

I suppose I could understand that. "I see. Well . . . I wish you'd stay a day or two longer." Not that I wanted to discuss those fateful words of his, but still . . .

Oh, curse it, I'd miss him!

Whatever did this mean?

"Thanks, but I've got to get back to work."

"I thought you had lots of vacation days saved up."

"Maybe, but I still want to get back to work. I need to do something normal in normal surroundings."

"Sure. I understand." I didn't like it, though.

Sam stomped off, and I went back upstairs to my room where I said a fond farewell to Gaffar after rushing into my room and grabbing my handbag. And then I pulled a page out of Harold's book and handed him a whole bunch of coins. I have no idea how many or how much they'd have been in American money. I guess I understood Harold in that instant, too. When you're pressed for time or under stress, you don't necessarily think through things like foreign money exchange.

259

At dinner that night, I wore one of the evening frocks I'd made for my spiritualist business. For some reason, I wanted to look good for Sam. As a matter of fact, I do believe this was the very dress I'd worn when Sam and I first met, an ankle-length black chiffon number with long fitted sleeves, a collarless wrap-over bodice that fastened on the hip with a beaded and embroidered (by my own very hands) clasp. A beautiful gown, I wore it when I wanted to look especially alluring and spiritualistic, although the latter wasn't necessarily my aim that evening. I just wanted to look good. Since the dress was made of sheer chiffon, even though it was black, it wouldn't be too warm to wear in the dining room. It hung on me kind of like it might on its clothes hanger, but that couldn't be helped. I aimed to eat lots of food in Turkey and to continue eating until I'd regained the weight I'd lost. Most of it. It wouldn't hurt me to lose a curve or two. Those bust-flatteners can be painful.

Harold knocked on my door at precisely seven-thirty. He was almost always punctual, something I appreciated as I, too, shared the trait. Since Sam hadn't come to my room, I presumed we'd see him in the dining room—unless the rat had stood us up and already lammed it out of Istanbul.

My heart did one of its recently undertaken loopy things when Harold and I walked into the restaurant and found Sam waiting for us. He'd cleaned up rather nicely, even if he still sported bandages here and there. But he wore another white suit, like the one Harold was wearing, and which, I'd come to understand, was standard tourist garb for males in those parts, and he looked quite spiffy. I smiled at him. He seemed a trifle nervous but smiled back anyway.

During dinner and afterwards, we didn't speak of love. We talked about Stackville's gang of thieves, and Sam filled us in on some more details about them, which I won't go into here. However, they'd clearly played havoc with the law in several countries and had smuggled gobs of antiquities out of Egypt before we'd caught them. They had proved to be brutal a time or two, as well, so it was lucky for Sam that we'd rescued him before they could do him in permanently. Good for us. And to heck with DCI Miller and his snooty attitude.

"The British and Egyptian authorities are going to be very grateful to you two for rounding up the gang," said Sam at one point.

I refrained from telling him it sure hadn't sounded that way to hear DCI Miller talk about our daring rescue and capture earlier in the day. I wanted the meal to remain pleasant.

And, boy, I did justice to that meal, too. My appetite had come back sort of like a runaway freight train, and I ate everything set before me, including something delicious made with lamb and eggplant, a vegetable I'd never cared for before, as I believe I've mentioned. It soon became apparent that I'd never had it prepared in its proper element before. Then there was a dish with cauliflower and chickpeas and I don't know what all else; more of those yummy *dolmas;* some of my favorite yogurt soup; a dish called rice pilaf, which was delicious; and for dessert we had some confections called *lokma,* which were kind of deep-fried fritters drizzled with honey. I wasn't sure how I managed to get it all down until I realized I hadn't had anything to eat since early that day when I'd had yogurt soup with *dolmas* and some flat bread and dip. Besides, it had been a very trying day, and I deserved to eat.

"Glad to see your appetite is back," said Sam at one point.

"You betcha," said I, struggling not to get honey all over me as I ate a *lokma.* "I don't think I've ever been so hungry in my life."

"Well, you haven't eaten anything for months," Harold reminded me.

I only sighed and continued eating.

Both Harold and I tried to talk Sam into staying in Istanbul for another day or two at least, but he was adamant that he wanted to get home to familiar surroundings. I guess I couldn't blame him for that, although I had a niggling suspicion that some of his eagerness to get away might have something to do with not wanting to think about those few words he'd let drop in my hotel room in the heat of anger. Come to think of it, I couldn't blame him for that, either.

After dinner, Mr. Ozdemir came to the saloon where we'd all taken ourselves off to, I to have a cup of tea, Harold to have a martini, and Sam to dare another cup of Turkish coffee. The hotel manager bowed low before the three of us and said there was a delegation of officials desiring to see us in his office. So we all trooped after him and, sure enough, when he opened his office and bowed us in, the room was packed with purposeful people.

As it turned out, there were the London coppers, Turkish folks from both governmental and policemanly branches, and even some Egyptians, who fawned over us as if we'd saved the entirety of Egypt's antiquities. Heck, it had only been one golden urn. I mean canopic jar. But after Harold went to his room, fetched the jar and brought it back to Mr. Ozdemir's office, those fellows nearly salivated with joy. Turned out they weren't just happy about the canopic jar, but, by capturing Stackville and the rest of his crew, we had not merely foiled a den of thieves, but we'd been the catalyst for their retrieving a whole bunch of other antiquities that had previously been smuggled out of Egypt.

Hooray for us!

After that, and after all the officials had gone and Mr. Ozdemir thanked us again and again—even though it wasn't

Turkish antiquities we'd rescued but Egyptian—Sam left us, and Harold and I went up to bed.

We enjoyed the rest of our stay in Istanbul, which lasted another three days. Mr. Ozdemir had clearly spread word of our heroic activities because every time we passed a hotel employee, he or she bowed and grinned at us. I noted that Turkish teeth didn't seem to be in as bad shape as the Egyptian teeth I'd seen. All things considered, and in spite of terrible tales of ancient and not-so-ancient Turkish atrocities Billy had read to me out of the *National Geographic,* I decided I liked Turkey a whole lot better than Egypt.

Because I was still reeling from those fateful words Sam had let drop, and also because I was once more healthy and even eating and we were no longer in danger of being besieged by thugs, I went kind of overboard at the Grand Bazaar. Still and all, my shopping spree pleased Harold, and I even managed to snaggle a Turkish cookbook, written in English, for Aunt Vi! I hoped she'd be open to attempting new ways of cooking eggplant.

CHAPTER TWENTY-FOUR

Harold and I arrived home to Pasadena three weeks after our adventures in Istanbul. We didn't stay long in England, both of us having had our fill of foreign travel by that time. Also, fortunately for me, I wasn't seasick at all on the voyage home, this time on the Cunard Line's *Berengaria,* although I doubt the difference in the ocean liner company had anything to do with my state of health. I was just getting better all around.

"I think this idea of yours was brilliant, Harold. About taking me to Egypt for a cure, I mean. I can't tell you how much better I feel now than when we left Pasadena."

Harold eyed me over his gin and tonic. "This has been the most disastrous trip I've ever taken in my entire life, and you're thanking me for it?"

I flung my arms out so that Harold could get a good look at me. "It might have been uncomfortable in spots—"

"*Spots?*"

"—but look. I'm ever so much healthier-looking now than I was when we left."

Tilting his head, Harold squinted at me for a moment before he said, "You do look better, Daisy. Much better, in fact. I hate to say it, but I'm afraid Sam Rotondo might be right about you thriving on chaos and pandemonium."

"He never said any such thing!" Mind you, he'd said just about the same thing, but not in those words, time and again.

"Well, he did to me."

"Hmph."

"It's true, Daisy. You attract trouble like honey attracts flies."

"Nuts."

Nevertheless, it was a Daisy Majesty refreshed in body and spirit who ran up the walkway and into the arms of my family—and neighbors and friends and assorted acquaintances—that hot September day when Harold's rented limousine dropped me off in front of my beloved bungalow on South Marengo Avenue in Pasadena, California. Harold followed a few paces behind. He didn't care to run even in cool weather.

Naturally, Spike was the first to greet me. He had, after all, four legs to everyone else's two, even if they were short. I squatted on the walkway and let him leap into my arms. From there he proceeded to kiss my face all the way to the front porch, where I set him down and he proceeded to frolic around me as if he'd never expected to see me again and was mighty happy I was back. Poor thing. First he'd lost Billy, and then he'd nearly lost me. But then the rest of the greetings began.

"Oh, Daisy!" Ma said, her face streaming with tears. "You look ever so much better than you did when you left home!"

"I feel better, too, Ma," said I, trying to hold my own tears at bay. I'd cried enough in the past few months.

"You look wonderful, sweetheart," said Pa, taking over hugging duties from Ma.

"Thanks, Pa. So do you."

He laughed, but I wasn't kidding. We always worried about Pa's heart.

"Oh, Daisy, it's so good to have you back where you belong," said Aunt Vi, giving me a hug, too.

"It's good to be back, Vi, and I have a really keen present for you!"

"Oh, go along with you. You shouldn't have bought me anything, Daisy Majesty. I swear."

"Nuts. I got gifts for everyone."

Then, sucking in about a gallon of really, really warm Pasadena air—which didn't feel nearly as warm as the Egyptian air I'd breathed a month or so ago—I glanced around, smiling at everyone gathered on our front lawn: the Wilsons, including Pudge, whose face beamed around his freckles and whose arm was still in a cast that he thrust slightly forward, I presume for me to appreciate; Mrs. Longnecker, who held out an entire chocolate cake as a welcome-home present; Johnny and Flossie Buckingham, Flossie looking as if she was about to give birth any second; and even Dr. Benjamin, who beamed at me as if he'd performed a miracle cure, although it had been Harold Kincaid who'd done that.

"As soon as I get my luggage sorted out, I'm going to be giving everyone their gifts," said I, pushing my hat back into its correct position on my head. It had been bumped about a bit during all the hugs.

So Harold directed the chauffeur, Johnny and Pudge in the unloading of my luggage. There was more of it coming home than there had been leaving it, thanks to all the gifts I'd bought. It occurred to me that we'd never once delved into the extra baggage Harold had bought, purportedly carrying clothes for me. That's probably because we'd nixed the Nile trip and didn't stay nearly as long away from Pasadena as we'd originally planned, but I didn't care about that. I was *home*.

I looked around some more. Lots and lots of happy, smiling people milled about in our front yard. I turned to Ma. "Um, have you heard from Sam?"

Ma's eyes paid a visit to the heavens. "Have we heard from Sam? I'll say we've heard from Sam. According to him, you had an entire gang of thieves pursuing you all through the Middle East and you nearly got yourself killed."

"It was only three men, and they only pursued me because

they thought I had something I didn't have. Harold had it. What's more, we didn't even know what it was until somebody told us at the very end. It was Sam who was in the most danger."

"Not according to him," said Ma, and it sounded to me as though she believed Sam over her own daughter. Huh.

"He'll be coming to dinner tonight," said Aunt Vi.

"Oh, good!" Then, when both Ma and Aunt Vi turned to stare at me, I decided I'd sounded a trifle too happy about a visit from Sam, whose presence I'd always before eschewed. Gesundheit.

Sorry about that. I can't help myself sometimes.

The gift giving took quite a bit of time, but there were lots of squeals of delight when people opened their parcels and saw the exotica contained therein. Face it, you don't find a whole lot of Turkish and Egyptian artifacts in staid old Pasadena. Aunt Vi took her Turkish cookbook, and her eyes grew round. She also liked her lavender bath salts, which I'd replaced for her in Paris, but I think she was happier about the cookbook.

"Goodness gracious, Daisy, what's this?"

I'd thought the title of the book was pretty self-explanatory, but I told her, "I loved the food in Turkey, and they fix eggplant in all sorts of delicious ways. I just thought you might like to try a couple of the *easier* recipes."

Her head went back on her neck and she stiffened. "The easier recipes?"

Oh, dear. "I mean, it's exotic foreign food. I don't know if the family will like it. But it's really good. I didn't mean *easier* recipes, exactly. I only meant you might want to try a couple that aren't . . . aren't too . . . exotic." I decided I'd probably be better served by shutting my mouth, since I only seemed to be flailing more deeply into the verbal quicksand.

Then Aunt Vi smiled at me, and I relaxed. "That's very

thoughtful of you, Daisy. I think I'll enjoy trying some Turkish recipes."

Thank God.

Pudge absolutely adored his Turkish dagger, although I'm not sure his mother and father shared his joy.

Ma and Pa exclaimed over the beautiful Egyptian rug and the camel blankets I brought back. And Ma was almost overwhelmed by the fabulous Turkish shawl and ceramic bowl I'd bought for her in Grand Bazaar.

Both Pa and Pudge loved their fezzes. I told Pudge I'd make him a Turkish costume just like the one worn by Ali, our guard at the Sultanahmet Hotel, and he thought that was a swell idea.

Aunt Vi loved the Turkish carpet I'd bought for her upstairs room.

Both Johnny and Flossie claimed to adore their embroidered Turkish slippers. I'd had to guess at the sizes, but they said they were perfect. And Flossie exclaimed in genuine delight over the fabrics I'd given her from both Egypt and Turkey. I'd been teaching her to sew, and I could just imagine their little bundle of joy—if it ever left its present cozy nest—all wrapped up in a beautifully woven blanket sewn by its loving mother.

I'd bought literally dozens of Turkish symbols said to ward off the "evil eye," whatever that is, and all the neighbors and assorted friends seemed pleased with them. My brother and sister were absent from my homecoming, but I aimed to give them, and Daphne's daughters, their presents the next time the family got together again for a holiday. Which, come to think of it, would probably be Thanksgiving. My, how time flies.

And then it was dinnertime.

A knock came at the door at a few minutes before six. I, after fortifying myself with a lungful of deliciously scented air—Aunt Vi had made her special beef Wellington for my homecoming—I nervously went to answer it. Sam. With a bouquet of flowers.

"Good to see you, Sam," said I, taking the flowers. "Thank you very much."

He hesitated for a moment as if ascertaining the validity of my gladness before he said, "Good to see you, too. Especially here in Pasadena."

"Oh, come on. Things weren't all that bad in Turkey."

"Good God."

I backed up in order to let Sam in, and he entered the house. I'd bought a gloriously inlaid vase in Turkey, and I went to fetch it, to hold the flowers Sam had brought. This time he'd come armed with yellow roses and baby's breath. I think there's something called the "language of flowers," and I'm not sure what yellow roses meant, but I was pretty sure that red roses were the ones you gave someone if you were in love with her. Or him, depending on the case.

They looked very pretty as a centerpiece on our dinner table, whatever they meant. Dinner was, as ever, delicious, and it was good to have some of Vi's cooking. Not that I hadn't enjoyed the cuisine on our trip—well, once I got my appetite back, I mean—but you really couldn't beat one of Vi's meals. She was an expert. In fact, if she were a man, she'd probably be called a chef. And if she were a man and called a chef, she'd make a heck of a lot more money, too, but don't let me get started on that.

Ma wouldn't allow me to help wash up after dinner, and before Sam and Pa set up the card table and broke out the cards for gin rummy, Sam and I stepped out onto the front porch for a breath of air.

So I handed him the present I'd bought for him in Egypt and at Istanbul's Grand Bazaar. "You didn't stay long enough in Istanbul to get anything for yourself, so I got you this." My face was hot and I knew I was blushing, but it was dark, so I don't think Sam noticed. "And I also got you a sphinx in Cairo."

He was slow to reach out and take the package I held, and he opened it as if he feared I might have brought back a coiled serpent or something. When he opened the box and removed the exquisitely inlaid letter opener I'd bought for him in the Grand Bazaar, I was pleased to see his eyes widen. Then he smiled at the sphinx and said, "Thanks! Thanks a lot. These are really pretty."

"I thought you might be able to use the letter opener at work or something, and maybe put the sphinx on your desk. And you can tell all the guys at the station all about your adventure in Constantinople."

"Yeah. I'll be sure to do that."

I almost laughed, but couldn't quite make myself do it. The notion of Sam regaling his cohorts with adventures of derring-do in foreign parts was pretty funny, though.

Then Sam took a huge gulp of air, as if he were bracing himself to say something he didn't want to say. "I don't know if you remember what I told you in your hotel room right after we got back from the police station in Istanbul."

Bowing my head to face the inevitable, I said softly, "I remember."

"Well, I meant it, but I didn't mean to blurt it out that way. And I'm sure you wish I'd never mentioned—"

"No!"

Sam eyed me slantways. "No? No, you wish I'd never said it, or no—"

"No, I'm not sorry you mentioned it. But I'm not sure how I feel, Sam. I mean, Billy's only been in the ground for—"

"I know how you feel. You hate me."

"I don't hate you," I said—and with a good deal of vehemence, if I do say so myself.

A pause ensued. Then Sam said, "You don't?" It sounded as if he didn't believe me.

"No, Sam. I don't hate you. At all. But I . . . well, I . . . you know. What with Billy's passing only recently, and—"

"For God's sake, I'm not asking you to marry me right this minute!"

Good old Sam. From words of love to a temper fit in a split second. Well, I guess I was used to it by this time. "I know that." I, too, could be irritable at times, and I was then. "I'm only saying that I think we need to take this slowly. If you know what I mean."

He let out a huge breath. "I know what you mean. And I agree with you. I won't push you."

I glanced up at him, a frown on my face. "You'd better not, Sam Rotondo, or I'll have Spike piddle on your shoes again."

And with that, we returned to the bosom of my family. It was so good to be home. I sat up a lot longer than I wanted to that night, petting Spike and talking to Ma and Aunt Vi, not wanting to go to bed because I just wanted to soak in the atmosphere of love that permeated the house. And I don't mean Sam's for me. I mean my family's.

I kind of staggered into the kitchen the next morning, Spike dogging my heels, so to speak, and found Pa sitting at the kitchen table reading the *Pasadena Star News*. I was so happy to see him there. The scene was so familiar, and yet so different from anything I'd seen for the past couple of months.

He lowered his newspaper and smiled at me. "You look good, Daisy. You've put on some weight, and it becomes you. You were kind of . . . um . . ."

"Gaunt? Skeletal? Skinny? Yes, I know. But I got my appetite back in Turkey."

"Good for Turkey. Speaking of appetites, your aunt made some really good rolls for breakfast. I've never eaten anything like them before, but they're delicious."

And darned if I didn't find a plate of *lokmas* on the table.

Naturally, since we were in America, Vi had also cooked some bacon to eat with them. And the coffee was American, too. It wasn't thick and black and tarry, but drinkable. Breakfast was heavenly. I only gave Spike, who'd managed to lose all the weight he'd gained during my starvation period, one tiny piece of my *lokma*.

Then the telephone rang. I looked at Pa. Pa looked at me. I sighed and went to answer it.

"Gumm-Majesty residence. Missus Majesty speaking."

"Oh, *Daisy*," wailed Mrs. Pinkerton. "I'm *so* glad you're home again. I *need* you!"

So there you are. Things change. People come and go. Relationships change. Good folks die and bad folks live. And life goes on.

ABOUT THE AUTHOR

Award-winning author **Alice Duncan** lives with a herd of wild dachshunds (enriched from time to time with fosterees from New Mexico Dachshund Rescue) in Roswell, New Mexico. She's not a UFO enthusiast; she's in Roswell because her mother's family settled there fifty years before the aliens crashed. Now that Alice's two daughters have moved to Roswell, Alice no longer longs to return to California, although she still misses the food. Alice would love to hear from you at alice@ aliceduncan.net. And be sure to visit her Web site at http// www@aliceduncan.net.